RENEE HAYES

THE GIRL WHO BROKE THE WORLD

A RIM WALKER NOVEL

Queensland, Australia

Cover design by Judith San Nicolas
Typeset in Goudy Old Style 9 & 12 pt/Harrington 28 pt
Printed and bound in Australia by IngramSpark
Prepared for publication by The Erudite Pen

A catalogue record for this book is available from the National Library of Australia

The Girl Who Broke the World ~ 1st ed.
ISBN Paperback 9780645587104
ISBN Ebook 9780645587111

Dedication

*For Summer. My happiest and most powerful memories
are all yours.*

Contents

Map of the Rim Territories

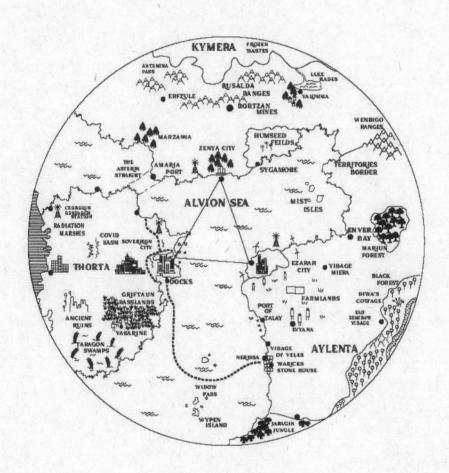

Part I

Part 1

Prologue

The fourth world war, later known as the Oxygen War, killed billions of life-forms in the year 2032. It ravaged the earth, destroying more than eighty per cent of the population and its man-made structures, after which the earth was reset.

In the lead-up, the world's resource limits had been reached, forests had been decimated and microbes in the soil had died out. Vital pollinating insects had perished from chemical poisons that lingered in the air. The rapidly expanding human population had reached beyond ten billion and was ridding the earth of its oxygen and food supply. With no possible way to remedy this situation, countries and nations panicked, and the global bombings culled each other's populations quickly.

On the 31st October 2032, two powerful bombs collided and ended the world's race to survive. Mother Nature, the life-giver of all on Earth, recycled the many bodies of her dead children, creatures and plants and used their collective energy to create a new land. This new land protected a small few from the poison of the bombs and the world's demise. For years afterwards, the rest of the earth was covered in a dense smog of concentrated chemical radiation from the bombs of the Oxygen War.

On much of the earth's surface, the smog was impenetrable by even the sun's sustaining rays. Unable to facilitate human life, the order of the natural balance before humans had disturbed it was restored once again. There was, however, a small circle in the earth's ozone, a pocket on the crust that could sustain life. The circle of light completely adjacent to the final blast, where the radiation hadn't quite taken hold, was where Mother Nature created what later became known as 'the Rim' and her outer Rim lands.

Within this shimmery circular wall of the Rim, three land masses separated by a large expanse of ocean was all that remained of the old earth. The strange force field that had appeared around the edge of these lands now held back the smog and darkness. None of the surviving humans knew how the Rim had appeared. Some figured it was a failsafe structure created by humans in case of catastrophic events. Others thought it some kind of natural phenomenon that had occurred to counteract all the radiation. All they knew was that they couldn't pass through this Rim. And that inside the Rim they were safe, almost as if Mother Nature had created the Rim world just for them. Unbeknownst to those inside the Rim, Mother Nature had also created Rim guardians, Rim watchers and new creatures in tandem to protect, manage, guide from afar and ensure the safety of the humans inside. In the outer Rim, creatures started to care for and repopulate the parcel of land outside.

Mother Nature or 'the Mother', having done what she could, returned to the earth in the forests of the new world to rest and to recover. She entrusted all of her remaining children and creatures to start the world anew, although this time, humans were to be much more closely watched over. The Mother was celebrated by the surviving humans inside the Rim every year on the last day of October – the day the old world died – at the moon festival.

Five hundred years or so after the Oxygen War, the three protrusions of land that now held the last flora, fauna and human life inside the Rim became known as Thorta, Aylenta and Kymera. The three territories were all that remained of the old, suffocated world. Humankind, by creating their own demise, had given Mother Nature a sigh of relief as billions were stripped from her surface. Somewhat like a dog being relieved of fleas that infested its coat and drank of its blood. Within the Rim, the now two-hundred thousand human population began to thrive and become grateful for their existence once again.

There were stories from the early days after the war of creatures that had emerged from the radiation smog in the outer Rim. Creatures that could enter in and out of the Rim as they pleased. These stories warned that these creatures would ravage the Rim's villages and cities, and take children from their beds at night. They alluded to men and women disappearing without a trace. But they had become just that: stories. Stories that deterred people from venturing into the outer regions of the Rim. The mutated creatures of nightmares were the only beings that roamed the dead lands, according to those inside the Rim.

However, there were actually other beings that were brought into existence by Mother Nature after the Oxygen War had decimated her surface. She recycled the energy of the departing lifeforms and used it to create others. These new beings were left to roam, live, protect and slowly replenish the damaged lands outside the Rim. The outer Rim became known as Lamiria, and the Temple of Lamiria was created for the Rim Guardians to reside in and watch over their fellow magical beings. For those in the outer Rim were indeed magical, and possessed supernatural powers bestowed upon them by the Mother herself.

On Aylenta, Kymera and Thorta, the people knew that their continued safety and survival depended on peace between all three nations. Peace above all was upheld and was the law. Each territory had a code and each upheld their own punishments for breaking those codes.

Thorta, the most industrial of the three territories with a population of fifty thousand, was west of the Alvion Sea divide. It was a harsh, wet, wind-stripped city that still contained the ruins of old buildings before the Oxygen War as well as museums with relics that had survived the blast.

Nestled in between these decaying structures were the new modern masterpieces. Living, breathing buildings and centres, some covered in greenery, all designed to benefit from Thorta's immense rainfall. It gave the city a sense of the present and past, moulded to convey the story of survival. And to never forget the past. Along with the rains came the intense electrical storms. The city thrived on innovation and its ability to capture and store the lightning for electricity and other uses, making Thorta's resources invaluable. The outskirts were made up of mostly factories, housing and laboratories created to study the Rim and its surrounding smog. For years the brightest minds had tried to somehow understand or reverse the effects of their ancestors, with no success.

Adjacent to Thorta, and to the southeast, was Aylenta. Aylenta had a hot, humid climate as it was situated where the sun's rays were most powerful inside the Rim. Hence, it benefitted from the angle of the sun that penetrated powerfully through the clean, crisp atmosphere at the centre of the Rim.

The heavily vegetated land gave life to many rare medicinal plants. Bountiful, edible crops were harvested all year round for its population of around fifty thousand people. Floods were a common occurrence for some villages in the low-lying areas, so they had houses and structures that rose up off the ground. These were safe from predators during the monsoonal weather and the elevation kept the dangerous parasites at bay. The structures withstood the surge of waters that came in downpours, sometimes lasting weeks. The ever-grateful earth would always drink the waters away within hours, as though the cleansing waters were never enough to quench the thirst of the poisoned foundation below.

Aylenta's warmth, old-world style and beauty contributed to it being the most peaceful of all the nations. Its people were deeply spiritual and connected to Mother Nature, with immense respect for their animals and lands.

To the north was the expansive nation of Kymera, with a much colder climate. Unlike that of its two sisters, it was a territory of ice and snow. Because of its position inside the Rim, Kymera missed out on much of the life-giving sunrays but had adapted accordingly. Its people were also adaptive and resilient, and had thrived in unique ways.

Kymera was a rich nation where many herds of large moscows roamed the frozen tundra. Moscows were huge beasts with thick fur hides and large fat supplies underneath, supplying Kymera's people with the means to keep warm and fed for generations in these harsh conditions. They resembled the ancient buffalos that used to roam the vast bush and swamplands of most countries in the old world. Moscows had thick dreaded fur, similar to that of a yak, and large metallic-like tusks that shone onyx against their white pelts, used for crushing ice to expose the humseeds contained within.

Humseeds were a remarkably tough, resistant plant that once exposed to the atmosphere would grow rapidly. The seeds could spread and lay dormant in icy conditions for years, preserved and just waiting for their opportunity to thrive. Long, straight, strong stems a metre or so high would produce small clusters of hard, nutritious seeds at the top of the stems and at the pinnacle of the plant. These seeds supplied the ice-hardened beasts with sufficient food throughout the winter storms.

Kymera, though resilient, had been more secretive and less co-operative with its neighbours. It had discovered many secrets from the past that were contained in its frozen lands and had kept the

knowledge that belonged there. The landscape was home to gargantuan trees growing so thick and tall as to reach the sun that didn't
grace its surface, spare a few precious weeks each year. These trees
towered over the herds of moscows and fields of humseeds below.
The trees were so ancient and solidly imbedded into the ice and
terrain that they had become the structures of which the cities were
built around.

Homes, transport stations and business centres were all connected and intertwined between the massive tree pillars. All were
positioned up and around the trunks, creating different levels of
civilisations reaching up to the cloudy skies. The tops of the trees
spread out with multiple sparse branches, no leaves, just small,
beautiful blue crystal-like flowers that bloomed all year round.

The capital city of Kymera was Zenya. Zenya comprised beautiful
floating tree houses, built into the massive trees, and was a glim-
mering city in the sky, all interconnected like an intricate spider's
web. Kymera was a nation of old and was governed by a royal line.
It was the only territory to choose this royal path, with its people
deciding that a royal line was a strong, decisive way to govern the
land after the tragedy of the war. A way to ensure a leader was born
who learned the best way to rule from their predecessor. The present king was King Ravaryn – a man shrouded in mystery. His
castle was situated in the middle of Zenya with the most amazing
views of the dark Alvion Sea that stretched out beyond.

Moon Festival

Zemira Creedence crept silently through the Aylentean forest under the massive ancient pines as they creaked against the gentle wind. Weaving her way over the fern floor, speckled light around her illuminated the small specks and seeds floating past. Without a sound, Wolf followed close behind. Wolf was Zemira's shadow, her closest companion. His thick, shining white coat and emerald eyes made his huge form stand out even more in the peaceful forest surrounds. Wolf's huge paws were stealthy and silent through the forest, and more than made up for his lack of camouflage.

Zemira, or Zee as she was known to most, was excited to be visiting Diwa Mumasumi. Diwa was a little old medicine lady who lived alone deep in the forest whom Zemira loved with all her heart. She had come into Zee's life at a young age but was cemented in every beautiful memory she had growing up. Diwa had helped raise Zemira - had adopted her as a granddaughter in a way. She wasn't

Zemira's relation, but she was family. Zemira's world wouldn't be right without Diwa in it.

The two rabbits Wolf had flushed out for her as an eighteenth birthday gift minutes ago now swung limply over Zee's shoulder. She couldn't wait to pry every detail of information from the old lady about the New Moon celebration happening in the village tonight. Zemira knew she couldn't go but she loved hearing about the decorations the villagers made, the extravagant flower wreaths, the painted stone pathways and the masks that the villagers fashioned and wore. All to celebrate the great Mother of the forest.

Unfortunately, Zee's own mother, Verena Creedence, worried deeply about everything; she was afraid that something would happen to Zemira if she were to go into town for the festival. Zemira knew that worrying was a mother's job, but *her* mother's anxiety was overwhelming. Verena had forbidden Zee from any if not all interactions with the village and had never let her attend the festival. Zemira imagined that it was beautiful; she could see the light from the massive fires that were set every year glowing like a beacon in the night from her small house on the hill. Diwa had also told her of the people dancing around the fires for hours on end, sometimes even till the sun brought dawn.

Zemira left the ferns and entered a narrow, worn path, now walking side by side with Wolf. His huge paws padded silently as they made their way down the path to Diwa's cottage. Zee was daydreaming, imagining the people dancing through the streets and around the fires, allowed to be free, allowed to be there, as a part of the celebrations. Singing and the sound of instruments filled her head. Ahead of her on the path, someone stumbled out of the thick ferns and onto the worn track. She quickly slid behind the trunk of the nearest pine without a sound. Daydream broken. Wolf followed her lead and crouched low, his eyes pinpointed on the figure, snout protruding through the tangled leaves, a low growl emanating from his throat.

'Shhh,' prompted Zemira. She slid the two rabbit carcasses from her shoulder to rest against the base of the large tree and removed her pack, circling behind the trunk to peer around the opposite side. It was a young man from the village, carrying a small sack on his back. His clothes were worn but fitted his tall frame well. Mid-length chestnut hair was tied back from his angular face. He seemed lost standing there, trying to figure out which way to proceed. She crept through the forest to come around behind him, gripping the knife that she always kept tied to her hip. Stealthily, and in one swift motion, she exited the ferns, stood tall and pressed the knife to his throat.

His hands raised slowly, palms opened wide. His breath was steady as he said, 'I knew you were around here somewhere.'

Zemira smirked. 'You should watch your back more, Pax. I could have slit your throat before you even realised I was there.' She pocketed her knife.

'Pfft, come on, Zee. I heard you coming from a mile away,' he countered with his eyebrows slightly raised.

'Surrre you did,' she teased. 'What are you doing out here, anyway? Shouldn't you be helping prepare for the festival?'

'I should, and I'm probably going to get an earbashing if I've skipped preparation on New Moon morning, but I had to see you. It is your eighteenth birthday after all, and I have something for you.'

It was now her turn to raise an eyebrow. 'Oh, Pax. You didn't have to get me anything!'

He swung the sack from his shoulder and produced a bread loaf-sized box, ornate with the most intricate designs of trees and little winged creatures – some holding fruit and others holding hands. A moon glowed down onto the carved forest with swirling beams of light connecting the figures around a central fire. It was so beautiful; the edges were even rimmed with gold flecks, and a small gem was in the centre of the lid. It must have cost him months of saving to buy this for her.

Zee's cheeks reddened 'This...this is really pretty, Pax. Thank you.'

His handsome face lit up with an adorable grin. 'The present is inside the box, Zee.'

Her face reddened further. 'Oh,' she said as she moved to open the box, curious about what could be inside.

'Wait.' Paxton Raker put his hands around hers just as she was about to open the lid, restricting her from seeing the contents. Warm sparks tingled up her arms as his large hands engulfed hers.

'I have to get back, but I want you to open it after I go. I don't want you to decide right now.' He leaned in close and pecked her on the cheek.

Her heart pounded. Wolf now standing right beside Zee. He growled at Pax and then forcefully squeezed his large body between their knees to separate them.

Pax laughed loudly, a deep and contagious laugh. 'Alright, alright calm down, Wolf.'

Zee's stomach felt as though it was going to flit off into the forest without her. She wasn't sure if she liked that feeling or not.

'Happy birthday, Zee. Have a great day, and I hope you like your present.' He flung the emptier sack over his shoulder and ruffled wolf's furry head. 'Seeya later, Wolf,' he said as he gave Zee a wink then turned back up the track from the way he came.

Zemira stood on the path and looked down at the box within her hands, her knuckles now slightly whiter than before. 'Ah... what just happened?' she questioned Wolf.

He prodded her leg with a curious whine and sniffed at the box still between her hands.

She sucked in a deep breath to calm herself. In all the years she and Pax had been friends, he had never kissed her or been... well, that nice. Paxton had been Zemira's only friend in the small village of Kali in Aylenta. They had met at primary school before her mother had pulled her out. He was warm and caring, and the two valued each other's company. Pax lived in the group home in the village. They didn't like to call them orphanages anymore. He had lost his parents to an illness called the silent sickness years ago and had no siblings. Pax was always teasing, joking around, and they often competed with each other to see who's hunting skills were better. He was, well, downright brotherly.

Zemira wasn't sure what to feel, but she loosened her grip, rolled her shoulders and opened the box. The lid was smooth, heavy timber; inside it was lined with a rich burgundy velvet, and nestled in the velvet lay a mask. It was beautiful – white, decorated with small stones that were clear and green around the edges, and the ears of a wolf curved up around the eyes. Spiralling ferns decorated the space within. It was the most stunning thing she had ever seen. This must be what the people wear at the festival! Even her imagination couldn't have crafted a more perfect mask for herself.

Wolf pawed impatiently at her side, and she lowered the box just slightly so he could see inside for himself. He spied the mask within and bared his teeth with a small growl.

'Oh, don't be jealous. I love the rabbits that you caught, too.'

Wolf made a scoffing sound and walked off behind the trees to retrieve his rabbits. She stared at the mask, and glow beetles filled her chest, bringing excitement and leaving it there.

'He wants me to go to the festival! To meet him there... tonight.' No one would need to know, not if she snuck out after her mother had fallen asleep.

Wolf returned with the rabbits in his maw. Zee retrieved them once more and slung them back over her shoulder as he whined at her and eyed the box. 'You could come with me, take guard, no one will even notice me. I'll just be someone else at the festival as the mask will cover my face. Don't you dare tell Mum when we get home or I'll never forgive you!' Her mother was overprotective in the extreme when it came to the other villagers, much to Zee's consternation. But she trusted Zee's hunting instincts in the forest.

Wolf looked away from her, then simply turned back and loped off in a huff towards Diwa's cottage.

Zee smiled. 'Good, so it's settled then.' The beam on her face made her emerald eyes shine. She nearly skipped off down the track to catch up with him, the excitement bursting within her. Excitement for the festival and to see Pax. But she would think how she felt about that later! Taking a deep breath, she calmed herself. After all, she was a deadly hunter in this forest, and hunters didn't skip. Well, except on their birthdays.

Zemira reached Diwa's little cottage with Paxton's gift heavy in her pack and the two rabbits warming her side. She loved the feeling of reaching the top of the track then looking down into the hollow that hugged the old cottage. Her shoulders relaxed as she took in the garden. The hollow was full of flowers and vines heavy with all kinds of strange fruit – from where they came, she had no idea.

Diwa was full of riddles, always joking and saying silly things when she wanted to avoid certain questions such as these. Zee didn't mind though; everyone deserved to have secrets. Sure it was frustrating as anything, but Diwa made up for it in spades with her bright, energy-filled vibe. Numerous herbal scents always greeted Zee on the stroll down the hill through the garden. Diwa's small cottage was wrapped around an enormous tree – its long, spindly roots had long ago started to encase the dwelling. The small, crooked chimney poked through the netting of roots like a blowhole on some ancient sea creature, smoke streaming steadily out.

If anyone were to stumble across the cottage they may think it abandoned if not for the smoke and vibrant gardens. Sometimes Zee would catch Diwa talking away and having conversations with the giant old tree, and she always wondered if it really replied. Could only Diwa hear the responses? Was there really some kind of magical connection that Zee didn't understand, or was the old woman just a little batty?

12

The morning sun was filtering through the canopy. A few glow beetles still flittered about in the shaded parts of the glen, yet to retire then return with their luminescent yellow glow once night had fallen. Zemira turned to Wolf, who was now beside her. 'Alright, let's go in and see what Diwa has to say about tonight. No doubt she already knows.'

Wolf looked back with a knowing nod and trotted off down the path through the heart of the cottage's gardens, leaving Zee to trail behind him scraping her boots. She knew Diwa would know what she planned to do. There was something about the old woman that Zemira was in awe of – Diwa just sort of knew things... like the kind of things someone couldn't even guess. She said she would feel things in her old bones and that the earth itself, and the birds, would speak to her.

Zee knew Diwa was a little bit crazy. As if living alone off the system in the woods so close to the Rim wasn't a red flag to start with, but Zee loved Diwa with all her heart. Her made-up stories of creatures and lands long gone had warmed every inch of her childhood. Some stories were magical, and some were terrifying. The story of the orcles was one of her favourites. Orcles were large almost transparent creatures that were the replenishers of distant lands. At night in the forests outside the Rim, they absorbed large amounts of water into their glowing bodies, and they had large, puffy arms and legs on big, billowed-out trunks. Small eyes at the top of the body where a head should be sought the way to the seeds that had dropped on the forest floor during the day. They would collect the seeds, absorbing them into their translucent, swollen bellies and travel to the outskirts before reaching the churned deadland at the edge of the forest.

They slowly plodded along the edges until all the seeds and water they carried were dispersed. Shrinking back to their original sizes, their glows faded as they retired for the night and headed back to their deep hollows in the fern floors to sleep and to do it all again the following night.

But as Diwa would always say, life needs balance, and along with the orcles would come the mud munchers. Mud munchers lived in the dead lands in the blackened, hard earth that the ancient humans had poisoned. Their long, armoured bodies were like steel, and they resembled huge earthworms as they munched through the actual earth, massive rows of serrated teeth in a large round mouth at the top of creature's eyeless head. They passed through the earth, churning it for the orcles, sifting out the poisons by absorbing them and dispersing them away with their magic. But they were also devourers, at times entering the forests to hunt and kill smaller creatures before returning to their burrows in the light of day. It was said that if a mud muncher scented you in the forests, there would be no escape from their viper-like speed and needle-sharp teeth.

Yes, Diwa's stories had fascinated Zee since she was a small child. When she was lonely or felt her isolated life was a burden and not a gift, Diwa had always been a spark of light and warmth, as these qualities somehow emanated from her. She just prayed the old woman would let her go to the festival tonight. That was if her guess was right that she already knew.

Zee wanted so badly to see the celebrations in the small village she was rarely allowed to enter. She loved her mother Verena dearly but couldn't understand her irrational fears. Why was she like that? What was she afraid might happen to her? She knew it would have been hard for her mother to raise her alone but Zemira had always tried to be good. She was always doing as her mother had asked. There was no give though; Verena was so controlling and wouldn't listen to reason. Was it so wrong that all Zee wanted to do was have some fun? To see the village illuminated with lights from hundreds of farmed glow beetles in their little lantern cages? Admire the neon paints made from Luna mushrooms that glowed all through the forest at night? The neon colours also adorned the small shop fronts and the paths throughout the town. Zee also wanted to eat the exotic foods kept and prepared especially for the festival, and to dance around the giving fires.

Lost in her wishful thinking, she followed the twisted path past the villa root vines, wild daisies and purple mistflowers to Diwa's misshapen door, where Wolf was waiting for her, tail wagging. The door opened before Zee had a chance to knock. Spices and a warm cinnamon scent wafted out behind the old woman standing in the doorway, her face crinkled with a grin from ear to ear.

'Happy eighteenth, my darling!' Diwa launched her fragile-looking frame at Zee, hugging her with a surprisingly firm squeeze. She was small, but Zee knew better than to think Diwa frail. She had seen the old woman wield an axe to chop wood for hours, and haul large pieces of meat from deer carcasses for drying with what looked like little effort.

'You've got something exciting to tell me! But before I hear about that, come in, come in! I've made you cinnamon tea and a mistflower cake with raspor's honey!'

'Raspor's honey?' exclaimed Zee. 'Where on earth did you find raspor's honey!'

How had Diwa done it? Raspors were almost the size of Zee, hummingbird-like creatures with the large stingers of a wasp instead of feathered tails. They had a proboscis from their sharp-pointed, thin beaks for collecting nectar from large forest flowers. Raspors roosted in small indents in the size of huge, craggy mountainside cliffs. Their nests were like tiny caves carved out in the rock, and the nectar they collected under their feathered wings was deposited on the walls inside these small nest caves to create a sweet, crystallised-type honey in preparation for having young.

Raspors were extremely beautiful creatures with their iridescent rainbow feathers, but equally as deadly if you were to be caught near their nests. You could be stung from their venomous tail, or skewered by their sharp-pointed beaks.

'Oh, I'm allowed to have secrets of my own, aren't I?' Diwa raised her eyebrows with hands on her hips.

'No, no you're not! If I'm not allowed to then you're not!' teased Zee.

Diwa let out a hearty laugh. The contagious sound always pulled a laugh from Zee too. 'Oh alright, I'll tell you where I got it from later, but first I have a gift for you, Zemira. You too, Wolf dear. Come on in, you handsome boy!'

Wolf, now wagging his tail profusely, nuzzled his head into the woman for a hug as she ruffled his large ears. Wolf stood nearly more than half Diwa's height, so she made the already large wolf look gargantuan. He was, in fact, actually gargantuan; he was far larger than any common wolf Zee had ever seen on rare occasions at the edges of the forest. His thick, pure white fur was unlike the mottled camouflaged coats of other wolves, and his eyes of clear emerald gave him a regal appearance. If he were wild, in a pack of his own, he would surely rule as the alpha on his size alone.

Zee was sure if Diwa ever wanted to go for a ride on Wolf, it would be no problem at all. That is, if wolf would let her, which she was sure he would as Diwa doted on him like another child. He practically melted around the old woman.

'Pathetic.' Zee rolled her eyes at her companion.

He scoffed at her and wandered over to his favourite spot on the old woven mat in front of the fire, stretched his huge limbs and curled up in front of the warmth like some overgrown house cat. Zee deposited her pack and boots just inside the entrance, and hung the rabbits from a hook just near the door.

'Very nice, dear,' commented Diwa.

'Birthday present from Wolf,' Zee said. She sat down in the warm, brightly coloured kitchen to wait for Diwa as she shuffled out of the main room and disappeared behind the trunk of the massive tree rooted right in the heart of the cottage's structure. She was off to her room to retrieve Zee's gift.

Zee looked around the small kitchen while she waited. It was enchanting and eccentrically resplendent with hand-painted vines, glow beetles, Luna moths and little flying lizards depicted under all the old wooden shelves. As well as forest sprites from Diwa's stories. Zee had helped paint them with Diwa one long, hot summer. Where Diwa had gotten the paints from, Zee didn't know (the old woman had always surprised her in more ways than one), but it was a fond memory.

Most of the paintings had faded and chipped over the years, but they were still beautiful. Along with the painted vines mingled real roots of the old tree, winding up and down the walls of the dwelling. This place was so familiar to her and felt like her own home when she entered, if not more. The chairs around the table were all different shapes, sizes, colours and patterns, collected over the years from bartering. Diwa's herbs and medicinal concoctions were sought after in the main village. Zee could smell the delicious cake and the tea brewing in the small kitchen on top of the large wood stove, and her mouth started to water.

At that moment, Diwa shuffled back into the room and handed a small bag to her, again wearing that mischievous grin, then turned to her stove to ready the tea and cake. It was a soft drawstring bag of deepest green with gold embroidered vines and leaves. Inside the bag was a necklace, not on a metal chain but on woven black thread, with a dark blue polished stone the size of a quail's egg that hung in the centre. It was intricately wrapped around by the black thread. The thread was woven in a pattern encasing the stone around the edges like a net.

'Diwa, it's beautiful. I don't know what to say. I love it! Thank you.'

'It's moonstone, dear, and very old, just like me.' Diwa winked. 'I've had it since before I came to be here in this forest and built my little cottage. But now I want you to have it. It will protect you. You must keep it with you always, Zee.' She said it gently, but Zee realised this was more of a command than a request.

'I will. It's stunning, Diwa.' The stone was a cloudy dark blue and not polished too finely, but Zee thought it was like Diwa – a little rough with hidden beauty inside.

Her old friend served Zee with the tea and cake. She then came around the table and stood behind her to tie the necklace around her neck, her shaky spider-like fingers making fast work of the intricate knots, sealing the two sides together. Diwa retrieved her own tea and a piece of cake on a small mismatched plate and teacup and sat adjacent to Zee, admiring the young woman now wearing the stone necklace.

'So you want to go to the festival tonight, I hear.'

'Argh.' Zee let out a frustrated sigh. 'Don't I ever get to surprise you with anything?'

Diwa chuckled. 'You surprise me every day, Zemira!'

Zee just rolled her eyes at the old woman and gave her a warm smile.

'So where is it? I want to see the mask he chose for you,' Diwa prompted.

Zemira had no idea how Diwa knew the things she knew. No one visited her in the forest, and she had no family that Zee knew of. She rarely ventured into the village to barter, or anywhere else for that matter. But she had always been here when Zee needed her.

'My little birds told me,' would be the only answer Zee would get if she ever asked how Diwa knew these things. So Zee just shrugged her shoulders and retrieved her pack from the door to show Diwa Paxton's gift.

The old woman opened the ornate box and picked up the mask, turning it over in her hands, a worried look frosting over her ancient eyes.

'What is it?' Zee inquired. 'Do you see something?'

Diwa placed the mask back in its box, withered hands shaking with a slight tremor. 'It's beautiful, Zee, and it suits you well. The wolf of the forest – I couldn't have picked a more beautiful mask for you myself. It must have cost the young lad an arm!'

Wolf let out a huff from his place in front of the fire. Diwa laughed.

18

'You don't like it?' Zee couldn't help but think Diwa wasn't telling her everything.

'No it's not that, dear. It's very beautiful, and I know you'll have a wonderful time tonight, but...' she hesitated, 'but you mustn't tell your mother as she will forbid you to go. I know you feel you should be honest but what she doesn't know won't hurt her.' A bit of that mischievous sparkle entered Diwa's eyes again.

'That's terrible advice, Diwa! What if she finds out I've snuck away? She'll be furious with me! But I'm eighteen years old now and the best hunter in all of Aylenta. I'm not a child. I shouldn't have to sneak around. Besides, I practically look after her now, not the other way around, so she can't stop me. Mother is so protective and I don't understand why. Her paranoia of the world is going to destroy her one day, and she needs to let go. I'll be grown up soon and then what does she think, that I'll stay and look after her forever?'

Zee's temples throbbed through her clenched teeth. 'I understand Mum knows I'm different in that I can do... things. But she never talks to me about any of it, like that I can move things around me, the way the forest feels, the wind, the earth beneath me. I feel it more and more like invisible vines connecting me to everything around me – the elements, the plants the trees. They're letting me into their energy, letting me move and manipulate them, like they are somehow a part of me, woven deep down into my being.'

Her eyes fell to her hands, where she had scratched a deep groove into her thumb. Zee tended to gouge at this whenever she thought about the growing distance between herself and mother. 'She doesn't understand me; she doesn't understand anything. She doesn't trust me.'

'Don't speak about your mother that way, Zemira. She's had a hard life and only wants to protect you, that is all. Don't fight with her; she... she worries. But I also know you need to experience more of life. So leave Wolf with her tonight. She'll sleep soundly and won't even notice you're gone,' Diwa said gently.

'Protect me? Protect me from what? Living? I've barely had a life! She may want to live isolated out here from the inner Rim for her whole life, but I don't.'

'Verena doesn't expect you to stay forever, just until you're ready,' Diwa soothed.

Ready for what? Zee could feel the heat rising inside her temple. She always got the same answer from her mother whenever she asked to go into the village, or heaven forbid the city: 'It's not safe.'

What wasn't safe? She never understood her mother's fears. Okay, most sane people were afraid of the Rim and of being too close to it, of the creatures that were rumoured to sometimes enter and take people at night or attack whole villages and then just disappear. But all Zee wanted was to go into the village every now and then. It was far away from the Rim wall.

Her head was pounding as she tried to refrain from showing Diwa her anger. After all, she wasn't a child about to throw a tantrum in front of her. Zee took a deep breath and wrapped her hands around the mug of warm tea. As she looked down into the cup, she could see the contents slowly moving, starting to swirl and boil within. She quickly withdrew her hands, spilling the cup's hot contents onto the table and all over Diwa's fingers.

'Diwa, are you alright? I'm so sorry, I didn't mean it. Did I burn you?' She wasn't sure why but she all of a sudden felt teary.

It's alright, Zemira. Sit, sit; it's just spilled tea.' Diwa didn't look at all surprised at what just happened. She only rose to retrieve a cloth to mop up the spilled tea off the table.

'Things will change very soon for you, Zee. They may not be the changes you are wishing for, though. So don't fight with your mother; she loves you more than life itself. But go tonight. Enjoy yourself. Be young. Be free. And dance with that boy by the fires,' she added with an all-knowing wink.

Zee reddened slightly. 'I'm sorry about the tea. I don't know what happened.' She could feel her body loosening off, the tension and heat slowly leaving her head and limbs.

'Tea schmee, lemon burgundy! I'll make some more. Now eat your cake and tell me the plan for sneaking out tonight.' Diwa clapped, mischief and excitement coating each word.

Zee laughed and felt herself relax even more, letting the calm warmth in again. With Wolf now contently snoring on the mat, Zee and Diwa chatted and laughed and planned.

The Explosion

Kali Village, Aylenta

After they had finished cake and tea, Diwa sat Zemira down in front of the fire and braided her long midnight hair into intricate patterns and swirls of tiny braids.

'It's tradition for the festival, dear, to celebrate the day that the old world ended and Mother Nature created this new one, saving us from ourselves. You'll fit right in,' she assured the young woman.

Zee couldn't wait. Energy was sparking through her body, and her stomach was all jittery. She could barely be still. There was something so exciting about the moon festival, not just the food, the music and the people, but it felt like she was meant to be there. Like she was somehow drawn to celebrate, to be around others. She loved the way her hair looked, so she'd definitely have to practise this as it was so nice to have her hair away from her face.

'Imagine this while I'm hunting, Wolf! No stray hairs to distract me, by the Mother I love it!' Zee pronounced, swishing her head around to show off the braids.

Wolf made a short agreeable 'rrruff' and nudged her side.

'Thanks, Wolf,' she beamed. What a beautiful birthday; she didn't think she could remember one that could match up.

'Alright, so it's decided on Diwa's orders that you're to stay behind tonight and sleep in Mum's room.'

A low growl slipped out of Wolf's maw.

'You know she sleeps so well when you're with her. Come on, pleeeease, it's my birthday, and you love me, and I'll give you one of my rabbits all roasted up just the way you like it,' she pleaded.

'Ohh rooora,' Wolf replied with an agreeable growl and a head tilt of defeat.

Zee lunged forward, wrapping her arms around Wolf's neck and giving him a huge squeeze. 'You're the best,' she admitted with a kiss on his large head.

Zemira left Diwa's cottage with the sun high in the sky, feeling full yet light as she always did when she left the dear woman. Her new stone necklace felt cool against her skin and seemed to hum with energy. She darted off through the forest leaving Wolf to sprint to catch up. The pair darted through the ferns and around large trees, until they thinned out and into a valley. A bank overlooked a large deep-blue and green expanse of river right on the edge of the Rim.

The strange almost iridescent sheen of the air in the middle of the river was eerie and deterred most if not nearly all people from the Rim's edge. It looked as though it almost cut the river in two lengthways, straight out from where she stood on the steep bank. Zemira and Wolf stood on one side with nothing but forests of a darker and misty hue on the other.

The outer Rim had never bothered her although she had heard the stories and even encountered some very strange, terrifying creatures in the forest while hunting. But that was her norm and though she had never told her mother what she had witnessed, Diwa knew. Diwa assured her if she just stayed out of their way, she would be safe and no harm would come to her.

Zee unloaded her pack and stored it safely away from the edge of the river at the base of a very large tree a fair way up with an overhanging root system. She liked to store her things here while fishing the river and checking her traps as sometimes, when it would suddenly bucket down, her belongings would be safe and dry, even if she was drenched. Not that it looked like that would happen today as the sky was a magnificent shade of mistflower. An interesting contrast opposite her where the sky almost appeared cut in two, with shimmering greys and dark clouds looming outside the translucent Rim wall.

'Okay, Wolf, fingers crossed we get something good to add to dinner tonight!'

Wolf always watched from afar while Zemira was at the river, usually lounging under the trees on the edge of the clearing. He crossed his front paws in reply and then fell to the side with a 'Huff', expelling a large breath then proceeding to have another nap.

Although Zee was unbothered by the Rim, she wasn't complacent. She never ventured too close to the edge of this river as she sensed it wasn't safe. She'd had more than once had something take a bite - a large bite - out of her catch before she even got to haul it out of the water. Zee swung a line with a small piece of rabbit foot attached to a large wooden hook carved from iron oak wood, strong as metal. She held the rope firmly between her fingers in anticipation. The young hunter was good at waiting; years of fishing in the river had taught her patience was the key to bringing dinner home.

After a short while, she felt a tug on the rough rope. She pulled back with a quick jerk of the line so as to plant the hook in whatever had taken interest. She pulled and pulled, the line becoming damp in her hands. A large tug responded, and her heart raced.

'Yess, I've got you.' Zee pulled harder, and the large force on the other end of the line fought back. She skidded, her boots digging into the ground on the muddy bank, preventing her from being pulled into the deep, murky water.

Pulling hard away from the edge, she backed up to a safer distance. The other end of her line took its chance with the slight reprieve. She could feel the creature pulling away, trying to dart in and out of the reed-mazed water and away to safety. The rope pulled suddenly through her palms with a hot stinging sensation, but she held firm, her hands burning.

'You're not getting away that easily,' she grimaced. Digging her heels in, Zee slowly but surely hauled in her catch with burning arms and sweat beading her brow. As she fell back onto the bank, she tugged with the last of her energy to drag the catch ashore. She was nearly spent, even though youth was on her side, but equally matched by the powerful river dweller. She groaned and dragged it the last few feet away from the river bank's edge up to where she lay.

Catching her breath, Zee sat up to see the thrashing creature and what she had accomplished, but her eyes widened when she laid eyes on the creature. It was monstrous. How had she managed to drag it all the way up here?

It had bulging black eyes, and its scales had a silver sheen while long whisker-like appendages sprouted from its mouth. The scales were massive, almost the size of her hand, and the iridescent silver shimmer coated the beautiful gold plates. Something else suddenly overcame her excitement and exhaustion. A deep knowing in her stomach sensed that this was not a normal fish. She had never seen anything like it before come out of the river. The large petal-like fins that protruded all down its sides were mesmerising as it thrashed around in the mud, wheezing for a breath of water.

'Aww, I'm so sorry, big guy. I don't need you. I meant no harm. You've lived too long for me to be the one to take your life away.' She reached for the knife from her side and grabbed the creature's large mouth, near where the hook had pierced.

'Please don't take any of my fingers off.' She braced herself. Using the knife's blunt wooden handle to force the sharp side of the hook back through the creature's lip, Zee pulled it through and out the other side. On her knees, she then spun his giant body around in the mud. His mouth could probably fit her whole head inside. His thrashing became less frantic, maybe having seen the river in sight again. With the last of her energy, she gave him a huge shove down the bank towards the water.

'I'm sorry,' she yelled after the behemoth that she had never intended to catch.

He slid and wriggled down the muddy bank to the water's edge then splashed back into the water, slowly disappearing into the depths. A shiver crawled down Zee's spine. She had never seen such a glorious but eerie creature come from within the river. Sure, in the forests and trees, but something about the water had always made her feel off. She gathered herself and set off back to the tree line and Wolf. That was enough of the river for today.

She reached Wolf still snoozing where she had left him under the large root overhang in her stash tree. His head perked up just as she reached him. 'No luck, just an extremely large and creepy fish. I let him go. Probably got radiation poisoning, or something.'

Wolf let out a small whine.

'It's alright, you still get a rabbit all to yourself. A promise is a promise.' Zee crouched down to retrieve her pack, yet hesitated. 'Best leave this here.' She pulled out the box containing the mask Pax had given her and gently wrapped it in a cloth so as not to scratch the beautiful paintings on the outside. Then she pushed it safely back into her hidey hole.

'Wouldn't want Mum to find it... at least until after I've been to the festival tonight.'

Wolf sighed.

'Come on, old boy, that's enough for today. Let's go home,' Zee said in a comforting tone. The sun was getting lower in the sky and starting to turn the trees and air around her a golden tone.

Zee and Wolf rounded the last bend on the track up the hill out of the river's valley and viewed the sun close to setting over the mountains far behind the village. She loved this view on the way back to her mother's small house on the side of the hill. The cottage looked out over the village, past the small intertwining stream through the centre and out over the many manicured fields, crops and farmlands. She wasn't really much a part of the village below, but at least she could see it and feel somewhat closer to society.

Just as she turned to leave, a loud, shuddering blast pulsed in her ears, and Zee fell to the ground. The sound pushed unbearably on her head, and a blinding light burned into her closed eyes, no matter how tightly she forced them shut, and the ringing inside her head was excruciating. She squeezed her hands as tight as she could over her ears to try and stop the agonising pressure. The blood trickled down her face from her nose and eyes, and her now-slick hands indicated blood was also pouring from her ears. She tried to move her legs to get up to run.

Zee had no idea what was happening, and this pain was not like anything she had felt before. Ever since being hit with it, she could feel Wolf grabbing at her shoulder, trying to drag her to safety. The acrid smell of smoke mixed with something stinging and more sinister burned her throat. A roaring blast swept past her body, and then she was in darkness. All alone she fell into the void, the noise gone, her senses blanketed. Numbed. The pain disappeared, so she welcomed the darkness, fell into it... and then there was nothing.

The Watcher

The Kali Valley, Aylenta

The watcher stood silently against the bark of the forest giant just outside the Rim wall. In his tree-wisp form he could stand still and completely blend into his surroundings for days on end, camouflaged completely from predators and prey alike. They could never detect his presence until it was too late. But he was not hunting today. No, he was watching the small human across the river on the inside of the Rim wall. She was hunting in the waters and hauling in her catch, a large catch.

He watched her silently as she struggled against the beast on the other end of the line. Surely the rope must be burning through her soft hands? As he watched, he thought she would certainly be pulled into the river's dark depths. He had seen others before her succumb to this fate, usually ripped to shreds beneath the water by the waiting water wisps with their needle-like razor-sharp claws. The water wisps would ensnare their victims, and a few moments later, he would see their spirits rise up out of the water and float away.

But he never felt anything akin to emotion as he watched them meet their fate. Why should he? He was a watcher. A warrior destined to guard the Rim and the creatures that inhabited the outer lands. Tasked by the Queen of the Forest, Kyeitha, the Rim guardian herself, to do so. These humans inside the Rim, they were all monsters. Kyeitha had said to stay away and observe only, yet the Rim itself was not to be entered. It was a crime punishable by death. But as he watched this one from just outside, he felt... a tickle of anticipation. What was she thinking? Was she so hungry inside the Rim's circle of protection that she was willing to risk her life for this catch? So close to the Rim this one always ventured. Was she stupid or brave? He wasn't sure, but intrigued, yes. Somehow this one was different; she produced an aura that suggested she somehow contained power. She slipped in the mud and nearly skidded down the bank into the dark water, only just catching her footing. He flinched and rustled some kind of bird nearby causing it to startle and fly off. He re-steadied himself; the small human didn't stray from her task. She hadn't seen or heard anything as she was too preoccupied by her catch.

The human didn't look that dangerous or vicious, unlike most of the other forest dwellers he encountered. Slowly but surely, he watched her haul in the old river god. Did she not know what she was doing? Did she not know the danger? He saw her fall backwards as she exhausted her last effort to pull the huge catch up the muddy bank. Her face went wide with surprise when she laid eyes on the river god. He was sure she was going to end him. This evil, dangerous human. But she removed her hook from his mouth and did the most unexpected – spun his large body around and directed him back to his home to protect and rule over his domain.

He watched her as she got up, looked down at the river and then walked away. He felt strangely liberated. She knew better. Better than to slay a creature of power and status. For if she had, the

30

next trip to the river would surely have been her last. The water wisps would have avenged their father and dragged her small body into the deep of the river. He stayed and watched for some time longer, processing what he had seen. A most unusual event.

He finally turned to stride off into the undergrowth of the black forest, transforming from tree wisp into his warrior form, when the ground shook beneath him. He spun around to see an explosion of light and intense sound waves emanating from over the peak of the forest on the other side of the river. The vibrations of destruction came through the earth and up into his being. He could sense the bad intentions. He watched for a moment longer, getting a sense of what may be happening before turning and transforming into wolf form, his black coat now a shadow racing into the depths of the forest, eastwards and far away from the Rim river.

Diwa Mumasumi shuffled through her small cottage and around the tree trunk, which was the pillar of her home, to her kitchen, and set about making some tea. The box on the worn wooden table caught her eye as she passed.

'It wasn't supposed to happen before the festival,' she said to herself. 'Too soon, too soon, she isn't ready, not ready yet.' Diwa filled the pot and placed it on the old wood-burning stove, then retrieved a mismatched teacup and plate from the shelf adjacent to the kitchen's little window that overlooked her gardens. The shelf had been brightly painted once with small, intricate colourful designs by a beautiful, smiling, fresh face with midnight hair and eyes of the forest. Zemira. The child had grown over the years and entwined herself into every corner of Diwa's heart, just like the old fig tree that was becoming a part of the cottage itself.

'She will need you, Orion. She will need you more than ever now. Zemira will need an anchor, something to hold her together and help her to understand her roots. Good roots are important,' the old woman said aloud to herself, to her tree.

The villagers had all thought her crazy, and that was the way she had liked it. They were less likely to try and communicate with her when she pretended to be insane, which was better than listening to them. But she could handle the young hunter and her mother Verena. Verena had been through so much, yet had raised Zemira on her own and raised her well.

Diwa had met Verena many years ago in the village markets, when she still visited them, and their relationship had grown. Verena, having no living parents of her own, had felt an instant connection with Diwa, and Diwa to her. But too many humans would wear on Diwa's soul. She couldn't tolerate their nonsense, and worse still, their lack of respect for the earth that gave them life. They had gotten greedy in the past, which had resulted in the war that destroyed most of the earth, except for one small, liveable space. They deserved far less in her opinion. They had all deserved to die, but as their luck would have it, they had survived... again. Safely contained for centuries now within the small circle of land they called the Rim.

But the girl was different. She would be the key. Zemira wasn't ready yet, but the old woman had faith. She could see the fire smouldering within, even if it had been reined in and controlled wisely by her mother all these years. But her mother wasn't with her now... and the fire was going to rage.

Diwa poured the tea into a dainty cup with wrinkled, shaking hands. She missed Zee already; the old woman pretended not to have such feeble emotions but they were in there for the girl. She sat and drank her tea in the small kitchen in the ancient cottage. The old woman loved the vines growing in and around her walls, the roots breaking through in some areas around the roof and along the shelves and walls of the dwelling. She had told this tree all her secrets, and it knew her better than any soul ever had. When she died, she wanted to be buried with her tree so she could always be a part of it.

Sipping her tea until the cup was empty, she looked down into it to see the message of the leaves from her brew. 'Yes, that will work, that will be good,' she said aloud to the tree. She placed her cup on top of the box, but it would have to wait till she returned. The blast in the village had shaken quite a few things into motion. The old woman had not expected such occurrences to happen so soon, but then timing was a fickle thing. She rose from her chair and shuffled out of the kitchen, using the giant pillar of the trunk for support as she rounded the corner into her small sitting room. She needed to rest in front of the fire in her worn old chair.

'Yes, yes, I'll wash the cup out later,' she said before she nodded off. The cup remained on top of the wooden box where Diwa had set it down, the leaves left in the cup still clinging together in the shape of a bird with its wings outstretched.

The Hospital

Thorta, Sovereign City

Brightness burned Zemira's eyes as she tried to open them, but they felt so heavy and the darkness felt so good, her weary body begged for more of it. Her brain pounded inside her skull, and a moan scratched its way up her dry throat like a glow beetle was stuck inside and trying with all its might to scramble out, scratching like mad. She tried to move to sit up, yet her whole body cried out, sending her pain receptors into overload. She cringed and forced her body to respond anyway, the pain and movement making her head worse.

Zee managed a look around at her surroundings through squinted eyes. She was in a hospital bed, a large window adjacent to her. It showed a blurry grey city below with crumbling moss covering some of the old buildings, dark green and grey vines weaving in and out of the cracks. Then there were newer structures, dark ominous structures that towered up, which were in stark contrast to the sleek, reflective glass windows. The windows of the tall buildings she could see shone with an iridescence that mirrored their surroundings, reflecting them in a dark, distorted way. Where was she? Not in Aylenta, she was quite sure of this.

Zee felt completely lost and so weak. This was nothing like her home or the cities she had once visited in Aylenta when she was very small. All she could do was wait in the bed, probably unable to move even if she wanted to, waiting for someone to come. Yet afraid to call out for fear of the pain it may cause her burning throat, and no doubt her pounding head.

There was a glass with water in it on the steel bench to her right. As she reached for it, cords trailed from her hand with fluids of different colours connected to needles in her skin. Zee reached for the glass, and it slipped from her flimsy grasp. Determined to get some soothing liquid in, she concentrated and tried again. Stilling her blurred vision, she reached for the glass, and as it slid towards her hand, she grasped it. She managed to down some of the contents, savouring the temporary relief of the burning inside her throat. Replacing the cup in its original place on the bench, she proceeded to take in her surroundings in the sterile white room. The room itself was cold and ominous. Zee tried to shake it off and counted the raindrops hitting the huge glass window that looked out onto the city, waiting for someone to appear. The raindrops slowed, then caught up with others, coming faster before finally making it to the bottom.

She was so tired, and everything ached. Zee tried not to dwell on the panic starting to creep up on her. She remembered the blast. But what had happened? Was her mother alright? Wolf? Diwa? Pax? Was the village gone? Where was she? She wouldn't allow herself to think the worst. Was her whole life gone in a heartbeat? Everyone, everything totally wiped away? No, there had to be a reasonable explanation for this. Maybe she had imagined the blast. She could have had some kind of blackout episode, from some underlying illness or something, and her mother had had to bring her to this place for treatment. 'Stop it, Zee, stop.' She calmed herself. 'There's no use working yourself up until you get the facts.'

As she watched more raindrops blurring together and the threatening grey city behind the window, someone entered and came to stand beside her bed. 'Hello, miss. Finally decided to grace us with your presence, have you?'

The woman had a beaming smile, rosy cheeks and brown hair tied back in a high bun streaked with a little silver. A croak was all that scraped out of Zee's throat as she tried to reply.

'Shh, shh now, young'un. Don't push yourself. You've suffered severe burns and smoke inhalation, and your throat may need more time to heal, love. Are you in pain?' she questioned, concerned.

Zee nodded her head, and it blasted with pain in response. She squeezed her eyes tightly at the sudden increase in pressure.

'Lay back, love, and try not to move too much. You have been through a lot. I'm going to up yer pain relief. But don't worry, I'll be here when ye wake up. I'm Jill Bloomfield, your nurse. You are in Thorta, in case you were wonderin'. In the sovereign city's hospital,' Jill informed her.

'Thorta?' Zee thought groggily, without bothering to try her throat again. That was all she grasped of what Jill had said as the drugs flowed through her veins, numbing the pain and sweeping her away into the darkness once more. As the darkness closed in around her, in her mind she saw a black bird with large wings descending on her, and she could hear herself screaming... someone screaming... to run...

It had been a week since Zee had awoken in a hospital bed in another territory, a foreign place, and her life had changed forever. Worse than the ache of grief was the guilt. Why had this happened? Where was her mother? Diwa? Wolf? She couldn't let the thoughts creep in, not now. It wouldn't help her situation as she had to be strong. The tears were stinging her eyes as she held them in, her throat feeling tight with the effort.

She had been told that the special Thorta fleet had been alerted to the blast through sensors installed in the town's vision centre. Every town had one, no matter how small. Everyone affected by the blast in her village, seemingly only children and teenagers, were in the children's ward in the hospital. No one had seen their parents and didn't know who had survived or who hadn't. There were so many questions that weren't being answered. The hospital staff had said that all patients would get told the situation once their tests had all come back. They also needed to be sufficiently healed, as the doctors and nurses didn't want to add any additional stress on them.

Rubbish. Something was wrong. Zee knew that Paxton was here too. He had found her room five days ago, searching for her in the ward when he had also awoken, throat swollen, eyes bleary and burns on his body. She knew Pax would be here any minute. He usually visited the same time every day since she had awoken. They were only allowed to roam free at certain times; the rules were very strict, and they had been told it was to optimise their healing. All patients affected by the blast in Aylenta were told to sleep and rest as much as possible. Zemira was finally feeling better. Her throat and face were healing, she could talk again and was grateful for Pax's company and a familiar face from home.

She didn't have any friends, couldn't really have any friends, as her mother had always stressed the importance and safety of not getting too close to anyone. Zee didn't agree, but as always, didn't want to upset her mother – so no matter how much it upset her, she deigned to be a loner.

But Pax had always been kind to her growing up, not like the other children in the village. Zemira and Pax had met one day at school, before her mother had deemed it not safe and pulled her out, just before she had turned ten years. Before this had happened, however, one of the boys in her year had been relentless in his bullying. Lawrence Shorecast. He had hated her fiercely ever since she had bested him in a silly sports race. Lawrence was the best at everything to do with sports in the small school until Zemira came along. She felt his jealousy simmer every time she was around. Or at least she guessed it was why he had taken a pleasure in bullying her.

His bullying got even worse after his parents attended the sports carnival and witnessed him being bested by her. She had told her mother all about him, and Verena hadn't even taken Zee's side, which just made her stress more.

'Stay away from him, Zemira. Maybe back off a little, let him win some. Don't get too close to anyone, honey, or they will notice your "differences",' her mother had said.

As always, Zee tried to be good and listen to her mother even though it made her feel small inside. She stayed away from the others, and they made little to no effort to get to know her either. 'Try-hard,' they would say behind her back.

Lawrence in particular would taunt and push her when no one was looking, and he even delighted in throwing the odd rock or two her way when he got the chance, always smashing her in the back of the head, back or legs – of course when no one was around to see. Zee tried to ignore the boy so he would lose interest and stop. Until one day she couldn't hold her temper any longer.

She couldn't get away from Lawrence after school fast enough this time. Her legs were aching from the previous day spent hunting in the forest far from her mother's cottage. She and Wolf had ventured far to the edge of the black forest near the Rim, searching for forest fouls. Her legs were weary and aching. The birds she had caught with her bow and arrow were worth it though. Her mother had roasted one for dinner that night, and Zee could remember the spices she had used, the smell filling her mind for a second. It was a short reprieve from the hospital's antiseptic tang. Zee was always amazed at what her mother could do with the meagre spices and herbs they were able to procure. A dull ache crept into her stomach. Her mother. Was she hurt? Dead? Would she ever see her again? The tears threatened again behind Zee's stinging eyes. But the memory continued on.

Lawrence had tripped her from behind as she ran. She fell hard on her face, smashing into the rough gravel path behind the old school house. She had tried and tried to ignore him just as her mother had said. 'Don't draw attention to yourself, Zee. We can't afford to be found, not here.'

Her mother's fears were always present, almost like she was paranoid that someone was after them. Verena was afraid that people would find out Zee was different and would ostracise her. She was always protecting Zee from something. 'This is it, darling, this is home, and we have to protect it. I won't let anything happen to you, I promise,' her mother had claimed.

But as Zemira lifted her bleeding face off the ground, tears streamed out and stung the cuts. Lawrence grabbed her by the hair and pulled her head up. 'What's the matter, little roach? Sad you don't have any friends? No one likes you here, you don't belong, you should just leave. Just like your dad probably did. He left because he couldn't stand to be around you. You're a little roach that should be squashed.'

His smirk grew as more tears fell. 'It's true, isn't it? I bet your mother can't even stand to look at you... that's why—'

Zee couldn't take it anymore, and she didn't care if she was seen. At that moment something inside her snapped, and she couldn't control it. Anger took over, consuming her small body, warming her insides. She twisted around and reached up, grabbing Lawrence by his throat and standing to look him face to face. Emerald flames flicked behind her eyes, and she squeezed her hand tighter. Lawrence started to panic, wriggling his scrawny frame about in a vain attempt to free himself from her grip. With her other hand, index finger outstretched, she motioned in small circles towards the muddy puddle on the ground. The brown water obeyed her command and rose into the air in elegant spirals, stopping before his widening eyes. He let out a muffled shriek of horror as she drove the muddy water straight up his nose, her nails digging into his neck to hold him still. His face was now slick with sweat, and he was spluttering muddy water out of his mouth.

She leaned in close and whispered into his ear, 'You ever touch me, speak to me or so much as look in my direction ever again... next time, it'll be down your throat.' Her face was like stone.

'Hey,' yelled out someone from the far end of the track that started at the entrance from the old school building. As quickly as she turned, she released her grip on Lawrence's throat, and he dropped to the ground like a heavy sack of grain. Spluttering and coughing out the dirty water, sheer terror in his eyes. He had actually wet himself. She gave him a sweet smile, the flames in her eyes extinguishing with a blink. Lawrence scuttled backwards on the ground like a crab before getting up and running away, tears staining his pale cheeks.

Zee turned and walked towards the boy at the end of the track who was jogging over to her. There was concern in his voice. 'Hey, are you alright? Your face is bleeding,' he said. 'I'm Paxton. But you can call me Pax. You want me to walk you home? You know, just in case he comes back?'

Zee produced a small smile at the offer and wiped the tears, blood and dirt from her face with the back of her hand. Pax watched, concern still on his face. 'I'll walk with you. I don't mind at all.'

'Um... nah, it's okay, he won't follow. But thanks,' replied Zee.

Pax looked over to where the boy had been, but there was no sign of him. She was about to protest but again stole a look at Pax. He was actually genuine; he had meant it. She grabbed her school bag that she had dropped as Lawrence had tripped her, then outstretched a bloody palm. 'Thanks, Pax. I'm Zemira. You can call me Zee.'

'Nice to meet you, Zee.' He grasped her small hand gently. They started up the track leading out of the village and onto the trail to her mother's small cottage on the side of the hill near the edge of the forest.

After she had left school, they had stayed friends and grown up together. Pax coming to the forest to hunt with her, explore and spend time within the safety of the giant trees. They had been the closest of friends for years now. She couldn't imagine her life without him. But Zee remembered the day they had met; how he had nearly witnessed her secret. He thought he had saved her. Little did he know. But he had cared enough to walk her home.

42

Time to Leave

The hospital facility was strange, sterile and cold, and Zee hated it. But Paxton was also stuck here and so were other teenagers from her village all around the same age. She had suffered burns down her neck and arm, and on the left side of her face. She was told they would take months to heal properly and disappear with treatment. But the pain was finally starting to disappear and the headaches were also easing. She hardened her features to show none of the underlying sorrow that beckoned to break out. She wasn't a child anymore, and she was sick of being treated like one in this place.

The nurses, including the only nice one, Jill Bloomfield, weren't giving her or anyone else any answers. They just kept saying to wait, concentrate on their healing and they would find out soon. Doctor Greymouth, the paediatric physician, was even worse. He barely spoke at all while taking blood, checking temperatures and checking pupils with a bright light. Zee felt like some monitored science experiment when he was around, not a human being in a hospital. Greymouth was always rapidly scribbling away in his note book, doing tests that Zee thought were redundant. The hospital was starting to suffocate her. She detested everyone except Pax and Jill.

Thorta was starting to wear away at her, and she had never been so miserable. The incessant rain was depressing her further. Sleep would have been a welcome distraction to pass the boredom, but the new nightmares that were there waiting every time she closed her eyes weren't an option either. She missed her mother dearly, but more so Wolf. Was he injured? How she hoped with all her heart that he was still alive. Would he come looking for her? He would be so lost here, and how would he even find her in this place? Or would he think she had abandoned him? No, her Wolf would know better than that, if he were still alive.

Zemira was so focused on the raindrops racing each other down the hospital window she didn't hear the door open. Pax slid silently into the room, whipped the privacy curtain back from her bed and roared, 'ZEE!' He then burst into laughter at her reaction.

'Farrr out!' she cursed him, placing a hand hard on her chest. Her heart skipped a beat and raced around in her chest. That awful all-too familiar feeling of panic overcame her. Her blood quickened as it coursed through her veins, and the pressure inside her head increased suddenly like someone was squeezing her temples with a vice. At the same time, the glass on the bedside table next to her spun along the smooth metal bench, fell to the floor and smashed into pieces.

'Got you that good, hey?' teased Pax. The smirk was plastered all over his face. The smug satisfaction of catching her, the silent hunter of the forest, off guard.

Zemira's scowl made her dark emerald eyes glow. 'You're a shit, Pax.' She laid a punch into his arm. 'Don't do things like that! It isn't a joke!' she whispered.

'Alright, alright, calm down. I'll clean it up before Jill comes for lunch rounds.' Rubbing his arm where she had hit him, he said, 'You're pretty strong for someone's who's supposed to be injured.'

'Yeah, well, you're pretty annoying for someone who's supposed to be injured,' she countered, both of them breaking into laughter.

Pax's infectious laugh warmed her and filled the small room. She didn't know how he was holding together so well. Zee wanted to know how he was doing but she also didn't want to push him. Why was he acting like everything was okay? She could see he was pretending to be cheerful, so was he trying to be positive for her sake? Each day it seemed more and more of the kids from the village were getting discharged, but no one was explaining anything to Zee and Pax. It didn't feel right; it was all too strange and secretive. She knew that they needed to get out of here, and soon.

'You're late today, so no cards, and get going while I clean the mess you've made!' she grumbled.

'I got caught up when I overheard some of the wardies talking,' Pax informed her. 'Besides... I made! You're the one who can all of a sudden smash innocent objects. Not me.'

'Shhh,' she warned. 'Not so loud! Jill will be here any minute, and you need to be back in your ward for lunch call.'

'Okay, Okay, I'll catch you in the morning then. And hopefully I find out something useful tonight.' He winked at her then slipped away behind the curtain near her bed to get back to his own room before one of the nurses arrived to escort him back. There were so many rules in this place, specific times for everything, with none of the freedoms of home.

Zemira let out a sigh, smiled and shook her head. She tenderly got out of bed, her body still a little stiff, to clean up the fractured pieces of glass now smashed on the floor like a booby trap beneath the miserable window. It was always raining in this dammed city. She tried not to think about Pax getting caught snooping tonight. Or what would happen to him if he did. She was unsure of the code in Thorta and the punishments that came with disobeying.

This whole place reeked of something, something off. She also pushed away the fact that Pax had now seen a smidgeon of the power she contained. They had been playing cards in their allocated 'free time' the nurses called it, when a poor bird smashed loudly into the window of her room. It had scared Zee, making her jump. Her heart began to race, and the air in the room around her started to swirl. At the same time, a glass slid from her bedside table and smashed on the ground. Just like today. Pax had made his own conclusions, and his mind had started to race to explanations. Zee just agreed to his conclusion that maybe the blast that brought them to Thorta had been radioactive and somehow altered her, giving her power.

Zee had been too panicked to say otherwise, remembering her mother's warnings to never let anyone see how different she was. She had needed time to think about what to say. How to explain. For now, he could think whatever he liked as long as he kept his mouth shut. She retrieved the pan and broom from beneath her bed and started to sweep up the pieces so no one could question her about a third glass broken this week. The old fear tingled in her veins. Truth be told, Zemira didn't know where her abilities had come from. She just knew she could manipulate water and air, the elements of her environment, moving them, using them somehow. As she got older, she felt more and more connected to the world around her.

She wasn't quite sure how old she was when they had started, or how, but as she grew up, she knew they were becoming stronger. The connections were growing, and she could actually feel the environment around her. When she smelled the air, she could feel how much moisture was in the earth. When she felt the temperature of water, she could sense the sun's rays charging it with energy – the same energy that also charged her when she sat still and breathed the rays in. Zee didn't know how to use these abilities or 'powers' properly, or what she was really capable of, or why she had them in the first place. She just knew she had to hide them.

Her mother had told her so a million times or more over the years. So Zee had never been able to trust anyone with the exception of Diwa and Wolf. Wolf because, well, he was a wolf and couldn't tell anyone. And Diwa, well, Diwa was something else completely. For some reason now though, it had become a daily struggle to control her powers. Maybe it was her weak state, or the head-fuzzing drugs she had been given since she had arrived? Zee wasn't sure, but she certainly didn't like it. Diwa would know what to do, she always did. It seemed she always had the answers to everything. And if her mother was gone...? Just thinking about it made Zee's chest feel tight and her breaths harder to take. Forcing the tears not to swell and overflow down her cheeks hurt the back of her throat. She tried to ignore that anxious, sick feeling deep in her stomach, uncomfortable like prickly caterpillars roiling around in a ball.

Picking away at her nails also wasn't helping. Her puffy eyes from the night before had told her she'd been crying in her sleep. Again. She felt so lost. And her poor mother would be absolutely melting down about this whole thing, that is, if she were still there to melt down about it. Surely everything would be alright though. Her mother had always been there for her and still would be. Zee had to leave this place, and soon. She would find a way home. Maybe there were some people left. Maybe, just maybe, her mother, Wolf and Diwa were still alive and searching for her.

The Scar

Zemira sat up in her bed, her bandages finally removed minutes before by Jill. It was afternoon now and still raining. The little gasp of shock Jill had released had said enough. Zemira knew half her face was probably badly scarred.

'A little bit of coverall on your brow, and no one will be the wiser, love,' Jill comforted. 'Very unusual though, dear. I-I've never seen anything like it.' She shook her head with a look of dismay but then smiled at Zee before waddling off to do her rounds.

Zee refused to look in the mirror just yet. What did she care about a scar. She sat and chewed her fingernail, when Pax appeared with a deck of cards in his hands.

'I thought I wasn't seeing you till tomorrow,' she said, anxious about what his reaction would be to her face.

Pax sat opposite her, dealing the cards, and had said nothing. That was all she needed to know - it must be bad. She tried not to be vain. *Just imagine the worst so when you see it you won't be upset.*

Pax's burns were contained to his chest, not his handsome face. If he couldn't even joke about her face – it must be bad. She refused to sulk. What do looks matter when she didn't even know if her mother were alive?

Taking a deep breath, she looked at the cards in her hand she had just been dealt. Pax would win, just as he always did. Zee had not gotten the idea of this game, even though it had been a week of playing. She was still no better than the day he had taught her. Truth be told, she couldn't even remember the game's name, that's how much it interested her. She stared out the window at the glowing lights while Pax took his turn. Outside was always lit. Like people here were afraid of the dark. She longed for home and the dark nights lit only by the glow beetles. How she missed collecting them in jars on warm nights and lighting the small cottage with their yellow-green glow.

Pax startled her daydream trail. 'The other night I was doing my usual rounds,' he said, staring only at the cards in his hand. Pax liked to sneak around at night in the late hours listening to any conversations he could find and checking to see who the other patients were. 'And I overheard them talking about Casey. He was transported to another facility or something, in Zenya!'

'Casey? Casey Shorecast?' Zee inquired, slightly panicked.

'Yeah, I guess, as there's no other Casey in our village.'

Casey was the butcher's son and Lawrence's older brother. Casey had always treated her strangely. Never cruel like Lawrence, but more suspicious of her. She had been afraid Lawrence would tell someone about the day she couldn't hold her temper and almost drowned him with filthy puddle water. But would anyone believe him? Casey made her wary though, and she had avoided him as much as possible.

'But Zenya? That's in Kymera. Why would they be moving any of us to Zenya? And not home? I don't like this, Zee, not one bit. Something's up, and I don't want to stick around to find out.'

'What else did you hear?' she pressed, her head had started to ache, getting the better of her again.

'Well, I asked Sam the cleaner about it, who works on this ward. And he said he'd never heard of anyone called Casey and didn't know what I was talking about. I've seen him coming out of the same room Casey was in. He lied to me.'

'I don't like the sound of any of this, Pax.' Zemira's anxiety about where they were and the real reason they were there made her momentarily forget about her damaged face.

'Look, we need to bust out of this nuthouse,' Pax whispered with a sense of urgency. 'Stop taking those pills they're giving you.

'What? Why? Which ones?' she stammered.

'All of them! I'm convinced there's something going on here, and that there's nothing wrong with us. They're keeping us here for ulterior motives.'

'But where are we going to go?' Zee was frightened but also elated at the thought of getting out of this place.

'You leave that to me, Zee, just be ready. Tonight, we go.'

'Tonight! Are you mad?' She didn't know how they would pull that off.

'You want to stay here and let them keep poisoning you? What about when they find out you can move stuff without touching it? Come on, Zee, you can't tell me the medicines are making you feel better? And where have all the others from our village been going? They still haven't told us anything at all. This is wrong, and you know it.'

'Okay, I know. You're right... but... if we're caught—'

'We won't be.' Pax cut her off.

She wanted so badly to trust him, to tell him. He'd already seen a tiny outburst of her power, and it hadn't bothered him at all. Maybe he wouldn't mind. Would he call her a freak? A mutant? These thoughts were enough to keep her silent.

'Just be ready tonight and don't take those pills. Stay awake and pretend you're sleeping. Ten minutes after first-round checks, meet me at the end of the hall to the left of J ward.'

'Alright,' she agreed. 'But how are we going to escape from here?' Her voice was the lowest of whispers.

'Just trust me. I've got to head back to my room. Be ready later.'

Zee gave an almost imperceptible nod.

'Oh and Zee, your face looks nice, ah, I mean fine. Good as ever.' He winked as he hopped off the bed, leaving the unplayed cards of their game in front of her as he left.

He had a winning hand again! By the Mother she hated bloody card games! She wiggled out from under the blankets, careful not to knock them all on the floor and cautiously walked over to the small mirror above the sink on the wall adjacent to her bed. Taking a deep breath, Zee peered into the mirror. She was utterly stunned at the reflection before her. She looked... she looked fine.

The melted and charred skin she expected that came along with being a burn victim were nowhere to be seen. Instead, there was a small, intricate black mark near her brow, like black vines creeping out from her hairline trying to reach her eye. The rest of her light-brown skin, like the earth of her forest tracks back home, was unmarred. Her face was slimmer, slightly darker around the eyes. But her eyes were brighter than they had been when she had awoken here, and the dark emerald forest shades of her home shone within. 'I'm going home,' she whispered to her reflection. A small smile in the sunken face answered back with glowing eyes. 'And I'll make sure nothing gets in our way.'

Paxton Raker left Zee's room in the hospital in Thorta, thinking about the burns near her eye. How on earth had they scarred like that? He didn't think they were ugly, just unusual, but then he didn't think anything about Zemira Creedence was ugly at all. He felt better than he had in days. He had stopped taking anything and everything they tried to give him. But Pax was unsure why he was still here and not already shipped home or to some orphanage in Thorta or something. He would surely flee and find his way home if it were the latter, but not without Zee.

They were in this together, and he had to look after her. Pax could feel a pull to her somewhere deep down. He didn't know how or why, but he wanted to be around her. The others from the village had all been discharged... or so he had been told. It was just Zee and himself left. He felt he was constantly being watched, monitored. And Zemira making things move, actually move, without a touch – he was sure it had something to do with all this. He had remained as calm as he could the first time he had seen her smash a glass when a poor bird had flown into the large window next to her bed, when they had sat cross legged playing cards on her bed. She had jumped in fright, and the glass had shot off the bedside table, smashing onto the floor. Her monitors had gone crazy, and a beeping started on one of the machines, alerting a nurse to come and check on them both. Maybe her heart rate went too high or something to alert the machines?

Neither of them was sure, but Zee hadn't tried to make excuses or given Pax a reason as to why it happened. He presumed she had no idea what to say, and was just as shocked as he was. Pax had jumped up and swept the glass under the bed with his slippers, quickly resuming his spot on the bed before the nurse could arrive and become suspicious for whatever reason. It had been Jill, thankfully, the only warm person who seemed to work in this whole hospital. She had just checked Zee's lines and monitors, then quickly turned off the beeping machine before anyone else could be alerted.

'Confounded things,' she had mused, 'always malfunctioning over nothing.'

The pair were glad she hadn't mentioned this to Dr Greymouth. Zee loathed Greymouth as he made her skin crawl, and she had correctly guessed Pax wasn't a fan either.

He was still replaying the memory, about to round the corner to his room, when he heard whispering voices in the next corridor. Pax stopped before the pair spotted him and listened as best he could without blowing his cover. It sounded like Jill.

'It's not right! These kids have been through enough, and I can't do this anymore. I have to say something, do something!'

'You can't, Jill.' The other voice was deeply male. 'You say anything, and you will disappear. And you know it. There's nothing to be done, no one will believe you... and what's worse, you know what they will do to you: put you in the radiation fields!' The gruff voice was filled with concern.

'I just can't live with what they're doing to those kids. What are they even looking for? There's nothing wrong with any of them! No mutations, no side effects, just scars and pain.'

The deeper voice answered with a sadder tone this time. 'It's not fair, Jilly, I know but... they're coming to get the last two in the morning, then all this is out of your hands.'

'I just hope... I don't know, I just wish I could do more,' she sniffled.

'You have, Jilly. You have been nice to all those kids since the day they got 'ere,' reassured the deeper voice. 'You've been kind to those kids and have made them feel as safe here as you could. There's nothing more to be done, and you know it. They'll be gone soon, and we can forget about this whole mess.'

Pax could hear footsteps walking down the hall from which he had just come. He was trapped. Did he dare stumble into Jill and the stranger? Would they know he'd been eavesdropping on their whispered conversation? He decided he would take his chance with Jill. She was now his best bet for getting out of here.

He casually rounded the corner before he could get caught by the oncoming footsteps. 'Hey, Jill,' he said.

She was a little startled but when she registered it was Paxton, it was replaced with a warm smile. 'Pax, what are you up to? Heading back to your room after winning again?'

'You know it,' he said with a grin. He didn't know the man she was talking to. The guy had a dark, bearded face with just a few stray greys streaking through. Small blue eyes but friendly, and underneath a healthy suntan and weathered skin. He almost reminded Pax of someone from home. Aylenta, where the sun was always at its strongest, not like this rainy city. He had not seen the sun once since he had awoken.

Just before Jill went to say something and possibly introduce the two, Dr Greymouth stalked around the corner from where Pax had seconds ago been spying from. The three were all quiet, and Jill's face went a little pale. The doctor approached, his beady dark eyes clear and focused behind the round glasses he wore. His pale skin and grey hair shone in the hallway fluorescence, giving him a ghoulish appearance. The whole temperature in the corridor seemed to drop a few degrees.

Greymouth was a tall and a slender man, middle-aged Pax guessed, who towered over people. His face looked like someone had sucked all the fat out of it leaving only the bags under his eyes, the skin drooping a little. His forehead was creased in a perpetual frown.

'Nurse Bloomfield, what is our patient doing out of bed when it is nearly time for your rounds?' His voice was crisp and clinical. He eyed the dark, bearded man Jill had been talking to. 'And visiting hours are over for the day.'

'Y... yes, Doctor,' Jill stammered. 'Come on, Paxton. I'll bring you back to your room before I start my rounds.'

Greymouth looked down through his glasses at Pax, his lips thinning. 'I'll see you in the morning with the last of your results, Mr Raker, and hopefully it will mean a discharge for you. You are looking rather well.'

Pax replied with a façade of happy ignorance. 'Feel great, doc, and can't wait to be on my way home, see what's left and all, you know.'

'Indeed,' replied Greymouth with a slight nod.

'Alright, off we trot, come on, Pax,' Jill said, resting her hand on his shoulder and turning him away from the overbearing doctor, almost protectively. 'I'll see you after work, Warwick.' She smiled at the bearded man and left down the hall with Pax, leaving Greymouth and Warwick alone.

'He gives me the creeps, Jill,' Pax admitted when they were far away down the next corridor and out of earshot.

The colour had now returned to Jill's face. 'Me too, love,' she revealed.

'Who's Warwick? I've never seen him here before,' Pax asked.

'Oh, he's just an old friend, dear. Warwick's a sailor, well, he's the captain of his own boat.' A proud smile bloomed. 'He transports between here and Aylenta, and all around the circle to the three territories. He's a well-trusted man, sometimes transporting very precious items. Warwick calls in to stay while he has time in Thorta, but I don't see him often as he's always away working. The man would be a fish if it were his choice, I swear. He loves the sea more than anything,' she explained with fondness, then added, 'He leaves tomorrow actually with a full shipment from the blue docks at 6 a.m. sharp. He's always on time and he'll be in Aylenta's west docks within a couple of days, the weather considering.'

Pax's mind started working overtime.

Alright, love, I'll leave you here as I have a lot of rounds to do, and I don't want to run into old grey again.' She winked, leaving Pax at the door to his room.

'Thank you, Jill,' he said more seriously than usual, looking into her warm brown eyes.

'You're welcome, dear, most welcome.'

She hurried of to the nurses' station to get ready for the dinner-time rounds, leaving Pax alone. He was ready and couldn't wait to get away from this place. He would miss Jill but that was all he would miss. He imagined the sun shining on his skin, warming his core, the sun from home. *If I had to be here any longer, I think I'd start growing mould,* he thought to himself, scowling as he looked out the window at the rain. A storm was beginning to dull the bright lights of the city, all blurring into blobs stuck in the darkness.

The Forest Queen

Lamiria

Wolf streaked through the Black Forest into the smog without stopping, past the visual border and through the translucent wall of the Rim. Into no-man's land, or the 'radiation fields' as the humans all believed was past the edge. He travelled through a boggy swamp, filled with mist and creatures that lurked to defend the edge. But Wolf was a warrior, so he was not afraid of the creatures here. Brothers, sisters – monsters – but kin alike. Wet, and drenched in mud and muck, his pelt was soaked from the swamp and rain. He paused to rest but once. Days passed as he neared his destination. How he longed for his young hunter and hoped she had somehow survived whatever had happened when the strange blast had travelled along the land. He had to get to Kyeitha, the Queen of the Forest, had to beg for permission to shift... to find Zemira.

Wolf would inform the rim guardian of the explosion. If the humans had reinvented weapons... if they were planning something... well, that would not bode well for them. If a war was brewing, Kyeitha must know and send watchers to find out. She must stop them before more destruction of this manner occurred.

He panted, his weary legs aching, the pads on his paws ripped and bleeding. But he didn't slow. He reached the valley in the midst of two giant mountain ranges – a narrow pass between the two. The only safe pass. Ferns coated the walls either side of the track, with moss rolled out like a carpet comforting his aching paws and leading the way through the eerie alley of rock and vegetation. The gates to Lamiria. Wolf slowed his pace. He felt the eyes watching him through the trees from above as he passed through, but proceeded on slowly all the same.

Wolf, the warrior, was still allowed here as it was his land too. If not exactly welcome, then tolerated. Kyeitha would listen to him, have to hear him speak. It was his right. For the hunter he knew and loved was not a creature of death and destruction as he had been told since her birth. No, she was kind, loving, powerful and never took more than she needed. He must find her, protect her. He padded through on the narrow mossy path. No one stopped him. No creature appeared. He knew he was safe to proceed and would soon be at his destination. Wolf would tell the forest queen of what he had witnessed and plead to investigate. He hoped *only* pleading would be necessary. But there was always a price to pay if you asked a favour of Mother Nature's Queen of the Forest. This he knew only too well. For she was the guardian of all things, and not easily persuaded. Balance above all was important to her, and he would use this to his advantage the best way he could.

He silently passed through the narrow valley and into the queen's land on the other side. When exiting the mountains, he found himself in a small clearing where the sun shone and life flittered all around him. Flowers bloomed, their scents intoxicating, and little forest wisps circled around him, their tiny wings fluttering and making a soft hum. Creatures of all kinds filled the clearing before him. It had been years since he had been in the queen's land, since he was banished, punished for a crime he couldn't help but commit. The years had not dulled the memory of Lamiria's brilliance. Everything glowed with a luminescent sheen, each flower and vine more beautiful than the last. He proceeded on his journey and would be there, soon.

Wolf just prayed she would be in a favourable mood. And his hunter... his aching legs picked up speed again. She was strong... she would be alright... as long as *he* didn't find her first. *He* had been searching for her, all this time, searching for Wolf's little hunter. Wolf was sure *he* was behind the blast; deep down Wolf just knew somehow.

Fury quickened his pace again. It was all *his* fault; he couldn't just let sleeping dogs lie. Wolf knew that the bastard was trying to unearth her any way he could, so he could use her powers, use her to do the one thing he couldn't: Break a curse that had nothing to do with Zemira. A curse that if broken would break more than just that.

Whiskey & Rain

Thorta, Sovereign City

Zemira lay still in the hospital bed feigning sleep, her heart already racing. She wasn't sure if she was scared as such or just excited about leaving. Letting her mind momentarily drift, she could smell Diwa's fresh cinnamon cakes, the crisp air of her forest and the sun warming her skin. Home. She just prayed Diwa was still there. Zee tried not to think about her mother, not now. The pair's escape would need concentration, not emotional distractions. She knew she could easily manipulate their escape from the hospital by moving the security cameras, but then what?

Pax had assured her he had a plan, but how could he know anyone or anything about this place, this city, this territory? It was nothing like home, and he had never even left their village until now. She could feel he wanted to protect her, and it made her feel safer, but Zee hadn't let him know that she was going to be the one protecting and looking after him once they got out of this place. Sure, he would slow her down, but she didn't want to be alone.

Loneliness was a vicious creature sliding in to take away the best parts of a person if they let it. She knew. Had witnessed it gnawing away at her mother for years after Zee's father had disappeared. Zee had scarce few memories of him – large, strong hands picking her up when she fell as a small child; a hearty, loud laugh; silvery white hair and not much else. She was four when he had gone missing. While Zee knew she would be fine on her own, she had realised she just simply didn't want to be.

The young hunter had started feeling much better in the last few days, so maybe this was something to look forward to. Maybe it was the thought of home, and that she had also now stopped taking any medication she was given. Zee was sure she could live with Diwa and have her forest and her old life back, no matter how badly the village had been destroyed or what was left of it. The village had never really been her home anyway. She didn't need it or any of the people who had lived in it, except for Pax.

The clock on the wall above the sink in her room was nearly at ten. She waited, growing more excited if not a little bit anxious. She was glad Pax had thought it was his idea to leave, not realising she had planned to get away anyway. Zee had played her part to see how committed he was to the both of them leaving together. It was a worrying feeling, but she was beginning to truly trust him... trust she had never given anyone bar her mother and Diwa, of course. Zee heard footsteps approaching her room and kept as still as she could, keeping her breathing even. The nurse came into her room, gave her a quick look-over and headed out again, with no monitors or IV lines to check. They had all been removed from her and the room days ago.

Slipping out of the bed, Zee wished she had better clothing to wear other than the hospital-supplied pyjamas. But she had nothing when she woke up here, and her dirty clothing that must have been hanging off her in shreds was obviously incinerated or binned. She padded down the corridors, turning the cameras away from her with her mind as she made her way to Pax's room.

'Pax,' she whispered.

He opened his eyes and sat straight up. 'What are you doing? I said I would come to you!'

'Yeah, and you probably would have alerted everyone in the place that you were up and wondering around.'

'What?'

'The cameras, Pax. I've taken care of them. It doesn't have to be such a stealth mission now.'

'Aww, I spent ages timing them all, so you could have told me that sooner!'

'Nah,' she said. 'Kept you busy. You ready? We just can't run into anyone on the way out, that's all.'

'What?' He looked puzzled and then recognition crossed his features. 'When we get home I want you to show me what you can really do.'

'Oh,' she said shyly. 'I haven't um... I ...'

'It's alright, Zee. I won't push you. It's not the time or the place right now, let's just get going.'

She was grateful for his understanding but he deserved an explanation sooner rather than later. The pair slipped out of Pax's room and headed for the stairs rather than the large silver box that was the lift to all the unknown levels of the enormous hospital. They didn't want to risk getting caught in there with no escape. Silently, the pair crept through the empty halls of their ward. Pax watched as the cameras slowly but surely all turned out of their line of sight as they passed, then afterwards slowly moved back into place.

'That's impressive, Zee.'

'You just wait,' she replied with a whisper, a little cockier now and enjoying the praise. Her pulse quickened, vibrating through her veins, and her chest felt open and light. No one had ever witnessed her using her abilities other than her mother, and she was never awed or impressed. Paxton seemed genuinely amazed. She had always carefully hidden any use of her powers over the years of their friendship, where they mostly hunted and explored in the Black Forest. It wasn't that she didn't trust Paxton, but she often felt a heavy weight in her chest when she thought about telling him. Her mother's voice would always intrude, warning her not to, and her guilt would make her obey. Sometimes after Pax would leave and head home into the village, she would sit alone in the forest, hug her legs to her chest with Wolf at her side and just try to breathe her surrounds in deeply, with her eyes shut tight. This was her way of feeling the forest around her and grounding herself before heading back to her own cottage and her mother.

Pax and Zee made it to the ground level and lingered in the stairwell. The front doors of the building were in sight but there was a night guard and a nurse at the reception desk mulling over some charts.

'What now? I didn't know there would be a guard!'

'Shit, neither did I,' Pax replied hoarsely. 'What about another way out through the kitchen or something?'

'Okay, I think that's a safer bet. I could get us out the front but not without a scene they would surely remember. And we can't get through unless the guard unlocks the door. I don't want to give them any reason to be looking for us after we're gone.'

'Good call,' agreed Pax.

They headed back up the stairwell to the floor above and down another set of shorter, more-twisted stairs past the empty cafeteria to the hospital's kitchens. There was one emergency door but it was triggered with an alarm.

'No way,' Pax huffed angrily. 'What now?'

Just as they were about to come up with another plan, a light flicked on and there was a figure standing in the door of the kitchen.

Zee quickly swiped her right hand through the air in front of herself and then in front of Paxton, causing the air to shimmer as she drew a finger to her lips and eyed Pax. Just in time for the person to look directly at them without even seeing they were there.

Pax looked a little shocked to see Jill looking straight past them, as if they were not there, but kept quiet as Zee had indicated. It dawned on Pax that Jill couldn't see them at all, and while he kept his amazement in check, it was written all over his face.

'Zee? Pax?' Jill whispered.

Was it a trick? No, Pax had too much trust in the woman, so he stepped forward and out of the thin shield before Zee could stop him.

'Oh, Pax,' Jill said, relieved. Then she did a doubletake as the two suddenly appeared in front of her. 'What are you two up to?' she asked, eyeing Zee.

'We're leaving,' said Pax. 'We want to go home, not wherever everyone else has gone from the village. We are not ending up there as well.'

'Oh... I know, I know... but what are you going to do? Wander the streets? Come on, come with me. My shift's over, and I'm going home. I just went to check on you both before I finished for the night, but you weren't there, and I guessed as much. You're lucky I found you and not anyone else. Can you do whatever it is you just did and follow me as I leave through the front door without being seen?

'Yes,' replied Zee, suspicious of Jill's calm reaction.

'Okay, that's good...' she trailed off more to herself then to them, and didn't look the least bit shocked at all at seeing them suddenly materialise in front of her, or the fact that Zee had made them invisible.

'Come on now, and once we get into the rain, we have to take the east train. My apartment isn't in the best part of the city; it's quite a hike but at least you'll be safe and dry for the night.' Jill didn't wait for a reply, just started off in the direction of the main entrance doors, maybe before she panicked and changed her mind.

Zee once again shielded the pair. They both looked at each other and said nothing, obviously agreeing it was their best bet as they couldn't get the guard to unlock the front doors without Jill. And the alarmed kitchen door was also a bust. She wrapped her arm through Pax's, and he looked down at her through sparkling dark amber eyes.

'Just a precaution, in case you get too far from me and some of you isn't shielded,' she whispered directly into his ear.

He didn't reply, the smug smile on his face saying enough now that he understood, while very much enjoying their closeness.

'Oh, grow up.' She poked her tongue in his direction.

They silently trailed behind Jill and past the reception desk as she signed out for the night. The guard checked her ID before nodding her forward and unlocking the main entrance. Jill raised the umbrella she had pulled from her oversized handbag and stepped off the curb and into the rain. She then turned left down the street towards the train station, not waiting for anyone who may or may not be following.

The pair followed a short distance behind. Unfortunately, Zee's shield wasn't quite as good as she had hoped, with two people to protect, and some of the heavy rain was making its way through. The icy drops soaked Pax and Zee's heads, and dripped down into their thin pyjamas. Pax said nothing as they trailed the nurse down the street, the trio all tense as they approached the station.

Zee was getting tired. She could feel the adrenaline wearing off, as it seemed they were in the clear, and her shield was beginning to waver. They followed Jill onto a streamlined-looking train, Zee's arm still wrapped around Pax. He was steadying her as she walked, and his body warmth was comforting. Though the pair said nothing the entire trip, they could see Jill looking around as if trying to spot them, the worry and panic clearly written all over her face. What was she so afraid of anyway? A couple of potential orphans from Aylenta leave a hospital? So what? Who would care? They weren't even from this territory. Who would even notice?

The pair stood still holding onto each other for support, swaying with the train's movements. The carriage was almost empty, possibly because of the time of night – not many people would be ending their shifts now, or travelling at this time. There was a man at the end of their cart with a weary face staring straight ahead and an old woman with a large flower-covered hat on, her head bent backwards on the seat, mouth slightly ajar and snoring. They felt pretty safe shielded in a barely occupied train carriage.

The news feed on the screen just below the carriage ceiling played on a constant reel. Zee had not seen any screens or heard any news while in the hospital, and it was so strange that they were absent from the building. She was surprised at seeing so many on a train but guessed it normal for this territory. Thorta had the technology that Aylenta lacked.

A pretty blonde news reporter was speaking, her voice a soothing tone. 'The tragic blast that had been caused by the unearthing of an ancient explosive pre-Oxygen War has caused the catastrophic loss of an entire village on the far-east of Aylenta, a small border town called Kali near the Rim. The only survivors from the village were air-flown here by Thorta's elite army, from the generosity of the sovereign city. They have all died in the ICU of Thorta's Capital Hospital. The bomb has thought to have caused a deadly chemical reaction and is being monitored and cleaned as we speak, the residual effects being to blame for the survivors' terminal conditions. Such a sad loss for Aylenta and all three territories alike. Not such a tragedy has been felt since the early days of inside the Rim.'

The solemn face of the young news reporter lingered a little longer on the screen before being replaced by clips of a village completely burned to the ground. Everything was blackened, with soldiers in biohazard suits clearing away debris and possibly charred remains through the smoke emanating from the ground. The images cut off, and the young news reader returned to other news. Mostly that trading agreements with Zenya to cultivate its own

69

crops into Aylenta had been approved as these two nations peace-fully worked together after such a monumental tragedy...'

'Holy... shit...' Pax whispered, turning to Zee to see her reaction. She paled and felt grateful there were empty seats behind them. She pulled Pax's arm so he could sit down closer to her. Saying nothing, the pair sat in silence digesting the vivid images of their decimated home and that fact that they too were presumably dead...

As the train glided into the last station, Jill hopped up fast. 'Come along,' she said quietly, looking straight ahead. She popped her umbrella open again and exited the train.

By now, Zee was feeling well and truly drained, the shield shimmering around them beginning to waver. They were both freezing and soaked to the bone, and her legs were like jelly after processing the news feed they had just witnessed on the vision screen.

Pax slid an arm around her to hold her steady, and she didn't reject it, needing the stability. He was like a strong tree to lean against. They round a darkened corner, and Jill fumbled in her bag for some keys. 'Nearly there,' she said aloud as if she was talking to herself.

Just as they stepped into the small entranceway of the old paint-peeling building, Zee's legs gave way and the shield vanished. Thankful Pax's strong arms stopped her from collapsing complete-ly, he half dragged her along bedside him.

'Jill, how much further?' he questioned, his voiced strained.

'Just up here, dear, last door behind the staircase.' She unlocked her apartment door, and a warm, gentle light filtered out into the hallway. She ushered Pax and a weary Zee inside before shutting the door. Several locking mechanisms could be heard sliding into place then Jill turned to face the two with a worried frown. Pax helped Zee onto a worn couch and wrapped her in a nearby blan-ket.

Jill let out an exasperated sound that echoed the stress she felt. 'Let's get you both out of those soaked clothes, and then we can all have a cup of warm tea.' She tried to hold it together after looking over at the dishevelled pair, their worried, heartbroken faces staring back at her. She shook her head and said, 'Oh stuff it! I think we all need a bloody whiskey instead!' and rushed off into her small dwelling to retrieve the dry clothes and whiskey.

Zemira and Paxton sat on the old, lumpy lounge dressed in numerous odd pieces of clothing that were all too large and smelled of musty glow beetles. As they clutched the old mugs full of warm whiskey, a hairy blanket covered the two and wrapped around their shoulders. The sharp unpleasant taste of the whiskey had made Zee nearly wretch, but the warm and relaxing after-effect was worth the bite. She had finally stopped shaking. Pax felt the same about the whiskey, and he made a face behind Jill's back on taking his first sip, making Zee want to giggle despite their horrible situation.

Jill Bloomfield returned to her small sitting room in the dilapidated old building with her own very full cup of the hearty brew. Opposite the two, she plopped her large self into an old armchair of woven brown materials, un-weaving in places, hands a little shaky as she took a long mouthful. 'Well, dears, where should we start?' Her voice was just as shaky as her hands.

Zee jumped the gun. 'The news reader, Jill. Is... is it true? Is everyone dead? Why did they say there were no survivors?'

Pax spoke after her. 'How Zee can do that stuff? Why aren't you more shocked? She literally made us disappear! Did you know? Are they going to come looking for us? What did you mean when you said, 'Oh, it's you,' back at the hospital? Is that place even a hospital?'

Zee cut him off. 'Why did they say it was an old-world explosion? Where did all the others from our village go from the hospital? Did they take them to Kymera? Why did they take them to Kymera? And where is everyone else? All the adults?'

'Okay, Okay! Calm down, loves! Take another sip and speak one at a time!' Jill protested.

'Jill,' said Zee, staring her right in the eyes. 'Just tell us everything. Please.'

Jill wiggled a bit in her seat, making the whole armchair move with her, and stared into the contents of her brown mug. 'I started working at the facility three years ago. I didn't know what they were looking for... or why all the patients were roughly the same ages. The first year, they were fifteen years old, the year after that sixteen, and now you lot – eighteen years old... and all from Aylenta. I'm just a nurse, but I treated most of them for burns. Some of the kids had amnesia, minor cuts and smoke inhalation from similar blasts like the one that happened in Kali, your village, nothing too serious. No parents were ever there, and after treatment they were shipped off to Kymera. I'm so ashamed of myself but I didn't 'ave much of a choice! They said that if I wanted to leave or spoke to anyone about the facility, they would ground Warwick's boat, take it away and send us both to the Rim's edge to shovel radiation waste.'

The tears streamed down Jill's face as she continued. Her chest was heaving as she thought of Warwick losing his boat. The sea was his life. If it weren't for Jill being such a coward, she would have told him how she really felt about him years ago, and they could have sailed off together, away from this depressing life altogether. Her cheeks bloomed red and her heart thundered in her chest at the thought.

'So I stayed and looked after them kids the best I could until, until they were moved on. I don't know where they were taking 'em, just that it was somewhere in Kymera, and not back to their homes... I don't know why but all I know is that they were lookin'

72

for someone, someone that reacted differently to the chemicals they were giving you, strange minerals all the way from the mines in Kymera.'

'I knew that stuff was poison!' exclaimed Pax.

'I'm so sorry.' Jill was now blubbering, and black mascara smeared down her cheeks.

Just then the door made a numerous amount of clicks and burst open, making all three jump. A large dark man filled the entire doorway, with a dark silver-sprinkled beard and small mistflower eyes. His eyes searched for the two on the couch and then moved to Jill's wet face, his own face contorting into a scowl. He made a deep growl as he entered the small apartment and shut the door firmly behind him.

As he passed through the sitting room, now made even smaller with his presence, and proceeded into the small kitchen to pour himself a cup of whiskey, he rubbed his forehead with his thumb and forefinger. They came to rest together on the bridge of his nose, and he seemed to decide against a cup and just grabbed the whole bottle, taking a long swig. He seized an old timber chair from under the tiny kitchen bench and brought it with him into the sitting room, plonking it down backwards and taking a seat. There he sat with his arms the size of tree trunks crossed over the back of the chair with the bottle still in his hand. Zee spotted a black mark on his right hand clutching the bottle... a tattoo of a black bird, wings outstretched. Her dream flashed before her eyes, and she remembered a voice telling her to run.

All three stared at him, waiting for him to speak. He eyed them all before taking another swig and assessing the situation. 'So I guess that you decided against staying out of it, Jilly, and as for you two...' His low voice grumbled like the thunder circling outside. 'You must be the brightest eighteen year old's I've ever met.'

Pax let out an unsteady breath, clearly relieved that Warwick must be on their side and wasn't going to alert the Sovereign guard.

Zee was still unsure of the situation and sat on the edge of the seat ready to bolt if need be.

'Oh, Warwick, honey, I'm so sorry but I just, I just couldn't have left 'em there.' She cried louder, her guilt overcoming her.

Warwick dragged his small timber chair over to her and leaned in, wrapping his giant arms around to comfort her, making her nearly disappear from view. 'Now, enough of that, love, it's alright. I had a feeling this may have happened one of these days, so I've got a plan. You need to gather your things. We're all leaving. And we have to go soon. They will be looking for you three. And by my guesses, they won't stop till they have you.'

He turned now to Pax and Zee. 'Which one of you is it?'

Pax and Zee looked at each other, not wanting to divulge anything to the burly stranger.

'Hmm,' he grumbled, 'doesn't matter to me. If you're important to Jilly, you're important to me. You've got two choices: stay here and let the Sovereign guard find you and deliver you to him, or leave now with me and Jilly. We'll sail you to Aylenta where Kymera hasn't yet dug its dirty claws in. You'll be safe there. I have a place on the coast, and after we arrive, you can be on your way.'

'Who is him?' asked Zemira, thoroughly confused.

Warwick looked over while helping Jill up, eyes like stone. 'The king,' he growled. 'The darned King of Kymera. He will be after you now. He's been searching a long time. You've got five minutes.' That was all he said, then trailed off down the hallway, helping Jill to her room, presumably to pack a bag.

Zee and Pax looked at each other, eyes wide. A loud crack of lightning made them jump simultaneously.

'The king! Zee, this is getting serious. Is that why those other kids were being shipped off to Kymera? Zee, he must be looking for you, your powers or mutation or magic or whatever it is!' Pax exclaimed.

'This is too much! How could he even know!' blurted Zee. 'But I think we can trust Jill and Warwick. Somehow I can feel that they really want to help, and besides, what other choice do we have? We clearly have no idea what's going on, especially why the king would want to find me. And there are no other options to get out of this damn city. Jill helped us escape that facility, and she knows what is going on, so they'll be after her too. We need her, and we need answers. Besides, if we want to bail, you can swim, right?' Zee flashed Paz a grin, breaking the tension, followed by a slightly unhinged-sounding laugh.

'No more of that for you! It's making you unreasonably calm and slightly loopy. This is serious!' Pax took the cup of whiskey out of Zee's hand and replaced it with his empty one. 'Go with the flow. Sure, we've got this. I mean, you now have magic powers, and I don't, but sure,' he said more to himself than to Zee. 'We'll be right. Have you ever been on a boat before?'

'Nope,' she replied. 'Have you?'

Pax shook his head.

'Oh, well, how bad could it be?'

Xavier Greymouth

Thorta, Sovereign City

Doctor Xavier Greymouth stalked down the halls of the Sovereign city research facility that he had worked within for the previous four years of his life. If only the simple fools at Cerberus Research Station could see him now. He had wasted half his life working in their research facility as a biochemical scientist, studying the radiation wastes and how they'd compounded hundreds of years after the Oxygen War. What they would do upon being administered to test subjects (mostly small animals) and how to reverse, if possible, their potency on human life.

As he strode down the halls of the immaculate, sterile white facility, his face glowed under the florescent lights. Years of studying and being contained to lab research gave his skin a pale, ghostly (some would say ghastly) glow. He still remembered when the king's guard had invited him to be head scientist and work on a new, secretive assignment. His sunken chest swelled at the thought, his head raising slightly with a small, proud smile on his stern face.

I, Xavier Greymouth, was chosen, not those other simpering fools. They are likely still working away back there, scratching their ignorant heads without me. Well, let them suffer. I work for the king now. I have my own facility. My own team that works under me. I'm in charge. They laughed every time I mentioned the possibility of other life forms, mutated, more advanced than us. Well, who's laughing now? We've found one. We've found her, we finally found the child we'd been searching for, for well over three years. How the king knew of the unnatural phenomenon, he still didn't know, but at least he wasn't alone in knowing the world was changing. He wasn't a lunatic.

The first project he had started for the king had been a success. The blasts that contained borenium and a cocktail of harsh but not deadly other chemicals were to render entire villages unconscious in a ten-kilometre radius, but mostly unharmed. This had been the triumph of his career. Except for the minor inconveniences of a few burns here and there, a dash of amnesia, disorientation, smoke and chemical inhalation. Oh, these were just minor and didn't dampen his success at finding a way to seize the children of Aylenta to test for abnormalities.

His heart sped up a little, and his clasped hands behind his back begged to fiddle as he reached the office that contained his private lab. He slid the card from his breast pocket and swiped over the door's locks. A green light flickered and mechanisms clicked before the door opened. He replaced the card, lifted his head high and entered his lab. This was the real research facility that he deserved, not like the shared mess back at Cerberus. The thought of the look on those faces when they heard of his success. That they had once laughed at the great Professor Greymouth. He may forgive a small few, maybe even offer them a pittance to come work for him again. Under him.

Greymouth folded his tall, gaunt frame into the familiar chair and slid to his station. Vials upon vials of coloured liquids were present in long glass tubes. Samples of children's bloods for testing, some he had already tested other things on. Like the effects of too much borenium in the blood system. Borenium mixed with other compounds injected into the nervous system. Oh, the children had suffered, but that was just another minor inconvenience. They were only dirty, poor little farm children from that wild territory across the way. The research he was doing was far more important than any one life.

He would be heralded as the greatest scientist of the age of the Rim! A chuckle left his mouth, accompanied with a breath of moths and decay as his shoulders lifted again, popping his chest forward. He slid the blood from the girl Zemira Creedence underneath the microscope for what seemed like the hundredth time that day. As his round glasses leaned in close and he peered through the microscope's end, a kaleidoscope of colour and movement filled his vision.

His heart beat faster. Incredible! The blood looked as though there were tiny creatures moving about within it, small snake-shaped ribbons swirling about into each other. No, more vine-like. Spinning and morphing into balls then rolling about as others came into view. By the Gods, he had done it! He had found the truth! There were others out there. Other types of beings that were not human.

A rapping came at his lab door. He ignored it. How dare he be interrupted. He was finally at a breakthrough! Bang, BANG, BANG.

'Enter,' the yell burst forth from his mouth, dislodging his small round glasses slightly as his body shook. He took a steadying breath in, trying to contain his frustration, and righted them. The door clicked and opened, and the front-door guard of the facility didn't enter but stood at the entrance to Greymouth's eerie lab. 'S-sir,' said Errol Parkins.

Greymouth scowled a little at him and the unwanted interruption. He didn't even turn from his desk to look at the large, plump, balding middle-aged man. 'What is it, Errol? Spit it out.'

'The... the kids, the two kids that were going to Kymera today, sir.'

'What about them, Errol? I haven't got all day. I'm doing important work here.' He cut Errol short with clenched fists upon his work bench.

'They... they're gone, sir.' Errol gulped as he ever-so-slightly stepped back a little from the entrance to the lab.

'Gone...' it came out quietly as though he misunderstood. 'Gone!' then erupted, not so quietly. Greymouth slammed his clenched fists down on the bench, rattling vials of liquid, and stood abruptly, rolling his chair back from underneath him. He came to tower over the top of now-shrinking Errol.

'What do you mean gone!' He was practically frothing at the mouth.

'They... they're not here, sir. We can't find them anywhere,' he stuttered, his neck bending back to look up into Greymouth's narrowed eyes.

'You search this whole place from top to bottom and find them! Or I swear you'll end up in the radiation fields shovelling toxic waste!' he spat into Errol's trembling face.

'Yes, sir. Of course, sir.' He spun and almost jogged off down the hall, his stomach not quite in rhythm with the rest of him.

She'll ruin me! That filthy, feral young woman! Fury reddened his face. I will find you, Zemira Creedence, and when I do there will be no comportment left in me. You ruin this for me, you cur, and you will regret it. Greymouth spun on his heel, fists and teeth clenched with such force as his reddened face broadened to beetroot. He marched off down the sterile hall. Off to inform the king.

Winifred 5

Thorta, Sovereign City

The huge metal triangular hulk rocked precariously side to side in the dark water. And it was indeed, to Zemira's disappointment, Warwick's boat. Zee had never seen such a menacing-looking thing. The large chunks of metal were roughly welded together like a giant patchwork of recycled parts from other dead ships – and they had to travel inside of it! The rain was heavier than before, and lighting flashed all around. Zee was too tired to use any shield of sorts to keep the pair dry, but Jill had given them both umbrellas and over-sized jackets. Jill had stopped crying but was still in a sorry state, and Pax, well, he was very on edge and sticking closely to Zee's side.

'Come on, you three,' bellowed Warwick over the pounding rain. 'Time to get on board ol' Winny.' He motioned to a tiny metal ramp attached to the side of the metal beast, bobbing to and fro with every wave coming over the edges of the dock.

Zee smelled the fresh rain around her mixed with the salty waves, feeling out this new environment and trying to connect with her surroundings. This was a very different world from her tranquil forest and still river back home. She eyed Old Winny to get a sense of the floating mass before boarding it. Spying the front side of the very old-looking metal bucket, she just made out the name Winifred 5 smeared in very messy writing with white paint dripping down from the letters like smeared bird droppings. *Winifred 5?* Zee thought. *What had happened to Winifreds 1 to 4?* She carefully followed behind Jill, trying to be sure-footed and not slip on the soaked, swaying ramp. Pax followed closely behind. Presuming Jill had been on the boat before and had obviously survived, this was going to be fine, just fine.

Warwick showed Jill, Pax and Zee to the cabin inside the front of the boat. It smelled of rotting seaweed, and a thin layer of some kind of fuzzy mould coated the roof and some of the walls. Items were strewn all over the place, some lying in a thin layer of water covering the floor.

'Aye, she's not much, but she keeps afloat. And that's all that matters.' He grinned for what Zee thought was the first time ever, eyes sparkling like little blue gems. 'Anyway, less leaks than Winny 4!'

Oh Mother, what had they gotten themselves into. Zee and Pax locked eyes with a reassuring 'This is going to be okay' look.

'Alright, ladies, you stay down 'ere. Laddie, you're with me.' Warwick slapped a dinner plate-sized hand down on Paxton's shoulder, steering him out into the storm and onto the deck of Winifred 5. Soon after, they left Thorta behind and sailed into the rough waters of the Alvion Sea.

'Um, are they going to be safe out there?' Zee questioned Jill.

'Oh, I hope so, love. I've never been on a boat before. What about you?'

Zee paled a little. 'No, but I thought you had.'

'Oh, no, I've never left the sovereign city, so I guess this would be kind of exciting under different circumstances.' Jill giggled nervously as she looked around the cabin. 'Mother's love! Look at the state of this place!' she exclaimed as if just realising the pit they were standing in. 'Warwick,' she tisked, and immediately started to pick up items while she swayed around within the small space.

Zee found a dry-ish seat and rooted herself there. She was starting to feel ill. 'Jill, I need you to tell me about the hospital facility, or whatever it is. Why were we there? And why on Mother's earth is the King of Kymera looking for us?' Zee asked.

'I don't think he's looking for Paxton, dear. I think he was looking for you. I don't know very much, but I know for a fact those blasts that have been affecting your villages back home. They... they weren't real. Well, they were real, but not from old radiation weapons. They were from some new technology and chemicals cooked up in Kymera to stage explosions, an excuse for the sovereign guard to come in and take 'survivors' and treat them here in Thorta. I think it was the only way the king could enter Aylenta untraced and without breaching the peace treaties. He has sunken his teeth into Thorta, and he controls almost everything from the government officials to the trading with Aylenta. It's not safe anywhere, love. I'm so sorry.'

Zee visibly blanched.

'I don't know why he was searching for you, but I do know he knows that you are... different... in that you can do things. That's what the tests at the facilities were for. Your blood is so different, like nothing I've ever seen, and the medications they made me give you, they affected you the most. Made you fuzzy, weakened your control. I knew you would be different but I never guessed you'd have actual powers,' Jill explained, not able to look Zemira in the eye.

'Great. So some king a million miles away is after me for some unknown reason, and somehow knows I can... manipulate things around me. And he has complete control over Kymera's and Thorta's armies...' Zee trailed off, making the water on the floor start to sizzle.

Jill jumped at the sight.

'Sorry, Jill. I have less control when I'm stressed.' She took a deep breath in, and the water stopped bubbling and continued to slop around side to side on the floor.

Jill waddled over to the flat, cushioned seat against the wall and plonked herself down next to Zee. Her large thigh rested up against Zee's leg, squashing her a little but also comforting her with the warmth. 'Look, love, everything will be okay. I didn't know when we would find you. I knew you'd be different but I didn't know you'd be... extraordinary. The few things I've seen you do... the glasses, the shield, the bubbling water on the floor. And the way you somehow made your scar shift and change into something beautiful. You're amazing, Zemira. And I'm a fool for not helping you sooner.' The tears threatened again. 'I'm just so scared, as they have so much control now... everywhere.'

'Don't fret, Jill. And thank you for helping us. Seriously, you're the best,' Zee comforted.

Jill leaned in and squeezed Zee into her large breasts, giving her a long, warm hug. Zee wanted to resist but didn't want to hurt Jill's feelings. She had had enough of watching the woman cry, so she hugged her back. It almost made her feel as though she were hugging her mother, or Diwa, or even Wolf. It reminded her of home.

Jill released her. 'Oh, I almost forgot.' she hopped up and went to the other side of the cabin where Warwick had put her bags. Rummaging through them, she found what she was looking for and headed back over to Zee just as a huge wave swayed the boat, nearly making her stumble into the seat. 'Ooh, it's getting rough out there!' Jill said, paling a little. 'I managed to save these for you when you came in. It's not much, but I thought they were important.'

Jill handed Zee a small cloth-wrapped parcel. She unwrapped her favourite knife and Diwa's necklace. This time it was Jill's turn for a hug. 'Jill, thank you, thank you! You are the best! They are important. A dear friend gave me both of them. Would you mind tying this up for me?' Zee held up the woven necklace with the dark-blue stone encased.

'Of course, love,' Jill replied, a warm smile on her weary face.

Zee spun back around after Jill had sufficiently tied the necklace on for her despite the rocking of the cabin. 'How's it look?'

Jill eyes widened as she stared at the necklace, now glowing a very luminous bright blue... just as a massive thunk hit the side of Winifred 5's hull, sending them both flying onto the slimy floor of the dank cabin.

Jill and Zee slid on the slick floor and crashed into the bench seat on the other side with a crunch. Zee felt her ribs sting and the wind knocked out of her lungs. 'Jill, are you alright?' she wheezed, crunched over and squeezing her tender side.

'I'm alright,' she said, sounding a bit wobbly. 'Lucky I've got a bit more paddin' than you, love.'

'I'm going to go up and check on Pax and Warwick. Stay here, Jill, and hang onto something.' Zee righted herself, the blue glow of her necklace dying down. She gripped the wet railing and headed up the stairs, swaying with each step. She reached the deck of the rocking metal vessel and searched for Paxton. The rain was spraying into her face like little needles and stinging her eyes, the lightning still zinging intermittently overhead. Zee made it to the back of the boat where Pax and Warwick were peering over the side at something.

'What's going on?' she yelled over the deafening rain.

'There's something trying to get at me Winny!' bellowed Warwick. 'Not today, you won't,' he yelled as he spun the boat in the opposite direction away from where he and Paxton had just been looking.

Pax made it over to Zee, grabbing hold of her arms to steady himself. 'There's something down there,' he said, wide-eyed and close to her face. 'Something big and—'

Just then, Zee's necklace lit up brighter than before. The stone glowed brightly enough for Zee to see a large blackish tentacle sliding onto the side of the boat behind her in the reflection of Paxton's widened eyes.

She spun around and grabbed Paxton's arm tight to balance herself on the wobbling metal deck. The slick black tentacles shone in the eerie blue glow of Zee's stone as they slid closer, becoming larger and larger.

'Do something!' yelled Pax to Zee.

'Like what!' She froze, her brain all fuzzy. The rain, the swaying of the boat, the information Jill had just given her all swirling around in her head, clouding her concentration. All while some giant tentacled creature slowly inched itself towards them, no doubt with food on its mind. Diwa's gift, her necklace, couldn't be a coincidence. Its glow had to be a sign; it had to mean something. If only she could focus – everything was flying around her mind like beetles in a cyclone.

'Zap it or something!' Pax insisted.

'If I zap it, I zap us all!' she screamed back, soaked to the bone from the water crashing over the sides of the boat. Channelling the lightning, yes, that would definitely fry them all.

Another large, slick black tentacle followed another and another, sliding onto the boat and making it tip to one side. Poor Winifred 5 was creaking and screeching her protests. Warwick was in the background clutching the helm and yelling something unintelligible into the storm. Pax and Zee slid on the angled deck towards the edge, their boots connecting with the side of the boat and just stopping them in time before going over the side. In the midst of all the tentacles, a large spider-like face with a gaping maw filled with razor-sharp teeth and fifty or so shiny black eyes popped its massive head up over the edge to stare very closely into theirs. It was so close that the smell of rotten flesh wafted onto them even over the pounding rain.

Zee's insides did a flip. She had seen things before in the forest, but none so closely and so terrifyingly real. The creature's massive head connected to a crab-like body with sharp spindly legs underneath the tentacled forebody. The creature seemed to focus closely on Zee's face, and she could swear all the beady, bulbous eyes focused on the blue glow of her necklace.

A tentacle slid forth, reaching for Zee's hair. It coiled around a dangling strand and sliced it off with one of the sharp pincers protruding from beneath its mouth. Zee held her breath, watching in horror. Within seconds, the beast recoiled, and all the dark, slippery tentacles withdrew from the deck, the large face disappearing from where it had come. The boat somewhat righted itself as they felt the creature detach. Still swaying and smashing around in the waves, Winifred 5 groaned with relief. Zee and Pax, both equally horrified, scrambled to get away from the edge and back to the helm that Warwick was still fortunately attached to.

'What was that thing!' Pax yelled to Warwick as they both reached him, grasping tightly on to the rusty railings surrounding the steering mechanism.

'A vipen!' roared Warwick. 'How did you get rid of it, girl?' He turned to Zee.

'I–I didn't,' she stammered. 'I didn't know what to do... I couldn't think straight,' she confessed.

A large wave sent the boat rolling as all three gripped on tightly. 'It's alright, love. 'Orrible things! Lots of beady, little black eyes, big crab legs and pincers and tentacles... lots of tentacles. They are hungry things, and sometimes latch onto the side of a boat without you even knowing, just waiting for someone to peer over the edge. I've heard rumours though – the king uses 'em for tracking ships. The first time seeing one of 'em is sure to melt your innards a bit!'

'But we've got to get rid of it! It'll be back. I can help!' yelled Zee over the deafening surroundings, slightly more confident than she felt. 'Tell me what to do.'

'You've got to take its eyes out, lass. My last crew and Winny 4, bless them all, were taken by a ruddy vipen bastard. This time, it was just seeing how many of us were aboard! But if they can't see, they're next to useless.'

A massive shudder vibrated through the metal bow of the boat, shaking everyone's balance even more, accompanied with a giant bang. A second later, a bloodcurdling scream could be heard coming from below that even the storm couldn't drown out.

'Jill!' Zee put two and two together. The vipen must have somehow made it into the cabin! She grabbed Pax's arm, dragging him with her as the pair tried to run across the deck to the cabin as fast as the waves would allow. Zee half-jumped, half-slid down the steep stairs into the boat's belly. Pax was right on her heels. The vipen's crab-like legs had penetrated the side of the boat straight into the cabin, forcing it open like a can of sardines. Zee took a look around and saw Jill clinging for dear life to the opposite side of the cabin, still screaming hysterically.

The screeching of metal and moaning of the hull grew louder as the creature parted the metal and started to slide its black snake-like tentacles in through the gaping hole. Zee turned to Pax. 'I need something, something small and sharp! I can take its eyes out but I need something to pierce them with!'

The two started searching frantically through items on a small desk and through the things lying on the ground in the now ankle-deep water. Pax desperately shuffled his hands around in the murky water on his knees, trying to bring anything useful to the surface. They found a few pens, some socks and an old communication talker. Nothing of much use.

'I could use the pens but there's not enough!' yelled Zee. More and more of the vipen started to appear, filling the cabin. The black tentacles were getting closer, all the while Jill's screams filled the air. Just as the massive beast poked two more of its spindly legs through, covered in sharp spines, its head appeared, eyes staring directly at Jill as it squeezed itself in through the hole.

'I've got it,' yelled Pax, ripping a soggy cardboard box open. More than 100 or so small screws now filled his cupped palms.

'Perfect!' Zee tried to steady herself and bring calm to her overwhelmed brain. She smelled the creature's rotten breath growing stronger, intoxicating the small space. Zee focused on the many black eyes, now focused directly on Jill. A tentacle wrapped around her ankle, pulling Jill's body closer to its numerous dripping teeth. Zee raised both her hands, elevating not just some but all of the screws in Paxton's hands into the air, rotating them all the same way. The air in the cabin started to swirl, her necklace filling the whole space with its luminescent glow. The creature wasn't stopping; it was prying Jill off the pole she had clung to so well up until now.

Just then Warwick burst down the stairs, causing Zee to lose focus, so all the screws landed with a splash on the cabin floor. 'Jilly!' he bellowed, the horror on his face plain to see.

Zee, knowing she had but mere seconds to save the nurse's life, raised her hands again, the swirling air whipping her hair around. It blew from behind her, taking all the floating screws with it, Zee's hands directing them where to go. They shot straight at the gruesome beast's face. Hundreds of tiny, sharp metal spears connected with the beady eyes, bursting them all on impact, like rotting fruit spraying the cabin with jets of black liquid.

The vipen screeched an agonising and ear-piercing sound, its head jerking back into its body. Releasing its hold on Jill's ankle, the legs and tentacles recoiled, sliding back through the hole in the hull, black liquid smears left in its wake. Zee was utterly astonished at what she had just accomplished, Pax's face telling her this was also what he must have been thinking. As the blue glow dissipated from his features, it signalled that the necklace was now dull again. It must be a warning system for danger.

Warwick rushed to pick Jill up from the now rapidly rising water on the floor. She was shaking and sobbing in his arms. He looked over at Zee and said with admiration, 'Love, whatever you just did was bloomin' amazing! But if you could do somethin' about that giant hole, it would be very much appreciated.'

Zee's legs wobbled, then prickled with static. Her heart was racing inside her chest like she'd just sprinted through the forest with Wolf. 'Pax, any ideas?'

'Warwick, do you have anything to fill the hole with? Metal patches or anything?'

'No, matey, I didn't have time to fully restock before we left the city.'

'Pax looked at Zee. 'You're going to have to try and bend it back together!'

Zee felt a trickle of panic streaming through her. She had never tried to manipulate something so solid before. 'I – I can try...'

The water was rushing in at an alarming rate. She gathered herself then stretched her arms out before her and willed the air around her to keep her upright and mend the metal. The cabin air rushed around in a giant whirlpool of items, water, wind and now a glowing light that streamed from Zee's hands. Her hair whipped her face, now in a grimace trying to control the forces from herself that were swirling around the cabin. The metal started to glow with the same white brilliance, so bright it was burning to look at.

Zee screamed with the effort as she slowly but surely bent the metal back into place, sliding backwards with the force it was taking her to push the water away. The glowing edges of the metal sizzled and joined together, melding into each other. Zee was actually welding the pieces back into each other.

As suddenly as it started, the air stopped swirling, objects started dropping all around and the white glow left her hands. Her body heaving, she panted for more air, dropping to her knees then collapsing into a heap on the ground. She was now lying in the clouded water tinted with black vipen blood on the cabin's floor, the darkness coming in all around her as Paxton reached for her and picked her up off the floor into his arms.

The Fairy-tale

Aylenta

A blurry view of Jill's bouncing behind came into focus as she hummed and cleaned when Zemira slowly opened her eyes, the familiar feeling of a pounding head and achy limbs accompanying it. She lay still on the bunk in the cabin of Winifred 5, feeling warm and dry. Oh, to finally feel dry. She lifted her sore body upright, making her head ring, and noticed that there was only a gentle swaying of the boat.

Looking around, the cabin was somehow homier and very, very clean compared to before. No smell of mould or rotting fish. The vipen. Zee remembered the otherworldly creature, a tingle tickling up her spine and making her cringe. And what she had done to eradicate it from the boat. She had used her powers in front of others. The old, familiar feeling of fear accompanied that thought, but didn't quite stick this time. So what? She'd saved lives – all their lives – and it had felt scary but great.

'Oh, love! You're finally awake!' squealed Jill, plonking her body on top of Zee's blanketed legs, sufficiently crushing them into the thin mattress as she gave her a long, suffocating hug. 'You saved me, Zemira! It was incredible. You're incredible! I've never been so scared before in my whole life. I thought it was the end for sure.' Tears ran down Jill's face again.

Zee shrugged it off. 'I'm just glad you're alive, Jill.' She offered a small smile, trying to ignore the pain the large woman was inflicting on her legs. Zee again looked around the neat, tidy and now-dry cabin, spotting the wall where huge, lumpy lines of metal all clung together like an inverted star. She had done that, actually melted the metal. Feeling a spark of pride and excitement, she wondered what else was she capable of.

Jill finally dislodged herself, wiping her face. 'I hope you don't mind, love, but I cleaned you up a bit and found some other clothes that fitted you a bit better. Some young sailor's outfit, I'm guessing. A baggy white cotton-collared shirt and some black tighter-fitting long pants.'

Zee didn't mind; she was just grateful to be warm and dry.

'You've been out for quite a while, and I was starting to get worried. But you're alright now, thank the Mother. We'll be in Aylenta before the day's out. If you're up to it, Pax is up on deck. He's been so worried about you, sitting with you the past few hours waiting for you to wake up. There's a lot of love for you in that boy's eyes.'

Zee's cheeks reddened. 'He'd just be upset if something happened to me, then he wouldn't have anyone to annoy anymore,' Zee said quietly, ignoring what Jill had said.

'Alright, love, I'll leave you to it.' Jill gave her one last squeeze.

The sun felt like embers of a warm fire shooting and whizzing into her veins as Zee reached the top of the stairs and stepped on to the deck of Winifred 5. She closed her eyes and breathed in deeply, feeling her face warmed and recharged after so long, her skin sucking in every ray. A caved beast waking after a long, cold winter hibernation. It was almost as though the warmth was strengthening her weary body.

'Zee!' Pax rushed over and gave her an unexpected hug. 'You're awake! I mean, I'm glad you're not hurt. How are you feeling? That was one wild night for the first time on a boat, hey! Warwick said he's never seen anything like it. Usually those creatures aren't anywhere in-sea so far from the Rim's edge.'

Pax took a breath. 'You totally saved all our necks, it was incredible.' He smiled, letting her go.

'It's sooo good to see the sun,' she replied, ignoring the praise as she had already had an awkward feeling receiving it from Jill.

'And look.' Pax directed her to the edge of the rough metal deck and pointed out towards what looked like a land mass far off in the distance, beyond the sparkling calm of the flattest water Zee had ever seen. 'It's Aylenta! We're going home, Zee!' he shook her playfully, a massive smile filling his face.

'I've missed that face,' Zee admitted, still a little worn but smiling back at the thought of home.

'Missed yours, too.'

The two soaked up the rays in the sun side by side, staring at the blue expanse of sea and sky. The smell of salt and metal taking on a totally different feel from the first night on the boat, one of promise and hope.

'Who knew being on a boat could be so wonderful?' Pax said.

Zee replied, 'I like you, Winny, but I hope I never have to get on another boat ever again.'

'Hey!' A large tattooed hand cupped Zee's shoulder and spun her around, making her feel miniscule and light. 'What did you say about my Winny?' Warwick's deep voice was filled with warmth for her. He pulled her in close and gave her a big bear hug. Then held her out in front of him at arm's length, both hands consuming her shoulders. 'You, lass, are bloomin' amazing!' he roared, then laughed, a hearty booming sound filling her with more warmth than the sun had moments before.

She could get used to this, maybe, and she loved that her small world was growing, that there were now two more people whose faces filled her with happiness and warmth. Who thought that she was actually amazing. Not a bother or a burden or a threat.

They reached the port of Talay in a small fishing village on Aylenta's shore late afternoon, earlier than expected due to the glass-like water conditions. The sun lit the little village with a gold-en glow, making it more beautiful than Zee had imagined. Warwick docked the boat and showed everyone the way through the cobbled paths lined with stone houses. They trekked to a small home on the edge of town that looked out over a cliff, the sea right below, giving the house a floating feel. A tiny garden in the stone wall ad-jacent to a larger-than-usual wooden door was filled with herbs. Zee imagined them all going well with fish, and memories from her own garden and Diwa's, of course, flooded her mind.

Peeling paint revealed a few different coloured coats from the past, but mostly a rusty orange colour. Zee thought this house suit-ed Warwick perfectly. Two small, mismatched windows full of puzzle-like pieces of coloured glass, mostly blues, greens and browns with a few translucent pieces sprinkled in were placed either side the doorway. The colourful windows were framed with weathered white timber frames. An old chair made from twisted wood sat in the paved space, and a twisted metal hook sprouted out from the wall above, curling upwards like a new fern sprout.

Warwick removed his thick leather hat and hung it from the black hook, in its rightful place, somehow signifying he had come home. Zee assumed even though Warwick must spend a lot of time travelling from territory to territory and all through the Alvion Sea, this must be his secret place of rest away from the world. He fussed with a large key in the larger ornamental brass lock on the door, shaped like a creature Zee had never seen, and opened it to a fair-sized sitting room, ushering them all in.

'It's not much, but it's peaceful and safe,' he said. 'And after a trip through the Widow's Pass like that, I think you all need a restful night.'

Zee took in the medium-sized space with its grey stone walls blending into grey stoned floors. It was slightly larger than the cabin on the boat, and definitely more organised. There was a large lounge chair opposite a blackened metal fireplace, situated almost in the centre of the space but closer to the back stone wall. A large pile of neatly cut wood was stacked high to one side. There was a small table and very simple timber kitchen opposite where they stood in the entrance. The kitchen had another mismatched glass window filled with more whites and blues compared to the front two. And on the wall behind the fireplace were books. Lots of books! All very neatly stacked, almost colour coded in timber squares, attached to the stone wall. Presumably in old stock crates from ships repurposed to house the books instead of supplies. Beautifully twisted pieces of bleached white driftwood sat atop some of the boxes, along with the most unusual shells and objects Zee had even seen.

Jill hung under Warwick's arm as he cuddled her to him, her head reaching just under his chin. 'Warwick, this place is lovely!' she beamed.

'Hmm,' he grumbled a little. 'It's not much, Jilly, but I hope it'll do for your new start, my love. I'm sorry you've had to leave it all behind,' he said unsurely.

'No, it's truly lovely. I think... I think I could be quite happy here.' Jill stared up into Warwick's deep ocean eyes. 'I've left behind nothing that I don't need right here.'

Zee watched the two, so content in each other's company, Warwick reaching down to plant a small kiss on Jill's lips. It made Jill's ruddy cheeks beet red, and her hazelnut eyes sparkled into his.

'Maybe you two were meant to cross our paths,' Warwick stated, breaking his moment with Jill. 'She's been trying to catch me in her net for years!' he laughed.

95

Jill slapped his large, barrelled chest playfully. 'You tell yourself whatever you want, dear,' she retorted.

The two clearly made for each other. Zee and Pax locked eyes with a 'this is awkward' glance, but both joined in with the laughter, the blissful vibes from Jill and Warwick filling the space. All were smiling, all were feeling better than they had in weeks.

After they'd settled in, the fire was lit. It roared inside the central hearth in the small stone house on the hill. Warwick had disappeared off into the golden glow of the afternoon and returned with three shimmering silver fish just as night fell, slightly amused to find Jill had busied herself by making herself quite comfortable in her new environment. She had happily hummed away, exploring the little cupboards of the kitchen, cleaning away dust and cobwebs, unearthing blankets, pillows and rugs for around the fire. Even finding flour and readying damper for supper. Not to mention making Paxton and Zemira numerous cups of unwanted tea. Jill was abuzz with happiness and comfort, whether it was to be out of Thorta's grasp, or just to be off of Winny 5.

Zee had busied herself with handling every book on the stone wall. Inspecting the covers and gazing over the beautiful illustrations. She finally decided on two books, one that contained old stories of how the three territories had come to be and how they had rebuilt after the war of 2032, centuries ago inside the safety of the Rim. The second was a collection of information on rare creatures that had been seen near the Rim's edge, and also the common inhabitants each territory had.

The hunter had started with the creature collection. The vipen still rattled her a little; she could still see its bulbous little eyes exploding all over the cabin on that first terrible night. Paxton had stuck near Zee most of the afternoon until he realised she was content reading and snuggling on the giant-sized couch, being spoilt by Jill with tea and blankets. So he ventured outside and found a chopping block, axe and wood pile out the back of the stone house, just between the house and the towering cliff behind, and proceeded to chop wood for the few hours left of sun.

The four then sat around the table, devouring plates full of delicious, fresh ocean fish, seasoned with a few herbs and salt. Simple but so tasty. Zee couldn't believe how hungry she was. She had seconds and dipped the damper Jill had made in the remnants on her plate. Warwick and Jill now sat side by side on the large lounge chair, with Zee and Pax either side on the stone floor with a mat and large floor pillows beneath them. They had finished the dinner in silence, all enjoying the feeling of fullness while staring into the fire's calming flames.

Jill had cleaned up after everyone, then returned with four mismatched coloured glasses and a bottle of some kind of brew she had found stashed away in the little kitchen. 'Warwick, dear, if it's alright?' she asked with a wide grin.

'Oh, why not! I was saving it for something special, but I think that this is the perfect time. We all deserve to celebrate survival,' he chuckled.

Jill handed him the brown bottle, and he flicked the large corked top out with just his thumb, sending it flying off in the opposite direction. He filled the cups with a generous amount of the mysterious brew. 'Raise your cups, comrades. To Zee!'

'To Zee,' Paxton and Jill replied loudly.

'May a vipen never try his luck again while she's around!' he roared, then took a large swig.

Zee sniffed her cup and took a sip, delighted to find no strong sting to the drink. Just a sweet, buttery flavour with a slight warmth that travelled down into her belly, making her feel light and fuzzy.

'Right, have you heard the tale of the first crossing of the Alvion Sea?' Warwick questioned everyone.

'No,' replied Pax, while Jill and Zee shook their heads.

Warwick proceeded to tell tales by the fire, enjoying the company and the flickering orange glow around the room from the numerous candles Jill had lit around the room as they all listened, laughed and drank. Warwick was a fabulous storyteller, having honed his skill from years at sea. As the night grew to an end and everyone's eyes started to become heavy, Warwick asked if anyone else had any tales of their own to share.

'Ah, my parents didn't really have time to tell me any stories,' said Pax, a little forlorn. He was orphaned when he was very young after his parents died from the silent sickness.

'Jilly?' Warwick nudged her a little with his shoulder.

'No, love. I like listening, not telling.' She smiled back warmly, clearly relaxed and totally happy in the moment.

He turned to Zee perched on her large square floor pillow, holding her cup with two wrapped hands, a blanket draped over her shoulders. She looked very snug in front of the glowing fire.

'I don't really know any stories like yours, Warwick, but I do know a fairy-tale that my mother used to tell me when I was a little girl. Diwa would tell me one too, similar, but in a very different way...' she trailed off when her heart started to ache for these two most important people in her life.

'Alright, lassie,' Warwick encouraged, 'a fairy-tale it will be. Just what we all need for a pleasant night's sleep to keep the nightmares away.'

'Yeah, give it a go, Zee. I didn't get many fairy-tales when I was a kid,' agreed Pax.

Jill just nodded and smiled, tucking her feet in under her body and snuggling into Warwick's shoulder.

'Okay, here goes,' said Zee. She finished the last of the strange drink, placing her cup on the stone floor to the side of her. 'I'll try to tell it like Mum did,' she said, saddening again. She then shrugged off the feeling, not wanting to think about that right now.

'There was once a young king in a frozen land who lived in a magical castle made of ice. He had hair as black as a raven. The king was all alone in his giant castle as his mother and father were both dead. But he was destined to marry a beautiful young woman when she turned eighteen, one his kingdom had chosen for him.

They had already met, and he instantly fell in love with her. She had the most beautiful green eyes he had ever seen, and he felt so happy at the prospect of sharing his once-lonely life with her.

'The young woman lived in a small cottage by herself, all alone as well, with a huge balcony that faced the giant ice castle, so she could always be thinking of her king-to-be. One night, a ferocious storm blew in, and waves of ice and snow blasted through the kingdom. She watched from inside, with no sight of the giant castle, just a blur of white snow. Suddenly, she heard a thud at her balcony doors. When she went to investigate, she saw a huge white snow eagle was caught outside in the blizzard. Immediately, she let the poor creature inside, rescuing it from certain death. It would have frozen in no time for sure.

'The king's maiden saw that the creature had damaged its wing, so she raced to retrieve a blanket to wrap the beautiful bird in. Just as she returned, the eagle transformed into a very handsome man with hair as white as snow and the darkest emerald eyes she had ever seen. Those eyes locked with her own just before he passed out from his injuries. The woman cared for the mysterious shape-shifting man in secret, for she knew the king would be jealous and not allow it. But she was so lonely, and the man would surely die without her help.

'She nursed him back to health, and he often visited after that in secret. They fell in love. The king became suspicious of her, and when they spent time together in the ice castle, he started to became angry with her. The young woman guessed he could tell her interest had wandered somewhere else. As time went on, she became afraid of his temper and no longer wanted to marry him. So the shape-shifter and the king's bride-to-be ran away together just before her eighteenth birthday. They ran far from the ice kingdom. They crossed mountains and rivers and many towns. After a very long time, they decided they were safe and stopped running. The pair found a safe village in the new land and built a house together. They had a beautiful baby girl and lived in a magical forest far away from the evil king and his kingdom of ice. The young couple and their daughter lived happily ever after. The end.'

Zee hadn't realised she had shut her eyes to concentrate on re-membering the story as her mother had told her. When she opened them, she was met with all three staring at her in awe. The whole room was alive with the candles now floating all around them, making the stone house glow magically.

'Ah, sorry,' said Zee. 'I didn't realise I was doing that.' She mo-tioned her hands downwards, and the candles floated down onto a surface, following her command.

'What a great story!' exclaimed Pax. 'Good fairy-tale, Zee.'

'That's not a fairy-tale, love,' countered Jill, sitting up.

'What do you mean?' replied Zee, confused 'My mum said she made it up when I was little to help me sleep?'

'Oh no, dear, that's the tale of the King of Kymera. He said a shape-shifter stole his bride-to-be, and he has been searching for her ever since. She was never found... and he still hasn't married any-one to this day. They say he's quite mad, actually. Hardly ever leaves his palace. Controls his armies from within and has plans to take over all the territories and to—'

'Well, well, Zee. You've given me a run for my talents once again! Time for bed, everyone.' Warwick cut Jill off, locking eyes with hers. 'Jilly's had too much brew by the sounds of it! We'll be off to the bedroom, then you two can fight over who gets the couch or the floor.' Warwick chuckled and helped Jill up, the two swaying together as they walked to the end of the small hallway to the back room of the house.

'What was that all about?' asked Pax, utterly confused.

'I have no idea,' replied Zee, repressing a very odd, cold tingle deep in her stomach. She shrugged it off, the tiredness overcoming her. She rose just as Paxton did, both eyeing the lounge.

'Fight ya for it,' said Pax, and Zee leaped onto the couch crash-ing into him at the same time, spinning her body around past him and burrowing into the back of the lounge, booting Paxton onto the floor with her feet.

'Owwwa!' he moaned, landing on the stone floor and barely missing one of the pillows.

Zee howled with laughter. 'What did you think was going to happen? I always win!'

'Yeah, yeah,' grumbled Pax jokingly in defeat. 'You don't think that's 'cause I let you win?'

'Pffft, you keep thinking that, buddy!' She laughed harder, then raised her hand into the air and pinched her forefinger and thumb slowly together, extinguishing all the candles in the room but leaving the fireplace alone. All without leaving her spot on the lounge.

'That is... so cool,' said Pax, making some sort of bed out of the pillows and blankets on the ground just under the lounge where Zee was resting.

'Night, Pax.'

Paxton kneeled and covered Zee in a blanket, tucking it in all around her and tickling her as he went, focusing especially around the neck.

'Stop, stop' she laughed. 'I'm all weary from saving your arse, remember.'

He leaned down near her face when she had stopped laughing. 'Okay,' he agreed, and looked into her shining emerald eyes, the reflection of the fire flickering within them. 'Night, Zee,' he said, before gently placing a soft kiss on her forehead.

Leaving Lamiria

Kyeitha had given Wolf what he needed, what he wanted. But there was always a price. She wasn't surprised to see him when he arrived filthy and exhausted. No doubt her Shadowrens, large bird-like creatures with the wings of bats and eyes of milky white, or other watchers of the Rim, had already filled her in. He had always assumed when they were around that she could see through their eyes in place of her own; hence, he was always weary of their appearance.

The Queen of the Forest knew about his young hunter, and that she was special. That she had elemental powers. The bargain Kyeitha struck was not fair. Curiously though, he had tried to see through it to the danger that had been twisted within the bargain. He needed to have his full strength to protect them, his hunter and her mother, Verena. He had never felt so much love for two other beings in his entire existence.

When he'd arrived at Lamiria, there was another there, maybe Kyeitha's new right hand. A sentinel in a large black wolf form. He had said nothing, only watched and listened. Probably in the same predicament as Wolf, he had done something to gain this place alongside the Queen of the Forest outside the Rim.

Kyeitha had been furious with Wolf all those years ago. She had come for him after he had disobeyed her, a ruthless force when one of her rules had been broken. But it could have been worse. It also could have been better. After his banishment, he had been free of her for so long... just not in the form he preferred.

Wolf trotted along the path, back through the ethereal valley, the entrance to Lamiria and Kyeitha's temple. He felt a pang of anxiety leaving. Was it a trick? Would he safely be able to pass through the mountainous entrance and head back to the Rim?

When he'd arrived in Lamiria, she had been there waiting for him in her stone fortress. Seated on a giant chair forged out of limestone and coated with moss, glowing fungi and tangled vines, with flowers blooming from the giant headrest. The stone throne was large enough to seat a giant. It was placed in a palace with few walls, just tree trunk-like pillars and a pergola of such, filled with plants and vines. The throne faced a lake-sized pond, filled with every colour of lotus and lily pad blooms. Millowisps danced and floated, playing with glowing orbs of light that shined with a life-giving essence. Some orbs would burst and land on a lily pad or blossom, the rupture causing them to transform into more miraculous rainbow-filled little life forms. Wisps of colour and light trailing behind their tiny floating bodies.

Kyeitha had sat immobile on that throne. Her ethereal beauty still amazed him, the years not dulling it an inch. With earthen hair tipped with golden sunlight, pale skin of a full moon's night and eyes that matched the most miraculous mistflower sky, speckled with flecks of white as if the stars had dared to stay out. Her greeting had set him instantly at unease.

'My dear son,' she had mused, a mulberry lip curling into a sneer. 'Whatever would cause you to drag your sorry carcass back into my temple? You're staining the floor with your filth.' She had the sweetest singsong voice, but her smile was malevolent. She was clearly revelling in the fact he had finally come back to her. Kyeitha had known the day was coming and wasn't going to let him off lightly. Of course he wanted a favour.

As he made his way back to the Rim, Wolf shivered at the thought of the wickedness she buried underneath the sweet and elegant mask. He ruffled his whole body, shaking his fur as if trying to eradicate himself of her presence. As he trotted along, the further away he got from Lamiria the better he felt; she had every inch of this place laced with her magic. Filling even the tiniest of creatures with the beautiful glow of her life force, but also her control.

It had been an enchanting place to grow up in a lifetime ago. But only if you had followed the rules. If only the humans knew what chaos would be in store for them, learning the truth of the world. That there was no radiation smog outside their cage, known only to them as the Rim. Maybe it was better this way. The less they knew, the safer from Kyeitha they were. The blissfulness of ignorance could keep them safe. Let them believe it was their own fault; the punishment had sufficed the last five centuries or so, so why would she change anything now?

Wolf approached the Rim river and stared at the shimmering wall reaching up out of the middle. The bank on the other side was where his young hunter would fish. The creatures kin to him wouldn't bother him on his passage back through, so he leaped from the muddy ridge into the cool dark waters and swam across the deep pass. The river and its depth beneath him still put him on edge, but he wasn't fearful. His brethren would only attack at the scent of a human. He passed through the middle of the river, feeling that familiar zapping tingle through his body upon swimming past the iridescent wall. Reaching the other side of the river, he climbed out, washing most of the muck from his white coat, which was now somewhat clean.

He would return to Diwa's. The old woman would be there, he was sure of it. She always knew what was on the horizon. He'd tell her what he had done, the deal that he had made. Her gifts of foresight were incredible. Diwa would know where Zemira was, and hopefully also her mother. Wolf didn't dwell. He knew that pondering on the unknown would only bring unhappiness. What will be will be.

He set of into the familiar forest, the trees almost creaking a greeting to him, filling his alert ears. He felt more settled than he had in weeks, possibly returning to the world inside the Rim that felt more like his home now. A rabbit darted in front of him further down the track; he ignored it. His destination at the forefront of his mind, another rabbit flittered past, zigzagging a way ahead of him. *Well, it would be rude not to bring Diwa a gift.* Sprinting off into the undergrowth, the small furry creatures had little if no chance at getting away once he had set his sights on them. His speed and accuracy were honed after years in this form. The rabbits were a well-earned distraction from the last couple of weeks. Diwa could wait another few minutes... surely also bringing her dinner would brighten her spirits.

The Woverbine

Aylenta

Warwick had instructed the pair on how to find woverbine transport on the outskirts of Nerissa, just up the cliff and onto the grassy plain that outstretched ahead. He'd given them a large oxel fish each, wrapped in a cloth-like sling so they could carry them around their necks and off to one side. The fish were absolutely huge, and they stank. Fishy ooze dripped down Zemira's pants, nearing her boot. She wasn't bristled by blood or mud or muck, usually being covered in it after hunting all day, or dismantling and processing a kill, but this was just... gross.

'You'll understand when you get there.' Warwick had chuckled at their puzzlement and screwed-up noses. Not giving away any further information and clearly taking pleasure in their complete confusion.

Jill had cried and squeezed them both numerous times into her warm and suffocating hugs. 'If you ever need a thing, you two you know where I'll be.' She had packed them both a damper lunch with a small amount of seaweed cheese that she had gotten from the market that morning, along with some chrysalis berries, small, clear berries that grew along the edges of the cliff near the beach. They were filled with clear, sweet liquid upon crunching into them with a pop. Jill had informed them upon leaving the market that there was news on soldiers invading Aylenta.

Unlike the overwhelming technology in Thorta with vision screens filling every wall, home, building and transport, Aylenta was lacking in this, and there was only a communal vision screen in the heart of each town. This kept anyone informed who wanted to be, but also kept a calm existence and lifestyle that Thorta certainly lacked. But now there had been riots in Ezarah. And all the small Aylentean towns were being invaded and citizens held against their will by the Kymerian guard.

'Stay wary and if you run into any trouble, just use your smarts, love. That shield you can do with the air, I'm sure it will do to keep you safe. Please be careful you two. Kymerians are not a pleasant bunch. And he's out there looking for you,' she had warned with a very worried expression creeping into her joyful face.

'What on the Mother's damned earth do you think these reeking fish are for?' Pax grumbled in disgust as soon as they were on their way and out of earshot of Warwick and Jill. Zee couldn't help herself. She burst out into a laugh at Paxton's disgust of the oxel fish's slime seeping into his side.

'Listen to yourself,' she wheezed, in between laughter. 'Oh, the fish slime is touching me. Oh, its sooo disgusting!'

Paxton's face was clearly not impressed with her mockery, but also happy to see her in such high spirits enough to mock him. He cupped a hand and nearly gagged as he slid it up the fish's enormous scales, gathering some in his palm – almost aborting the act with the absolute vile sensation of it seeping in between his fingers.

But then he slung the handful of putrid smelling slime straight at Zee's face.

She saw this at the last second and countered the slime ball with a blast of air, sending it spraying in every direction back onto Pax, and showering him with it. Zee howled, almost falling to the ground with laughter, trying to suck breaths in.

Pax roared in disgust. 'Zee, you're in for it now!' He launched at her, tackling her into the long grass. But he laughed along with her at the ridiculous situation, digging fingers into her ribs, making her laugh even more. Their laughter finally died down, and Pax helped Zee up off the ground with the enormous weight of the fish slung around her body. At least they were both covered in the smelling slime, now with grass seeds sticking to them all over. Paxton pulled her up, and they came face to face. He looked into her eyes, turquoise flecks standing out in the sun's reflection, mixed in between the sea of emerald.

Zee stared back, her heart starting to race as she thought of the kiss Pax had unexpectedly placed on her forehead the night before. Her pulse quickened, and she became quite uncomfortable being so close to his face. The glow beetles' wings fluttered in her stomach and crept up into her throat as she took in his gorgeous tallowbark eyes flecked with pieces of gold in the sunlight. They matched his thick chestnut hair that filtered the sun shining down on her face. Pax leaned towards her just as a thundering roar pounded the air behind them.

The roar snapped the two out of the moment. Zee spun around as fast as she could with the giant fish's weight still attached to her. A huge, hairy creature stood out on the plain before them, bellowing at the pair. Its massive moscow-shaped head had four large horns, black as onyx, which protruded from its skull outwards, almost like a crown. Its large trunk-like hooves ended in a stump with three toenails, and a large flat tail flopped behind the beast, swaying side to side. Its fur was a multicolour of fire tones, and earth-brown hair dangled half over its face.

The creature had small dark blue eyes, though they didn't seem menacing. It bellowed again towards the pair, making them jump. 'Ah, is that what I think it is...?' asked Pax.

'I've seen this creature in Warwick's book!' replied Zee. 'It's a woverbine... ohh.' Recognition clicked in her brain. 'I think this is what Warwick meant when he said woverbine transport.'

The pair looked at each other with worried faces and then back at the gargantuan beast slowly plodding towards them, bellowing once more.

'What! I thought he meant like a train or a cart or something?' Paxton said, very unsettled.

'Well, it is better than having to risk trusting more people not to turn us in to the soldiers,' said Zee. 'Maybe it's worse than what Jill and Warwick are making out. Look, we know that blast was definitely to do with the king, so what else is he capable of? I definitely don't want to run into any soldiers. I want to get home.'

'I know, I know, me too, but what do we do with this beast?' Pax grumbled.

Zee approached the massive animal, and a thick, swirling blue tongue extended from its mouth, wrapping around Zee's arm and then licking up her entire face, covering her with yet more slime – this time warm slime. Great. The woverbine sniffed with its wet brown nose towards the oxel fish on Zee's side. She unslung the cloth hammocking the fish from over her neck and shoulder, removing it from the material, letting the large, repulsive-smelling fish slide out onto the grass.

'I think this is for you,' she said aloud to the woverbine. The woverbine roared and wrapped its giant tongue around the fish, sucking it up whole. 'Well, that was disgusting,' Zee said.

Pax gagged again.

'Your turn,' she said, coaxing Paxton over.

'How do you know what you're doing? What if that thing decides that we will taste just as good?' questioned Pax.

110

'I can feel it... like how I can feel Wolf. I don't know how to explain it but I can feel that this animal is calm, patient and gentle.'

'Gentle? Did you just see what it did to that fish?' Pax almost squeaked.

'Oh come on, it's no vipen. We'll be fine,' Zee assured. 'What's the worst that can happen? Besides, my necklace has no glow to it whatsoever, so my assumption must be right.'

Pax removed his fish sling and dropped it onto the grass, the fish sliding out towards the giant, woolly beast. The woverbine sucked it up again, just like the first oxel, in one go. And bellowed his thanks in a very ripe-smelling blast of air.

'I guess we get on now,' Zee announced. 'Hey, we're going to try and climb on you now, so please don't eat us, buddy.'

The woverbine in return plodded up beside them, waiting with his side facing them. Zee grabbed onto the dread-woven pieces of fur on the side of his pelt, using them like little vines to scale a steep forest cliff. The animal stayed steady, reassuring Zee that this was indeed what Warwick had intended they do for transport. She only wished he had been a little more explanatory. He was surely having quite a laugh to himself about this by now.

Pax followed uncertainly, but always confident to follow Zee's lead. They sat up on top of the beast and could see out past the grass fields.

'See this isn't so bad!' said Zee, full of confidence again, feeling proud she had somehow figured out what to do. The beast's back was huge. Zee's legs barely reaching the sides as she sat astride him and reached for the black horns stretching out either side of his skull. The woverbine suddenly shot forward, Zee in turn hanging on tightly to the shimmery dark horns while Pax held on to her waist. It was moving at breakneck speed, all four of its feet taking a turn at pounding it forward on the solid ground. The fact that the slow and docile creature was now travelling at a marvelling speed was proof not to judge anything at first glance.

'How does he know where he's going?' Pax yelled.

'Ah...' she faltered. 'I guess we tell him?' Zee leaned forward between the large black horns and yelled out, 'Hey, can you please take us to Kali?'

The pounding woverbine changed course, swinging violently to the right, nearly unseating them, with both sliding close to the edge of the flat of its back.

'I guess that means he understands us?' Zee confirmed.

'Your guess is as good as mine, but seeing you know what Wolf is thinking half the time, I trust your judgement more than mine!'

Zee glowed a little inside. She loved the newfound feeling of Pax's encouragement, and she loved being right. More than that, she loved the air coursing over her body, through her hair and whipping at her face. She felt so free. She almost couldn't wipe the smile off her face as they travelled at what felt like breakneck speed through the grassy plain. She would choose a woverbine over Winifred 5 any day. Pax's closeness didn't feel uncomfortable at all; it felt warm and safe. They were together, and they had each other. Together they could make it through anything – the perfect team. Paxton made her feel whole, and he was almost beginning to feel like home. His warmth made it easier to ignore the constant gnawing in her stomach when her mind drifted to her mother, Diwa and Wolf. She forced herself to breathe, driving the worry to the back of her mind for now and leashing her anxiety the best she could. They would have answers soon.

Atop the woverbine, the pair came to the edge of what Zee guessed was the southern part of the Black Forest near the outskirts of Kali. The creature raced along the edge of the trees, not entering the forest and slowing a little, but still making the land blur by. As they encroached the edge of a hill that stretched into the forest, with large pines covering its expanse, Zee knew exactly where they were. As if on cue, the Woverbine slowed to a trot then a very slow plod, coming to a stop just inside the forest where Zee's house was nestled in the hill another kilometre or so away.

Zee and Pax slid down from the hairy hide, and she felt her legs nearly give way when they hit the ground far below. Her muscles were aching from the ride, legs wobbling slightly. Incredibly, the journey had not even taken a whole day. It was a few hours past midday, but she marvelled to be here so soon. She gave the woverbine a rough scratch on his forehead, the dark blue eyes watching her.

'Thanks, buddy, you're amazing.' She reached into the small pack attached to her side and pulled out some of the chrysalis berries, holding them outstretched in her palm. The large blue tongue pulled her hand into its mouth, sucking all the berries in and leaving Zee's hand dripping with saliva.

'Eww,' she flicked her hand dry and stepped towards Pax to wipe the rest on his clothes. He just gave her a deadpan look.

The woverbine bellowed again loudly as if to say his goodbyes, then turned and plodded off in the direction from which they had just come, leaving Zee and Pax to make the rest of the way on foot.

They made it to Zee's house, legs weary and hearts racing. The door was open... but her mother wasn't *here*. Zee just knew it. There was a smashed teacup on the stone floor of the cottage with dried splotches following it... indicating what? Had there been a struggle? Had her mother been affected by the same blast as herself and Pax? Where was she!

A sudden uncontrollable rush of rage hit her, and her palms ignited with brilliant green flames. Her body shook, and she let a scream rip from her throat. Zee aimed the fire balls and thrust them directly into the large fireplace at the opposite end of the cottage, sending dust, soot, ash and pieces of charcoaled wood blasting out all over the place. Then she let the tears fall, the sudden sadness taking away her anger. What had she expected to find? She knew her mother was probably not going to be here, but as always, she had let herself hope. Just like she had done her whole life, wishing, hoping for her father to return.

She sat down in a colourfully painted chair worn with age, put her head in her hands and wept. Paxton watched her outburst from the doorway and solemnly came to rest a heavy hand on her shoulder, with wet eyes of his own for her.

'Hey, it'll be okay. Everything will be okay.' He wasn't sure it was going to be, but he couldn't think of anything else to say. Time felt as if it slowed down in that moment for the both of them. After a long while, she rubbed at her wet face and stood up as Paxton wrapped her in his arms. A safe, reassuring hug brought her back to real time.

Zee disentangled herself and headed to her room, searching through her belongings and gathering a few things she thought would be useful. The pair then stopped to have some of the hard, dry bread Jill had given them, along with the seaweed cheese. Despite its name, it was actually delicious with the damper and chrysalis berries. She didn't feel hungry at all but knew she needed to eat.

'Time to go see what's left of the village,' Zee said after what seemed like an eternity of silence for the two. Pax was unusually quiet, just hovering about, obviously giving her the space she needed to digest the gravity of situation. At least the blast hadn't reached her house. It was still standing far from the village, safe in the Black Forest.

When they reached the village, they were shocked to find it still standing and undamaged, save for the festival decorations that were strewn around the simple buildings. The painted chalk stone walkways were now smudged images that blended together with dull colours. The large fire pyres were still assembled, unburned. It was like the village was frozen in time, untouched, but where was everyone? Did all the inhabitants desert after the blast?

It was eerie, and Zemira had the feeling they were being watched. 'I don't like this at all, Pax. Let's check your building and get out of here. Hopefully Diwa is still okay.' Pax just nodded, sticking close to Zee as they walked down the silent pathways through

114

the empty village. Dead flowers blew around on the ground, and the decorations hung weeks ago were slightly torn and faded.

Once they reached the orphanage or communal home, they headed up to his room. They were the only two in the building. His room consisted of a very plain bed, made to perfection, unlike Zee's knots of blankets left on her own bunk. A tiny window shone into Pax's small room with hardly a thing in it. Zee remained silent, just taking in the sense of Pax's bedroom. He was such a light-filled soul. How could he have lived in such a bland place for so long?

Zee asked gently, 'Pax, what happened to your parents? I know you've lived here for a long time, but you've never told me what actually happened to them.'

'My parents...' he stumbled. 'They died a long time ago, from something called the silent sickness. I came here to this 'care home' when I was pretty young. I can remember small things about them, but that's all.' His back was now facing her while he forced some clothes into a pack, his head hanging low between slumped shoulders. Pax then let out a long, deep breath.

'I never told you before because I just didn't want you to feel sorry for me. Everyone else in the village treats me so differently than you do. Every time I think about my parents I feel like I can't breathe. My chest gets so tight, like a knife is being twisted into it. It was so long ago but it's just so painful to feel like you're all alone in the world. I miss them every second of every day.

Zee stood there watching him pack, completely still. Her arms hung at her sides heavily. Her throat tight, she opened her mouth but closed it again as no words came to mind. How dare she feel upset. Pax was an orphan, both his parents were gone at the same time from some horrible disease, and all she could think of was herself?

'I'm so sorry, Pax. I knew that you lived here, but not what actually

happened to your parents. I'd never treat you differently.' Words finally reached her.

115

'It was a lifetime ago. I just guess it's easier to not think about it.' He swung the pack over his shoulder wiped at his wet eyes and turned to face her, a small smile accompanying his shining eyes. 'Some things are easier to leave in the past.'

'You're not alone, Pax, and you'll never be alone again. You've got me... you'll always have me... no matter what.'

'You promise?'

'I promise.'

He slung an arm over her shoulder, turning her into him, and she gave him a long, reassuring squeeze. Pax took one last look at the dull, empty room. He finally felt like he was leaving the emptiness behind. Zee let him squeeze her back tightly.

'Come on, let's go and check Diwa's cottage.' She squeezed his hand with her own and leaned closer into him. What if Diwa wasn't there? What if they were completely alone? The town felt ghost-like. What would they do next? They were relying on someone to be there, anyone to explain what was going on. What was happening. To help steer them towards their next destination.

As they headed back into the forest, it seemed eerily quiet. Both felt uneasy, and Zemira was concentrating on forcing that dark feeling of sadness and desperation deep, deep down into someplace she could deal with later – much later. *Please let Diwa be alive. Please let her be there. Please let Wolf be with her.* Zee knew this path well, but never had she hoped so much on the way to Diwa's that it was still all there.

A rustle from beside the path stopped Zee in her tracks. Her hand reached out and slowed Pax beside her. 'Something's watching us,' she whispered.

She rounded the next tree, creeping into the ferns with Pax following closely behind, like they had done so many times before when hunting. Zee stood after scanning the forest ahead.

'I think it's clear. There's nothing there.' She replaced her knife back in its sheath at her side and turned to head back the way they had come, just as a giant object flung her into a large patch of ferns, all white fur and wagging tail, licking and yipping profusely.

'Wolf! You scared the life out of me!' Zee clutched her arms around him, roughing him up then sliding her hands around his giant head for a hug. 'I missed you so much.'

Paxton let out a deep breath; he must have been holding it. 'Hey, Wolf, are we glad to see you.' Wolf finally left Zee and let her get up out of the ferns, loping over to Pax to give him a big nudge with the side of his body. He looked up at Pax with a nod of his large head.

'Yes, you're most welcome,' said Pax, accepting the thanks. 'It was hard, but I managed to look after her this whole time.'

Zee threw a punch into Paxton's arm. 'You're full of it.'

Pax laughed. 'Nah, Wolf, as per usual she was the one saving the day.'

Wolf just watched the way Paxton looked at Zemira, as if taking note. He sniffed at Pax, giving him a snort, then sneezed into the ferns around him.

'I know, Wolf, we stink.' They both set off after Zee.

Zee held her breath at the top of the small hill that led into Diwa's beautiful burrow. The tree-intertwined cottage had smoke coming out of its small, bent chimney. Wolf was now on one side of her, Pax on the other.

'Have you seen her, boy? Is she there?' she asked Wolf.

He just nudged her hand and sprinted off down the track as happy as ever. From the far side of Diwa's beautiful twisting gardens, Zee saw the old cottage door open, and then the little old woman was standing there with arms outstretched. It was now Zee's turn to sprint, legs aching but heart full of hope once again. She made it to Diwa and bent down to crush her in a hug, tears overflowing just at the sight of her.

Zee breathed in cinnamon and lavender as she looked at Diwa. It felt like an eternity had passed, so much had happened in such a small space of time. Paxton hovered behind her.

117

'My dear, I've been waiting on you. I even saved you the last bit of raspor's honey!'

Zee laughed through her tears.

'And what is this?' Diwa motioned to the black vines reaching towards Zee's brow.

'Oh that...' Zee had almost forgotten about the irregular scar.

'It's beautiful.' Diwa smiled, rubbing her small, spindly fingers over the black markings.

'Diwa, this is Paxton,' Zee explained, wiping her happy tears away.

Paxton held out a hand to the small woman, taking in her size and wrinkled grin.

'Oh, I know who you are, dear boy,' she said, pulling him in for a hug. 'So handsome, Zee.'

Zee interrupted. 'Diwa, where is everyone? Where's Mum? Have you seen her? Anyone?' Zee asked desperately.

'I haven't seen anyone, Zemira, I'm so sorry. But I feel that your mother is still alive.'

Zemira let out a sigh of relief. Diwa always knew far more than she let on, so if she felt that Verena was still alive, then her mother was undoubtedly still alive. Somewhere.

'Now, both of you come in. But before anything else, you both reek! Smelly, melley, rotten, cotton!' she crowed. 'Baths for you both. Wolf's already had his.' Diwa smiled at Wolf standing next to her, nearly the size of the old woman.

Upon entering, Pax took in the colourful, crooked, mismatched cottage. It was just like Zemira's bright home, and he loved it. It all looked interesting, like it had a story. The vines hung down from the ceiling, some tickling across his head.

Diwa commented, 'Been a long time since I had such a handsome young man in my house, and so tall!'

'Diwa, really, first Wolf and now Pax,' Zee complained.

'Just noting the obvious, dear.' Diwa raised her eyebrows towards Zee as Paxton took in the surroundings of the little cottage.

Zee's widened eyes begged at Diwa to stop. 'Diwa, please. Do you have any idea what's been going on? Can you tell us anything? Don't you want to know where we've been?'

Pax turned back around and acted as if nothing was amiss. 'You've got a beautiful place Diwa,' Paxton said genuinely.

'Thank you, dear.' She then turned to the distressed Zee. 'Oh, yes, I do, and I will. But first, baths for you both! You want one together or you want to take turns?'

Wolf growled, realising what she had just said, the pair both extremely embarrassed. Paxton was blushing, and Zee was trying to hide the absolute horror she felt, hoping it wasn't plastered all over her face.

'I take it from that comment we're not getting any answers until you're ready. Diwa, you're wicked! And just for that, you're stuck with her, Pax. I'm going first. Torture him all you like,' she called out to Diwa as she stormed off out of the awkward situation.

Zemira realised with certainty that Diwa knew something about her mother, yet wouldn't tell her till she was ready. By the Mother, the old woman infuriated her sometimes. Stepping into the bathroom, she could see the bath was full of warm water sprinkled with petals of all sorts from Diwa's garden. A relaxing aroma of rosemary and lavender filled the air, mixed with a lemony scent. A towel was set out for her, and a set of her own clothes clean and folded were laid out off to the side on a large tree trunk slab used for a stool.

She let out a long breath upon seeing the bath. If Diwa knew they were coming, she must also know what had happened to her mother. Diwa could be infuriating at times, but she always amazed her. The woman was magical inside and out. She was so glad her dear friend was alright. It also meant that Zee and Paxton weren't alone anymore.

The little bathroom was full of plants and vines, giving it a warm, relaxing atmosphere. She stripped off the vile clothing that was coated in all kinds of grot and slid into the water, her aching legs almost sighing in relief. She was annoyed she had to wait a little bit longer for the answers she wanted right now. But she felt warm and safe again. Her body felt totally relaxed for the first time in weeks, and her muscles healed. *Thank the Mother*, she thought... *Thank the Mother that Diwa was alright.*

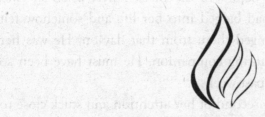

Diwa's Cottage

The Black Forest, Aylenta

Zemira had forgotten how amazing it felt to be clean. She had taken her sweet time, washed her long thick hair and scrubbed the numerous layers of dirt and crusted slime off. The herbs Diwa had placed in the bath for her had done the trick, and she was totally at ease, her muscles no longer aching and her head feeling light and peaceful.

Sliding into her old familiar clothes felt good, just not as good as finally making it back home. Paxton hadn't taken as long cleaning away their latest adventure, but when she refilled the bath for him, and went to tell him it was his turn, he was very eager to get away from Diwa. Clearly uncomfortable passing her in the hall with an awkward smile. What they had been talking about, Zee had no idea, but no doubt it was something horrifyingly embarrassing.

Zee cuddled up to Wolf, feeling as though she hadn't fully given him the love or proper greeting to show him how much she had actually missed him. He had been her shadow since the day she had come across him in the depths of the Black Forest when she was only six years old. He had barged into her life and somehow felt like he had always belonged there from that day on. He was her double, her constant hunting companion. He must have been so worried about her these past weeks.

Wolf lapped up every second of her attention and stuck close to her side as she got up and ventured into Diwa's quirky kitchen. The sun had set and there were glow beetles buzzing about outside in the dark. A few were hanging in the kitchen in little woven cages, lighting the place with a bright yellow glow. The rest of the cottage was lit with candles. Diwa always felt bad and would let all the glow beetles out before she went to bed.

The canny woman must have known they were coming back today as she had so many things ready for their arrival. The bath, Zemira's clothes, dinner cooking in the wood-fired oven and the fireplace was alight with a large pile of wood ready to go. There were even mats set out on the lounge room floor with pillows and blankets.

'Diwa how do you always know everything?' Zee asked, giving her a hug. This time a clean one.

'You smell glorious, Zee! How do you feel?' Diwa deflected the question, as usual.

'I feel better, so much better,' Zee said, looking Diwa in her stormy, sparkling eyes.

'And also, only a fool knows everything, dear girl. I'm just... well-informed,' she rattled off with a wink. 'We'll wait for your handsome young Pax, then well have supper. There are a great many things we need to discuss, I think?'

'A thousand things, Diwa, and can we please start with you telling me if mum's safe!' Zee pleaded.

'Yes, dear, please calm yourself. She's safe and alive, I promise... just not here in Aylenta.' Diwa stroked Zee's long, still-drying ebony hair.

Zemira felt the tension leave her body even further, and she let the rhythm of Diwa's fingers lull her into peace and quiet within.

As always, the food Diwa made tasted amazing. The herbs spices and numerous vegetables from Diwa's garden were delicious, beyond compare to anything Zee had ever tasted. Saying that, she had not really left Kali until recently, but remembered the hospital's bland sludge she'd had to endure. Zee now understood that her tastebuds knew what a good thing was – she had been spoilt with good food her whole life.

Judging by Paxton's reaction to the feast Diwa had laid out for them, including rabbit and fowl, boiled eggs crusted in something heavenly, roasted root vegetables of all kinds and two crisp, colourful salads, she was indeed spoilt.

'This is delicious, Diwa!' You're a food wizard!' commented Pax, devouring the meal.

'Witch, dear, and thank you, you're most welcome. Eat up as much as you like. You two deserve it, as you've been through a lot to get back, I'm guessing.'

Zee and Pax told Diwa of Thorta and the hospital/institute where they had been looked after then tested. Of Dr Greymouth and his creepy demeanour, how Jill helped them escape. Of Warwick, Winifred 5 and the vipen. How Zee had saved them all from the vipen and of it sinking into the Alvion Sea.

'Wonderful,' Diwa had commented when hearing of Zee using her powers. 'Well done, dear.' She had a proud, knowing smile on her face. But Diwa couldn't hide the worry coating her voice, no matter how unruffled she tried to seem. 'What happened next?' Diwa didn't judge or reprimand Zee for using her powers in front of the others like her mother definitely would have. She praised every move the pair had made. She laughed at the woverbine story.

Zee had let Pax tell that part, also laughing at him recalling his disgust at the oxel fish.

Zemira cleared up all the dishes and plates after they had had their fill. Even Wolf seemed like he had been sufficiently fed, which was a rare feat. He lolled to the side, rolling on the floor with a groan and a yawn.

'Getting out of the doing the dishes as always,' said Zee to him, giving him a ruffle on the head as she stepped over his large body into the kitchen. He had not left her side since she had come out from her bath. How lost he must have been after the blast. Poor boy. She was still so happy he had known to come and find Diwa. Such a smart creature.

Zee had so many questions she was holding in. They all helped clean up Diwa's tiny kitchen, stepping around each other, wiping bowls and stacking dishes as Diwa brewed tea on the stove. After cleaning up, she had sat them down with a mismatched cup each, Zee's purple with little creatures dancing along the sides of the cup, some throwing pink berries at each other – the worn and chipped paintings still so beautiful. Paxton's cup had black vines travelling up from the base of the cup, the ends of the branches blooming with crystal-like flowers. Black birds perched all around with small white eyes.

'Diwa, do you have any idea where the villagers are? Where my mother is? Why there was so much effort into making out the village had been blown to bits? We saw it all on the vision screen in Thorta,' Zee questioned when they were all seated, drinking the mysterious tea with small pieces of flowers and herbs floating around in the translucent blue liquid.

'Yes, Zemira, I'm afraid I know where they all are.' Diwa took in a deep breath, slumping a little in her chair. 'The villagers have been taken to Kymera, where they have ended up in the slave mines, like the rest of the villagers north of here. King Ravaryn has slowly and meticulously been taking villagers hostage from small villages, searching for you and your mother for years now. No one knows as he covers his tracks well, but his soldiers are ruthless and cunning. He has your mother, but he has not harmed her... yet. But that's all I know. He's been searching for you, Zee. I didn't think he would find you so soon but I cannot always see when things are going to take place. Only what is going to take place.'

'The king? What? Why, Diwa? Why has he taken my mother? What does he want with her? None of this makes any sense! She's been a hermit her whole life. What could the king possibly want with her?' Zee asked all at once, feeling lightheaded, as her eyes filled with tears.

'I'm not quite sure why he has her, but you must find her. You can save her from the king, but you will have to be wary. He plans on you coming to save her. You have to use your gifts, no more hiding. You'll need them to stay safe.'

Paxton's mouth hung open in shock. Zee was unsure what he was thinking of all this, this no doubt very odd, mysterious old woman, and how she had so much knowledge of what was happening around them. The tea was making Zee's body heavy and her eyelids sleepy. She struggled to think straight, her brain slightly foggy. 'How in the Rim am I supposed to find her? Let alone save her from some king who wants Mother knows what from me?'

Diwa raised her hands above her head, motioning them in circles in towards her. She blew out a long breath that swirled in the air changing colours, a cloud of grey morphing around the colours like a serpent entangling into itself, changing into dark purple and then white.

Paxton's eyes were huge as he slid his chair back from the table slightly. Zee just stared, mesmerised by the cloud. Inside the swirling cloud, a blurry image appeared and a woman started to form. She was inside a room where the walls shone as though made of ice, and a giant bed with golden threaded blankets and majestic furnishings surrounded her. She was dressed in a beautiful, shimmering silver gown that draped from her shoulders, with white crystals woven into her hair. The woman sat on the bed and turned to face the cloud Diwa had projected high above her table, her face beautifully familiar. A worried look saddened her features.

'Mum,' Zemira breathed.

The cloud started shrinking, smoke spinning in on itself and swirling the image of Verena away, before dissipating altogether. Diwa rested back in her chair, eyes closed for a moment, composing herself.

'Diwa that was unbelievable. You're like me...' Zee trailed off, feeling the exhaustion catching up on her.

'Umm, wow.' Pax just stared at Diwa then at Zee. 'That was blooming awesome.' His eyes also looked weary.

'I'm so sorry I couldn't have told you more growing up. It was your mother's wish to not enlighten you about the gifts that we both share. She wanted a peaceful existence for you, and was only trying to protect you. But it seems the time has come for you to protect her. I am a seer, Zemira, and you have elemental powers from what I've seen so far. You're able to manipulate all the natural elements around you.'

Zee now felt absolutely worn out. 'How, Diwa?' Her head was spinning after seeing her mother safe but clearly in Kymera, no doubt with the king.

'Your father will help you, Zee. We'll talk more in the morning. I think it's time we all had a well-earned rest. I'm feeling achy in this old body.'

'But what? My father? Wait? What do you mean, Diwa?' Zee's mind exploded through the fog inside her body.

Diwa shuffled around the table to Zemira, barely having to bend down to place a kiss on her forehead. 'In the morning, dear, I promise. Too much information for one night will set the glow beetles on edge.'

'Diwa, that doesn't make sense!' Zee complained.

'It's not supposed to!' She laughed. 'Goodnight, you three. Oh, and leave the teacups on the table, please.' With that, she headed off up the hallway to retire for the night.

Zemira was frustrated with her but not surprised. Diwa had always done this to her. Silly riddles or avoiding questions was nothing knew, but her father? It couldn't be true. Verena had said her father had disappeared many years ago before they came to Kali. Zee peered into the dregs on the bottom of her cup. The tiny black pieces all clung together in the shape of a wolf's head.

'Hey look, Wolf,' she said, feeling lightheaded and all of a sudden giggly. 'It's you, boy. What did you get, Pax?' she asked, yawning.

'Hmm,' he looked down slowly, obviously feeling the same lightheadedness and blurred cognition that Diwa had clearly intended by the tea. Mischievous old thing she was. 'It looks like a star,' he said, twisting the cup and his head around at the same time. 'No, more like... a snowflake. So that was all extremely strange, right? Not just to me?'

'Very strange,' replied Zee. 'Definitely not just to you.'

'I thought you told me your father had died or disappeared or something,' said Pax as they both got up and crawled into beds on the floor in the lounge area in front of the fire place.

'I thought he did,' she replied quietly, now staring at the roots dangling down through the ceiling above her.

Pax rolled over propped up on his elbow. 'I'm feeling wrecked. Goodnight, Zee.' He lent in to give her a kiss when Wolf, out of nowhere, squeezed his huge body in between them. He circled around and plonked himself right in the middle, his huge head towards Pax, letting out a giant yawn and wafting his breath into Paxton's face. Forcing Pax to roll over and away to the edge of the mat, far from Zee.

She laughed and cuddled up to Wolf. 'Goodnight, Pax,' she said sleepily.

'Gee thanks, Wolf,' Pax yawned, closing his eyes.

They both quickly fell into a deep sleep.

Zemira dreamed of her mother needing her, ice freezing up her arms and her body, creeping up her limbs in beautiful snow-flaked trails. Over her skin and into her mouth, freezing her. Verena reached out to Zee, her body turning to ice... then she swirled away into the darkness.

Her mother was gone, and Zee ran through the forest – lost, searching. Fear pounded in her chest while a giant creature followed, snapping at her heels. She searched everywhere for her father – where was he? Just as the creature knocked her to the ground, she flipped around and it was on her, above her. As it was about to devour her, its maw dripping onto her face from above, the beast's face transformed into a man's face. A man now stared back at her with dark eyes, pale skin, curly black hair and a wicked grin. Then Wolf appeared and ripped at the man's throat. Black blood poured out from him, and he disappeared into a cloud of swirling black smoke. But Wolf stayed. He watched over her, keeping her safe, a beautiful, glowing light surrounding him.

Crossing the Rim

The next morning, Zemira awoke to Wolf's wet kisses, coaxing her up. Pax was already up and helping Diwa chop firewood out back. Zee felt so rested, yet so worried about her mother and still rattled by the dreams she'd had for what seemed like the longest sleep. There was a cup of tea awaiting her on the table with scrambled eggs, a seeded slice of Diwa's special bread, small ripe juneberries and fruit in a bowl. There was a plate of greens from the garden and a few pieces of leftover roasted vegetables from the night before.

After demolishing the breakfast, Zee felt amazing and full of energy. She cleared the table and headed out back to where Diwa and Paxton were. The sun beamed down and warmed her face as she approached the back of the cottage, and she drank in the rays on her skin.

'Morning, dear. How are you feeling?' Diwa questioned gently. She was perched up on a tree stump, sipping at a cup of tea and watching Paxton chop wood.

'Energised, but I had some strange dreams last night though. What did you mean last night, Diwa? When you said my father will help? Enough with the nonsense and riddles.' Her jaw ached from clenching. 'Please, can I just get some straight answers? Where is my father, do you know? How do you know? Have you seen him in a vision or something?' Zee's heart was racing as she fired off one question after the other.

'All in good time, Zemira. All in good time.' Trust Diwa to de-flect her questions again.

Zee tried a different tack. 'Pax said he felt fabulous this morn-ing too. Funny that. What on Mother's earth did you ever put in that tea?'

'Secrets, secrets, only the tree knows. Ha!' was Diwa's only an-swer.

'You are kookier that a brustlehen after winter!' Zee retorted, still annoyed.

'Diwa, queen of the brustlehens!' Diwa cackled.

'Oh, Mother.' Zee just rolled her eyes and shook her head. 'Can you just act worried and distressed like the rest of us? Act like a normal person for once?' Zee asked.

'Where's the fun in that?' retorted Diwa.

Seriously, it was like the old woman was ten years old some-times, not probably one hundred. Zee brushed off her quirky mood. 'I was thinking of going for a wander down to the river, I just want to... get something, see if something's still there, I mean. And clear my head a bit, you know.'

'Oh yes, the gift. I see it,' said Diwa, closing her eyes for a mo-ment. 'Still there, no moss hair,' she sing-songed.

'Do you ever get bored of being a know it all?' asked Zee.

'No, dear, I told you only fools know it all,' said Diwa. 'Okay, but take the boy and Wolf with you. I don't want you going alone, and when you're back we have to make some decisions. You will need a plan, Zemira. We will get her back.' She eyed Zee more seriously. Onyx stared into emerald.

'Whatever have you got in that tea?' was Zee's only reply, unable to wipe the smile off her face. With that look, Zee felt stronger. She knew of Diwa's confidence in her. They held each other's gaze for the moment, Diwa conveying unspoken answers, as the thwack, thwack of the axe in the background echoed around the quiet glen.

Diwa gave them both very long hugs before they left for the river. 'We're just going for a walk, Diwa. We'll be back soon,' Zee assured her.

'I know.' She smiled and watched the three leave up the path through her gardens and over the hill.

They wandered through the peaceful forest path, the tallowpines squeaking together and swaying gently. Zee had her pack on and knife at her waist. The two walked in comfortable silence with Wolf scouting ahead.

'So Diwa's nuts, right? And also, where are we going?' asked Pax after a while, breaking the quiet calm.

Zee let out a little laugh. 'Yep, totally fruity,' she confirmed. 'I just wanted to check on something down at the river, and take a walk. Think about everything crazy that's happening,' she explained, eyeing the ground in front of her.

'I know. Everything's so... different,' agreed Pax.

They reached the edge where the forest thinned and opened up to the clearing where Zee's favourite fishing spot was situated. It all looked exactly the same, the large tree that Wolf was wondering off up to concealing her hidey hole. Off in the distance, the cool, deep blue waters flowed steadily, the unforgettable iridescent shine of the translucent Rim wall towering up out of the middle of the river. It was then she heard it, the shuffling sound behind them, and rustling in the brush all around them.

'Something's wrong,' said Zee, just as she turned to see soldiers materialising around them, their shimmering black armour tight on their large forms.

'Run!' She grabbed Paxton's arm, pulling him into a sprint alongside her, out of the edge of the forest towards the other side where Wolf was. They were fast, but the soldiers seemed to glide towards them, closing in around the pair in the middle of the opening. There were so many of them, ten or eleven or so, Zee quickly tried to count.

The tallest soldier approached her, his shimmery black helmet concealing most of his face. 'We've been looking all over for you. All this trouble for a scrawny little village feral,' he said with a deep, uninviting voice. 'You've given us the slip quite a few times now, it seems. But your fun's over. You're both coming with us.' He moved towards Zemira, and she swiped her arm violently forward, conjuring a great blast of air that should have knocked the soldier ten feet or so away from her and into the dirt. Yet he only slid back slightly, boots scraping into the ground.

'Something's wrong,' Zee whispered to Pax.

The tall soldier just laughed a deep rumble and motioned his hand forward. The rest of the soldiers encroached on them. Two soldiers grabbed Paxton's arms and forced them behind his back. He managed to break free and swing a punch, connecting up under one of the soldier's jaws. The soldier recovered quickly. 'You'll pay for that,' he bristled, smashing a fist into Pax's stomach. Pax doubled over, nearly falling to the ground.

'Pax!' Zee screamed, so loud that the air pulsed around them, the soldiers clutching at their ears.

'Enough of that!' the tall soldier roared, his fist connecting with Zee's face. Splintering pain shot through the side of her jaw, just as a savage set of jaws ripped into the tall soldier's arm. Blood sprayed as Wolf's teeth tore into the strange, thin metallic material.

'Zee, run!' Pax wheezed out a yell. She twisted both her arms towards the ground, grinding her teeth against the throbbing pain that blasted from the side of her face. Not stopping, she raised two large rocks from the earth and swung them through the air, pummelling the two soldiers either side of Pax in the face. Zee lunged to help free Pax, but the soldiers surrounded him. Wolf released the tall soldier's arm leaving it in pieces, and grabbed for Zee. He pulled her ferociously away by her pack.

'Wolf no! Pax!' They had him, his arms twisted behind his back, with one of the soldier's boots on Paxton's head, forcing his face into the dirt. The tall soldier lunged for her, but she blasted dirt up into his eyes and ran, following Wolf's lead down to the river's edge. Zee slid to the edge and looked at Wolf, her eyes questioning him. Then he reared up and pushed her in. Frigid water engulfed her, and she sucked in a gasp as she surfaced from the icy water. Wolf was close behind, heading straight for the middle of the river towards the Rim wall.

'Wolf, where are you going?' she spluttered after him through the water; she definitely was not the best swimmer. The tall soldier was now furious.

'You're dead, dog,' he seethed behind them, jumping into the river with his arm dripping blood. He pounded towards them with incredible speed, the injury not slowing him down in the slightest.

Zee could see the Rim wall getting closer and closer and panicked that Wolf didn't know humans were unable to pass through. He might be safe, but the furious soldier was going to get her. He was so close behind her, she could hear his pounding strokes in the water and his breath blasting in and out. Yet she was so close to the Rim, its shimmery iridescence an arm stroke away.

Then Zee was swept backwards as the soldier grabbed the top of her pack. 'Got you,' was all she heard as he forced her head under the water from behind. She tried to hold her breath as long as she could, the bubbles bursting out. She kicked and thrashed in the water, seeing a golden flash before her eyes. Then the soldier ripped her up out of the water and started to drag her backwards. Wolf paddled back towards them just as a giant golden creature leapt out of the river. The huge fish's mouth stretched open to reveal teeth that hinged forward from within. In a split second and in one smooth motion, the river god flew directly towards the soldier's head, engulfing it whole and ripping it from his body in one swift movement.

Zee felt the pull of the soldier cease and didn't dare to look back. She scrambled ahead with Wolf reaching her side. They closed in on the wall, and Zee reached forward with her hand fully expecting it to feel like a solid, impenetrable force. To her surprise, her hand slid straight through the air into the wall with a tingle. Her body followed, a sparking sensation zapping through her as she paddled franticly through to the other side, utterly shocked she had somehow passed through and away from the cruel soldiers' grasp. The dark façade of the other side of the wall disappeared as soon as she passed through it. There was no smog; the sun shone as it had on the other side. Was the dark smog just an illusion? Zee tried to focus on her surrounding situation, looking around for Wolf.

Instead she saw the tall soldier's headless body floating by on the other side, seeping red into the water, a little fuzzy through the veil on the other side of the Rim wall. She cringed. The soldier was well and truly dead. How on Mother's earth was this all possible? No human had ever passed through the Rim. It wasn't possible. Wolf was paddling in front of her and now circled back to Zee's side, letting out an anxious whine – clearly very uneasy in the water. He nudged her on, closer to the bank. The air outside the Rim wasn't blackened and there was no smog. In actual fact, the forest and river looked exactly the same on both sides. She was so confused.

Zee had just made it to the steep bank when her necklace started to glow bright blue. Wolf jumped in front of her, shaking the excess water from his pelt, and reached down to help pull her up. As she reached for him, a sharp scream ripped from her throat. Something felt like knives raking down the back of her calf. She twisted to see the cause of the sudden pain and there was a creature digging its thin needle-like claws into her leg. Its revolting little face flowered with flapping fins, scaly blue-green skin and two very large, shining black eyes. A wicked grin spread across its horrid face as it peered up at her.

Wolf let out a savage growl before grabbing Zee by her pack and yanking her towards him. Upon being pulled from the river, the water waif still attached to Zee's leg screeched and detached itself, tearing out its claws and darting away into the depths. Wolf dragged her up the bank and out of the water. Hissing through her teeth, Zee took her pack off quickly and dived through it for a spare cloth to wrap around her stinging leg. Blood poured from the gashes, and green slime coated the edges where the waif's claws had sliced through.

She quickly wrapped her pulsing leg and got the hell away from the edge. Standing up, Zee leaned against Wolf to look back and see the soldiers inside the Rim on the banks of the river watching her. A pair of them were now dragging Paxton away. His body was limp, head bobbing to one side. The tall soldier's body floating in the river suddenly jerked into the deep, some giant unsettling creature surely smelling the blood. She thanked the Mother it wasn't her.

But Pax. They had him, and it was all her fault. She was so angry with herself, at the soldiers, at the stupid king! And her leg. Mother, it was burning. Wolf gently nudged her hand. Time to go, his eyes seemed to say. Zee felt utterly and completely lost, and scared, entering the forest on the outside of the Rim! What next? At least she was safe from the soldiers for now, but a new question was growing like a vicious weed in her gut: How had she passed through the wall? What was she?

She followed Wolf, limping into the forest away from the river. She had to get back, had to help Pax. Had to find her mother. But not through that river; there was no way she was ever getting in there again. The cold was starting to work its way into her bones, the adrenaline rush clearly wearing off. The large pines and ferns of the forest felt the same as inside the Rim. There was no evidence of radiation, smog, fog or anything horribly different. The air was clear and smelled, if anything, sweet. The only thing Zee could note that was any different was that the outer Rim was possibly even more beautiful. Every mushroom seemed to have a slight glow to it, there was no deadfall, and all the ferns were fresh and green. There was no decay anywhere. And it was very, very quiet. Hardly the hum of a glow beetle, the caw of a raven or the shriek of a shadow-ren. Not even the creak of a breeze through the trees, it was so very still.

She wanted to stick close to the edge of the river so as to cross back through when it veered away from the edge, but Wolf was trailing away deeper into the woods in the opposite direction. She gritted her teeth trying to keep up, her leg on fire. 'Wolf!' she called after him. 'Wrong way, boy. Come on.' Zee motioned back towards the river.

He ruffled his fur and shook his head, circling behind her and carefully nudging her in the direction he wanted to take.

'No, that's not the way, and I'm not going further in there. Who knows what other horrible creatures live in this forest.'

Wolf spun in front of her, eyed her and made a 'rufff'.

'I can't. I have to get back and see if Diwa is alright, mend this leg, find Pax...' she trailed off, feeling drowsy.

Wolf whined and pulled at her. It was going to get dark soon, and she had no chance of getting back before nightfall. Even if she did, would there be more soldiers along the Rim waiting for her? She wanted to cry with frustration.

'Fine,' she snapped at Wolf, his whining getting to her. She couldn't think straight. Hobbling after him, through the eerily perfect forest, they came to a very clear stream. After following the stream for a while, they came to a small cave. Zee's head was now swirling, the forest moving on its own around her.

Wolf quickly and carefully inspected the cave before returning and nudging Zee inside. He kept watch like a sentry while she sat down and removed her pack, noticing a large golden hand-sized scale attached to the front pocket. How had she not seen this before? Her head was swimming, like the feeling of drinking too much of Jill's whiskey, but much worse. So much had happened in such a short amount of time. Setting the scale to the side, the young hunter unravelled the cloth around her leg. And gagged. Most of the bleeding had stopped, but the edges were now coated with thick green slime and puss. It must be some kind of poison.

She started to cry, finally letting the tears stream out. Zee had Wolf back, but Pax was gone. He would know what to do, he'd have a plan, or at least he'd look after her. Or make a stupid joke and somehow make her feel better. She lay down hugging her knees to her chest, letting all the dark and miserable things in her mind come to the surface, crying like a child into the dirt.

Her leg screamed with pain, rattling through her whole body. Zee felt the darkness coming for her again but didn't care. She knew this time she wouldn't come back, and that she was useless even with her gifts. Her tricks and manipulations wouldn't help her now, her cocky façade was useless. Who was she kidding... she couldn't help anyone, not her mother, not Pax, and she couldn't even understand why this was all happening. Why would some king of another territory waste all this time, cause so much pain and destruction, just to find her?

Jill and Warwick should have left her there in that hospital bed, ready to be delivered to Kymera. Let Greymouth experiment all he liked. She pulled her knees up tighter, shivering, wanting to pull them so close she could disappear. The tears kept coming, and she let them all fall. After some time trying to process it all, Zee finally stopped crying, all the tears used up. She just lay there staring at Wolf's silhouette and slipping into the peaceful dark place that promised to take her away from the blasting pain. Why fight it? She was lost... in more ways than one. There was nothing she could do. The shimmery image of Wolf at the entrance of the cave glowed bright, Wolf disappearing, morphing... his form changing, twisting and blurring into the shape of a man... the dark creeping in towards him, swirling around him and swallowing him whole...

Ice & Stone

City of Zenya, Kymera

King Ravaryn's long black leather boots clipped down the large glass-like hallway of ice and stone, echoing behind him and ricocheting in the silence. His curly black hair shone, perfectly in place above his dark eyes and sharp, angled jaw. His hands were clasped behind his back, and his shoulders were held taught. He reached the shimmery, metallic black door and entered the massive room at the end of the hall. The woman stood, arms crossed at the far side of the room. The room's metallic and ice-lined walls were joined to a high ceiling covered with numerous ice chandeliers, their crystals shimmering all around like an artificial starry sky.

She stood in front of a huge window that stretched the expanse of the whole southern wall of the room, staring out towards the rough sea that stretched far into the horizon before her. Ice and snow crusted the land around its edges, large chunks of ice rolling around in the waves before crashing into the shore. Her crossed arms were wrapped in front of her tall, slender body, now covered in a glittering gown that trailed down over the floor. Silver fabrics and woven pieces like spider webs cascaded from her shoulders. Her dark brown hair was laced with intricate crystals and trailed down her back.

'Verena, you look simply stunning. It's been far too long...' the male's deep, smooth voice crooned behind her.

She shivered, and not just from the frigid temperature that suddenly seemed to plummet all around her.

'I told you that one day I would find you, and here you are. Did you not miss me at all?' He stood just behind her, towering over her from behind.

'No, Ravaryn, I did not. And if you somehow think that keeping me locked away in here will bring you into my favour, you've truly gone mad.' She spun around to lock her verdant eyes on him.

'Verena, my long-lost love, still so fiery.' A wicked grin illuminated his pale yet extremely handsome face. 'Well, if that's how you feel, you'll have plenty of time to change your mind, my dearest. And I haven't heard any news of that mongrel who stole you from me all those years ago. Gone into hiding like a coward, has he?'

She didn't reply, her jaw muscle tightening at his words.

'And you've been busy... a child... a daughter, I hear. Tsk, Tsk, so many things I have to find out through the Juneberry vine.' His honey-toned voice would have been a sweet caress if not for the hard edge simmering underneath.

Verena turned away from him, rubbing her arms as if her skin was trying its hardest to crawl away, to once again stare out at the dark ocean.

'What, nothing to say? I thought you'd be happier to see me. After all, we have so much to catch up on.'

There was a knock at the door. 'Enter,' he boomed, catching Verena off guard. She recoiled at the sudden burst of his deep voice.

A guard entered the room and approached the king. 'Sire, we have word on her location.' He handed Ravaryn a small piece of white cloth, which the king unwrapped, smiling at its contents.

'Thank you, Caden. That will be all.'

'Should we take action?' Caden questioned.

'No, not yet. Let them return and see if she leads us to the shift-er.'

The soldier eyed Verena then nodded to Ravaryn before heading off and closing the door behind him with a thud. With the soldier now gone, the king took a step closer, his body so very close to hers. She could feel the heat of his breath in her ear as he leaned his tall, muscular frame in closer to whisper, 'How I've missed you, my queen.'

Verena didn't move a muscle, although she wanted to run. To get far away from him and this palace and this whole territory, but she knew better. He was cunning and powerful, and there would be no escaping him this time. She hadn't forgotten how controlling he could be.

'So quiet, my love.' He trailed a hand down her face, fingers twisting in a length of her hair.

Verena turned her face away, cringing at his touch.

'Well, I have other things to attend to at present,' he said, pulling away from her. 'I know you'd love me to stay and catch you up after all this time. I'm afraid it'll have to wait, but I will leave you with a parting gift for now.' The king reached around in front of her, his face very close to hers.

She didn't move an inch.

He laughed – a deep, unsettling boom. 'My queen, you have no idea how happy it makes me to see you again.' Ravaryn placed the piece of white cloth that Caden had handed him on the window-sill, directly in front of where Verena stood, and watched as her eyes left the horizon and peered down to see what he had presented her with. Within the piece of cloth was a small tuft of shiny, straight, midnight-coloured hair. Unmistakable to Verena, it was the same hair she had brushed and braided for almost eighteen years.

Her composure fled, just as Ravaryn had hoped. 'You do anything to her and I swear I will cut you to pieces myself!'

Verena spun round to rake her nails over his face. The king caught her hand in mid-air, pulling her roughly into him, her face now just below his chin. He stared down into her glowing emerald eyes. 'Now, now, my love, that's no way for a queen to act...'

Part II

Part II

Orion

Blurry light entered Zemira's stinging eyes. She squinted, only allowing a small amount in to let her eyes gently adjust. Her head was still spinning slightly, and she could feel something softer than the dirt floor of the cave underneath it that she had cried into and drifted away on.

The cave. She was still alive then. Just as the recognition of the river events hit her, she felt her leg stinging as if on cue. But it was not the agonising roar of the night before, when she passed out on the cave floor, giving up all hope. No, it was now a dull thud, not sharp anymore. Just achy. Trying to open her eyes more against the brightness of the cave, she opened her mouth to speak, but it was so dry.

Zee pushed herself up on both arms and swivelled around to look at the state the water waif had left her leg in, and what she found surprised her. There were newly healed black claw marks still swollen and red around the edges, but healed nonetheless. Completely closed together, no oozing green sludge. It must have been a poison. But how had she healed? And so quickly? Had it been quickly? How long had she actually been lying here in this cave? Three thick black lines appeared and sprouted tiny tendrils of vines as she looked intensely at them, becoming more like beautiful tattoos. The mesmerising, twisting lines crept into place then set still around the scars. Amazing, how did she manage this? Was this what Jill had witnessed upon opening her bandages at the facility in Thorta? While she was captivated by her calf and newly beautified scar, a deep voice permeated her ears from a dark corner of the cave behind her.

'That's incredible, you know... how you do that.' The velvety male voice rolled around the cave, bouncing from the walls, sounding positively ancient.

'Who's there?' Zee replied, sounding way more confident than she felt. Her sore throat groaned in protest. The voice gave her a sharp jolt of shock. She wasn't alone. There was someone in the cave with her, and it wasn't Wolf. Still in a sitting position, she twisted around, instinctively reaching for the knife at her side. Her eyes adjusted to the light at the back of the cave. A man... a large man was sitting on a pile of rocks, his face staring towards her, his hands entwined, clasped together in front of him. Dark arms similar to the brown shade of her own rested on his knees, and his shining, glowing green eyes reflected the light from the entrance.

'Don't be alarmed, little hunter,' soothed the voice. 'You're lucky the river god felt so kindly and gifted you that golden scale. Or you may not be so fortunate to have kept that leg. I may not have been able to... to save you,' he finished.

The scale. Zee remembered the soldiers, Paxton. The river crossing, entering through the Rim and the giant fish that had decapitated the tall soldier trying to drag Zee back with him. A tremor slid up her spine. There had been so much blood in the water... and then the grotesque little water waif.

'The scale... is that how my leg has healed?' Zee asked, trying to understand how she was still here, utterly surprised that the poison hadn't finished her.

'It was a gift, I presume, a very powerful gift. A life debt owed, maybe,' replied the stranger from the dimly lit back of the cave, his voice like silk. He rose from his spot, silver pieces of long hair framing his face, having come loose from the rest tied at the back. He was well built, extremely muscular, and his face... it seemed somehow familiar.

'Don't come any closer,' Zee said in a calm, authoritative voice. Her knife extended in front of her, but the thought of her inflicting the stranger with any damage seemed laughable in her state, and with her size.

'Please,' his voice soothed. 'I mean no harm whatsoever.' He proceeded forward, open hands out in front of his tall form.

His body was covered in black marks... tattoo-like marks – just like her own now entwined around the scars on her leg. How could this be possible? Were there people beyond the Rim? Alive? And the smog the radiation... had it all been a lie? She had to know. And Wolf, where was Wolf?

'How is it possible?' Zee demanded. 'That we're both breathing outside the Rim. Are there others out here? Where have you come from?' Her head was now swirling with questions. And Wolf? Where was he? Why had he left her? Maybe the stranger had done something to him, injured him or worse? Fear caught in her throat, and her heart raced.

'Why are you here? Why help me? And where is my Wolf!' she demanded, getting slowly to her feet, ready for a fight. Her leg trembled slightly but took her weight. Zee dropped the knife as an afterthought... after all, she had a better weapon... herself. She extended her hands towards the stranger, suddenly feeling furious as a flame started to flicker behind her pupils. There was also some kind of shield at the entrance to the cave. To keep her in?

'Answers, now!' Zee ordered, feeling completely not herself, but this seemed like the only option as she had been backed into a corner... literally.

The man seemed to see her notice the shimmering shield at the entrance of the cave and said, 'It's not to keep you here, I assure you. It's to keep the Rim watchers from scenting you. It's to keep you safe in here while you are healing,' he explained.

The flames grew...

'Whoa, please calm down, Zee.' The stranger's deep voice and serious face tried to do his best to de-escalate the situation, and he raised his own hands in surrender. That act just made him look even more dangerous, as he seemed to tower over her.

'Get back. How do you know my name?' Panic flickered in her stomach now, and she couldn't think straight. Where on earth was Wolf? She felt the green flames ignite in each palm. Her breathing evened; she was ready.

'Zemira, it's me! I am Wolf!'

Her mind was playing tricks on her. Had he just said he was Wolf? Was the poison lingering? Distorting her reality? Everything was happening so fast, overwhelming her. The flames in her palms grew to the size of shadowrens, just as she was ready to direct them at the strange, ominous-looking man. She was so disoriented she didn't think to check her stone necklace for reassurance for whether or not she was in danger. It didn't even cross her mind. Zee was being careless, letting anxiety and exhaustion take the lead.

Within a split second, the man sensed the oncoming attack and spun around, a blue/white glow of light coming from within his form. It glowed through his skin, illuminating the black tattoo-like marks with white. There was a flash and then standing before her clear as day and more familiar then her own face... was Wolf.

The flames encircling Zee's palms shrank as the utter shock of what she'd just witnessed paralysed her for a moment. She stood there dumbstruck and staring at Wolf. Dousing the flames immediately, her emotions see-sawed and her eyes regained focus. The flames within them disappeared to be replaced by tears.

'W... Wolf...? How...? How can this be?'

Wolf trotted over to her, clearly sensing the change in her. Zee brought his face to hers and stared into his eyes. They were indeed the glowing pine eyes of the man who had just been standing before her. He turned his face to the side of her, nuzzling into her for a long hug. Still unsure of the situation, Zee couldn't resist. She needed the hug, the warmth, the reassurance of the familiar. To know she wasn't alone. She wrapped her arms around Wolf's neck and held him for a moment, collecting her thoughts. Wiping away the tears, she composed herself. The pair sat together on the floor of the cave for a while.

After a while of looking at him and sorting through all the possibilities in her mind, Zee finally said, 'You're much more handsome as a wolf, you know.'

Wolf scoffed and tried to fain being offended. He whipped his large head up and to the side, away from Zee, the action making her laugh.

'I knew there was always something strange about you, that's why Diwa loves you so much, right? The pair of you are weirdos.' Zee broke the tension in the cave.

After some time, Wolf got up and walked away to the other side of the cave... and shifted. Zemira watched as her friend, her hunting companion, her Wolf, transformed back into the man she had awoken to before. His huge form made the cave feel small. His large, tattooed hands led to corded, muscled arms. His face was stern, but not menacing. The man had a strong, angular jaw, and silvery white hair framed a handsome face with eyes a very familiar shade of emerald green.

Zee took him in, her eyes wide. Was this for real? She tucked an arm around her stomach and shifted to pull her uninjured leg up in front of her, wrapping the other arm around it. The man didn't say anything, just sat opposite Zee in the musty, cold cave and waited... giving her the time she needed.

She took in a long breath. 'I think you've got some explaining to do. Because I've either gone mad from the waif poison and am hallucinating all this... or you, my Wolf I've known for twelve or so years... just transformed into a man, and has made this all very weird.'

She paused. 'What is it then?'

The man grumbled, just as Wolf would. 'It's a long story...' he volunteered.

'Well, lucky for you, I've all of a sudden got some free time on my hands.' She was not letting him get out of anything.

He seemed to mull something over in his mind, then after a moment replied, 'Alright,' in his deep voice. 'But you need to drink something first, and I imagine you are hungry after all you've been through. He eyed her. 'I'll make you a deal. I will go find something for us to eat, and you make us a fire. You must stay near here for now, relieve yourself if need be, but do not wander far from the cave. The creek out front has fresh, drinkable water in it. I was serious when I said that shield was there to protect you... every creature outside the Rim is designed to harm humans. They are... controlled, compelled to do so. They can smell your human scent and will attack you, unprovoked, and they will try to end you. Do you understand?'

'Geez, you're a bit of a downer as a human,' Zee muttered.

'I'm serious,' he growled, sounding more like Wolf.

'Okay, I get it. I won't go anywhere until you're back.'

'Thank you, Zemira. I don't want anything to happen to you. I'll tell you everything when I get back, little hunter.'

Zee just nodded, the whole situation extremely strange. And Wolf was now in charge somehow? He left the cave and proceeded to shift outside then sprinted off into the forest without looking back, leaving Zee to tend to her needs. Alone. On her own, far from her home, outside the safety of the Rim.

Upon his return, Wolf shimmered and filled the cave momentarily upon his arrival, shifting into his human form. Sitting by the small fire in the centre of the cave opposite one another, they shared a meal like they had so many times before, but also like no other. The pair ate the most colourful foul Zee had ever seen, and she was so tempted to keep every single iridescent rainbow-coloured feather. She almost felt guilty for eating such a beautiful creature when Wolf had returned with it, but she was ravenous, so ate every morsel from her portion.

After eating her fill and tucking a rainbow feather into her pocket, Zee felt much better than she had upon awakening and was now impatient for answers. Wolf was quiet.

'You going to start or do I have to keep waiting?' Zee questioned him after some time.

'I haven't spoken for a long time,' he said gruffly. 'You'll have to bear with me. Where should I start?'

'Umm, I don't know, maybe with the obvious - like how my best friend has been a Wolf my whole life and now is suddenly a giant warrior man!' Zee replied, losing patience and throwing her hands in the air.

'My name is Orion, and I am the son of Kyeitha the Forest Queen. I have always been a shifter, just not always been allowed to shift,' he started.

Zee made herself comfortable, feeling this would be a long sit. She closed her wide-open mouth and just concentrated on listening

'I did not grow up inside the Rim, and I'm not from within it. I was a watcher, designated to simply 'watch' the humans inside the Rim. I could come and go as I pleased and was tasked to make sure no war, famine or any other dire situation were to occur from the humans inside, and to report back to the queen of the forest, Kyeitha, and inform her of the goings on within the Rim. To make sure the humans did not destroy themselves, or commit any major catastrophe as had happened in the past. There are many other watchers, and all are under the command of the Rim guardians, but Kyeitha is now the only Rim guardian.

'I was told that humans were evil, could not be trusted and had to be watched, kept and contained. They were still creatures of Mother Earth, but Kyeitha - she wanted nothing to do with them and did not want to be near them. But she had a job to do, given to her by the Mother Nature herself: She still had to watch over humans, contain them and keep them safe.

The humans inside the Rim believe that the outside world is polluted from their ancestors. And they are not wrong. Most of the lands to the west are too far gone to be recovered, even by Mother Nature. The Rim is to keep the outside world safe from humans. To allow nature to thrive and the balance to naturally keep itself in line. The humans are disrupters to this balance. They take too much, they kill too much, they pollute and they fight. And they spread.'

Zee just listened, having heard similar things throughout the years from Diwa... a few ramblings here and there. Zee could understand a little; she had had her run-ins with people who were not so desirable... Lawrence, Greymouth, the soldiers at the river, the king.

'About twenty years ago, I was on watch and keeping an eye on a certain ruler, one that was making plans... growing forces... scheming. Kyeitha had ordered me to keep a close watch over him and his land. Kymera. There was a huge ice storm, and I was still in the form of a snow eagle, when it suddenly surrounded me. I couldn't escape the powerful winds and return to my own land. I was blown around, finally smashing into a dwelling's veranda, fracturing my wing badly. The cold was intense.' He pointed to a particularly beautiful tattoo on his upper arm that had striking snowflake-like markings intertwined in a pair of delicate little hands.

'That is where I met her, the most caring, beautiful woman I had ever laid eyes on. She took me in, cared for me without a moment of hesitation.' Wolf paused, watching the recognition bloom in Zemira's eyes.

'Her mesmerising eyes went deep like cool and calming waters, and I couldn't help myself. I fell for her... hard. I had disobeyed every rule Kyeitha had against the Rim insiders. Do not interact, do not be seen and do not speak or form relationships with any humans inside the rim. I knew I would be punished. But I also now knew that Kyeitha was wrong. Humans are not all destructive and consuming. This woman, she was light, air, hope – the sun itself.'

A smile stole across his face, the first one Zee had witnessed. Despite her not knowing how to feel about Wolf all of a sudden becoming a man, she couldn't but notice how extremely handsome he was when he spoke of this woman. It filled her with warmth.

'But she was promised to another, one that I knew had ill intentions. He didn't really love her, and she knew it. He was becoming dark towards her and would suffocate her light if I had left her there, so I stole her away. We were so happy. We had quite a few, happy blissful years together on the run. She was so young and free and made me live like I had never dared before. Then we found somewhere safe... and... we had you.' He smiled this time at Zee.

'My world changed forever. I had never felt a stronger bond or love before. I thought this was what it must be like to be human, to be a father.'

Zee was rendered speechless. She just stared at the man, at Wolf at...

Her father's eyes watered as he said, 'Zemira, I've waited so long to be able to speak with you, to tell you, to finally meet you in my real form. You were so little when I was taken away, my young hunter. My little wolf. The punishment I received for my betrayal when Kyeitha finally came for me was to never return to you, and if I did, I would be stuck in one animal form for the rest of my days. But you were worth every minute as Wolf.' He smiled proudly at her from across the fire, his emerald eyes – her emerald eyes – not leaving her gaze.

The Borztan Mines

Kymera

The whip was now slick with his blood, and tears pricked at the edges of his eyes, crushed shut with the force of every blow. The wind swirled frigidly at the entrance to the Borztan mines in Kymera. Paxton's back was in ribbons of flesh, blood and muck as the soldier, without a care, slid the black whip through the mud before delivering each shuddering blow. A contorted smile carved his dirty face, flashing black and yellow jagged teeth.

It's nearly over, Pax thought to himself. *Hold on.* His fingernails dug into the mud. *Hold on, hold on.* Thwack. *Hold on.* Tears slipped down his dirt-stained cheek, black with Borztan soot. He felt no shame. They were all watching, the other prisoners, and they knew that he was strong for not having passed out yet. He wouldn't give the soldier the satisfaction. Thwack. He ground his teeth together, his body shaking on his knees in the mud. One more... He'd been counting. His head burst with the pain, his back on absolute fire. The whip slid through the mud, the soldier arching his back to put as much force into the last blow as he could.

Thwack. Paxton's arms shook but still held his reeling body up out of the mud. Retching and vomiting into the mud, it sprayed onto his hands. He sucked in breaths trying to slow his pounding chest. He had done it. He had won... this time. The soldier wandered over to him as the crowd watched, wrapping up the blood-soaked whip tipped with a small dark metal barb, and attaching it to his side.

'Take note, this is what happens when you filthy gutter rats disobey the king's orders.' He planted his boot into the young man's side, sending him sliding into the mud clutching his stomach, tucked into foetal position.

'Nine for the first punishment as a warning,' the soldier continued out loud, 'and after that it's up to my discretion.' He grinned evilly at Pax as he raised himself up out of the mud. More quietly, he said, 'Next time you cross me, boy, I'll make sure you don't get back up ever again.' The solider spat in the mud near Paxton's face and stomped away towards the entrance of the Borztan mines.

'Get back to it, you maggots! I've got plenty more in me if anyone's asking!' he shouted into the crowd of powder-covered teenage boys, all covered in black dirt and soot. They scattered like roaches under a flashlight. The soldier turned to continue back up to the entrance of the mines, to enter into the hole, the pits, where they were all expected to dig and to die.

A skinny boy quickly ran forward and bent down to help Pax, who was bleeding into the mud. He wrapped an arm around Pax's waist and grabbed his arm, placing it around his neck, and helped him up as gently as he could without disturbing the sliced ribbons of flesh hanging from his back. Paxton grimaced and more tears slid down his face, his legs like jelly.

The smaller boy struggled to hold up the taller more-built and muscular young man. 'Hang in there,' he said. 'You did so well.

I've never seen the blacksmith so furious, but you didn't give up. And I've never seen anyone not pass out before.' A few more steps. 'Hang in there, I'll get you to the healer.' A few more steps. 'Stay with me, Paxton.'

Paxton's eyes opened, and he concentrated on the blurry form in front of him. Pain blasted his back as he became more conscious. 'Zee,' he croaked, his voice shaking. 'Zee, is that you?'

The light from behind the figure blurred their face, with Pax's fuzzy eyes trying to come into focus. He tried to steady himself through the immense pain radiating from his body where it now lay on a hard cloth stretcher.

'Pax, thank the Mother you're awake! You scared the life outta me!' said another young boy sitting vigil at Paxton's side. He could feel the boy's hand tightly wrapped around his own now, slightly crushing it. He tried to sit up.

'Be careful! Do not stress your back too much, please. I spent hours patching it all back together.' The younger teenage boy hopped up, helping Paxton to carefully sit up while he placed more brown-stained pillows behind him for support.

'Where... where's Zee?' he asked groggily.

'Oh Pax, you're still here ... you're in the infirmary of the hole... the Borztan mines. In Kymera,' the young boy said in his most soothing of voices, taking up his stool again beside the stretcher Paxton was on. 'It's me, Tye.'

'Tye,' Paxton said, recognition dawning as the last few weeks clicked back into place in his memory, unable to hide the defeated tone in his voice. He stared at the small-framed teenager with fiery red hair, teeth he had not yet grown into and bright blue eyes.

Pax was still here. It hadn't been a nightmare. He hadn't seen Zee for what felt like weeks. Months. Mother, he missed her. He needed a joke, a smile from her, anything. An 'It'll be okay... or a 'What's the worst that could happen?' with a wink would surely suffice right now.

He didn't want to think about being in a worse situation than the one he had landed himself in right now. But he knew better than to think that it was the worst thing that could eventuate out of this festering pit they called the hole. Pax had seen things on his arrival here, things that would scar him for life. Bodies piled up, from exhaustion or disease, he didn't want to know. But his peaceful, simple existence back in Kali was definitely a thing of the past. He couldn't imagine a worse place than the mines. The king's soldiers had dumped him here after they had captured him that day at the Rim river. He had tried to fight back, but he'd had no chance. He was smart and a fit fighter, but he didn't stand much of a chance with a fight against ten Kymerian soldiers.

They had held him and flogged him until one of the soldiers landed a good blow to his head that had rendered him unconscious. The last thing he had seen before he had passed out was the tall soldier's body floating in the water and Zee swimming frantically beside Wolf towards and somehow through the Rim wall. How had she done it? Had it something to do with the powers she had acquired after the blast in the village? What on Mother's green earth had happened to the soldier? Had Zee..? Had she killed him? Did she do that with her powers? Accidentally? Or did she actually mean to kill the soldier?

He felt a gnawing in the pit of his stomach and hoped she was alright. He hoped she had made it safely away and that there weren't worse things on the other side of that wall than the soldiers and the Borztan mines. His imagination ran wild every night, so he had to reel it in, of the monsters ripping Zee to shreds, of Wolf not being able to help her. 'It's all in your head, Pax,' he would tell himself. 'She's strong, she's a fighter, she'll be fine.' His vision became blurry and his back throbbed, the pain rattling up into his brain. He was finding it hard to thread thoughts together.

'How long have I been in here, Tye?' he asked the concerned face opposite him, watching his every move with eagle eyes.

'A few days, not too long. Your back... it's—' Tye tried to cover the worry creeping into his alert eyes '—getting better every day, I promise. I've been tending to it myself,' he replied with a bit of pride and a small smile. 'I help out here whenever there is an incident in the mud yard,' he explained.

'And Pax, I...' the boy stammered. 'I don't know how to thank you... for what you did for me. No one's ever stood up for me before, and I'm so, so sorry about your punishment. It's all my fault.' Tye grabbed his mop of hair and pulled at it in complete and utter frustration. 'It's all my fault! I'm so sorry!' He was in tears, rocking back and forth on his seat near the bunk.

'Hey. Hey!' Pax soothed through his own pain. 'You did nothing wrong!' He tried his hardest to connect with Tye's watery eyes, grabbing his hand and squeezing it hard. 'Stop that, mate, stop. You did nothing wrong.' He said more quietly, 'This place is wrong. These soldiers are wrong. Not us.'

Tye calmed himself. 'I'm still so sorry,' he said, taking deep breaths.

'That's it, Tye breathe, and don't be sorry. It's not your fault. We'll get out of here, me and you. We'll get out of here and when we find Zee, they will all pay for what they've done to us. We'll make each and every one of them pay.' Pax's golden eyes shone with retribution. He stared at Tye, still squeezing his hand as his pounding head forced him to shut his eyes.

Pax eventually drifted off into another fitful sleep. No doubt to be filled with the worrying dreams of Zee. At least the dreams were better than being awake... in Kymera... in the king's torturous, festering mines.

Wolf Explains

Lamiria

Zemira didn't know how to feel. This was - this was unbelievable. She had dreamed for so long to have her father back from wherever she had imagined him being. Her mother had never told her anything about him, and she had stopped asking as she grew up. Because of the pain her young eyes saw it had caused her mother, clear in her face. So she had just stopped. It was what it was, and after all, she had met Wolf and he had somehow filled the void. Wolf... who was actually her father all along...

She felt so confused, so overwhelmed. Tears brimmed in her eyes as she stared at him across the small fire between them. 'How can this be? How have you now been able to shift?' The word felt strange coming from her mouth, like it belonged in a fairy-tale not real life.

Orion stared at her, his beautiful girl, his brave, kind, smart, powerful hunter. He clasped his hands and looked down, almost shamefully. 'I knew I couldn't follow when the blast happened. I knew the soldiers would catch me in wolf form and deliver me to him. I couldn't help you. I couldn't help your mother.' He paused, a grief-stricken look creeping into his handsome face.

'So I ran. I ran for the land outside of the Rim, from where I was born, the land called Lamiria. I ran all the way to Kyeitha's temple. The Queen of the Forest, the guardian of the Rim, had raised me on her own after I was born, hundreds of years ago. I have no idea what happened or who my father was. I knew my love for you and your mother had enraged her, but I knew I had to make a deal with her to regain my full strength and powers to save you both.'

Zee took all this in. Her head was still rolling around in an emotional tornado. But why, if it was so easy, had he not done it years ago? Made a deal? Gone to see his mother, Kyeitha. Her grandmother. Oh, stars. Her grandmother was the Rim guardian? The queen of the forest?

'But you, it seems, my little hunter, don't need any saving.' His face morphed into a proud smile.

'Why did it take so long?' she asked. Zee had to know. She still felt the loss, the abandonment from all the years she thought he had left and never returned... because of her. 'Why did it take something like the blast to happen for you to make a deal to shift back?'

His smiled faded. 'There is always a price to pay when you make a deal with Kyeitha. I'm so sorry that you've felt alone all these years and that you thought I wasn't there. But I was always with you, watching over you and your mother, keeping you safe,' he explained, noting Zemira's change in demeanour. The hurt in her voice was not hidden from him.

'Mum... did she know all along that Wolf was really you – Orion?'

Zee recalled the day she had found Wolf, or more likely now she thought about it, that he had found her.

A sweet six-year-old Zemira was on her way to Diwa's, the old lady in the woods, as she used to call her. Her mother had met Diwa in the village, seeking her out after hearing of the old woman's remedies – she could fix anything. Zemira had been having nightmares... of places she had never been to... a forest alight with colour but full of creatures that made her scream and roll around in a fitful sleep until her mother shook her awake.

'They've got him, mummy. The creatures, they took daddy.'

Verena just hugged her small child, tears spilling from her own eyes, and lied. 'No, my darling, he's safe... no creatures have him. He's just gone away for a while, but I know he's safe.'

The old lady at the markets had commented on Zemira's beautiful dark hair and stunning eyes. 'Such a precious child,' she had exclaimed. 'No payments, dear, but this will help her sleep and keep those dreams away.'

The old lady with the radiant smile winked at Zee as she told her mother the correct amount to give her before bed. 'And you, my child, you are welcome to visit me in the forest anytime you like. I have hundreds of flowers and fruits in my garden that I'm sure you would like. If you come to visit, you can pick anything you want.'

Zee remembered her mother thanking the old woman, and the tea did indeed help with the nightmares. Verena and Zemira visited the old lady in the forest with a gift. She'd had the most amazing gardens and cottage Zee had ever seen. She had picked nearly every single flower she could carry, and her mouth was stained purple with all the juneberries she had managed to stuff in there. After that, it had seemed she'd been allowed to visit whenever she wanted, Diwa's cottage becoming her second home.

The day she'd met Wolf on the way to Diwa's, she had gotten distracted in the forest looking for floxels, the small, fluffy creatures that made burrows in between the fern patches, and were as fast as lightning. They popped their little heads out if a large stick was shoved into one of their doorways, as Zee had discovered. She was kneeling down and trying to coax one to come flying out so she could attempt a capture. A shadow blocked her path of light from the sun that she was using to peer into the floxel's hole. As she turned around to see what was in her way, a giant creature's head slid towards her, its flickering tongue outstretched. Its large, legless, black-scaled body was wrapped around the trunk of a tallowbark tree, its mouth now making a clicking sound... and the creature's four shining silver eyes were all pinpointed on Zemira.

Zee was as still as possible for a second, absolutely fear stricken, then her sharp mind had told her to run. She scuttled backwards in the ferns... the giant creature's flat, wide head sucked its tongue back in and opened its mouth, recoiling – preparing to strike. The glistening razor-sharp serrated teeth were a gleaming dark amethyst within. Just as the creature sprang forth towards her as she ran screaming into the ferns, a flash of white flew through the air.

The huge wolf's maw connected with the black creature's neck and ripped it away from Zemira's path. Completely terrified, she crawled backwards, found her jelly-like legs and ran. She ran what she felt like was the fastest her young mind had told her she had ever run. Zee was getting further and further away and dared to look back to see if the horrid black creature or the giant wolf were after her. But there was nothing. As she turned her head quickly back, she slammed into something solid... and soft. It was the wolf. Before she could scream, he was on her, licking her cheeks, her neck, his giant tail wagging profusely. Zee was so shocked at what she thought was going to be her end, but now there was a massive, terrifying-looking creature acting... like her friend. He had saved her from the monstrous black tree creature. She almost immediately trusted him.

'You saved me,' was all she could muster as her huge eyes took all of him in for the first time, her little fingers feeling his soft fur. 'That was... that was absolutely brilliant!' she concluded.

The wolf did not leave her side that day. She showed him around her forest, carefully explaining where all the floxels and rabbits liked to live, where the best glow beetle spots were, how to find them hiding during the day and where to catch them best after the sun had gone down. The best spot to collect fallen mist fruit from the trees bordering the edge of the river, her favourite fishing spot and her new-found hidey hole nearby. She couldn't believe he was following her, listening to her. She was so happy to have found a friend all of her own. Other than Diwa of course.

The sun was getting low, and her eyes were growing tired. 'Okay, Wolfie, I've got to go now. See you tomorrow?' she yawned, but he wouldn't leave her side.

'No, don't follow me, my mum will freak out! She'll never let me into the woods again.'

But he wouldn't budge. She tried to walk away again after explaining... but he was her new shadow. She tried everything to shake him, becoming more and more tired and frustrated.

'Oh fine! But my mum's not going to like this! She's not going to like you, and I'll never be allowed out again!' she had stated, frustrated.

They made it to the small cottage on the side of the hill, and she took a large breath in. 'You stay here, for now,' she ordered, with a hand gesture. 'I'll explain everything before you come in, okay. I'll tell her about you gently, then maybe she'll let you stay.'

Miraculously, the giant white wolf had nodded, actually nodded.

'You understand me? Or am I just imagining things again?'

He sat down as if patiently waiting. 'Ok,' she said to herself 'this will work,' before she opened the door to the small cottage, her mother sitting by the fire in the comfy lounge.

'Mum, I'm home!' Zee had said like she would normally, before spinning around to shut the door behind her. Wolf then flew in like a shot. He quickly assessed where Zee's mother was and ran towards her, his two large paws pinning her by her shoulders, profusely whining and licking her face... his tail going mad, almost ready for lift off.

'ZEE! What is this? What have you brought here?' her mother screeched in shock.

'WOLF! I told you to wait!' Zee said, panicked. She had rushed over to help get him off her mother, but Verena was quite capable and stood up out of the chair, pushing the animal away, her book falling to the floor. Her face was wet with kisses and her hair now dishevelled.

Wolf was still going nuts, now spinning his huge body around the cottage and knocking stools, pot plants and books off places all around his circle with his large powerful tail.

'Mum I can explain, he – I – we were in the forest and there was a tree monster. Wolf saved me. He's my friend. Can I keep him? Pleeeease?' she begged.

Verena, completely caught off guard at the whole situation, just stood there for a second looking at the massive wolf in her sitting room. As if knowing she was about to make a swift judgement, he sat very quickly right in front of her at her feet but still nearly face to face with the woman, and stared at her, his green eyes shining. Verena stilled, staring at the wolf as if noticing him for the first time.

'His eyes are cool, hey, Mum? Kinda like mine. Can I keep him? He kept me safe. He followed me. He's good, I can tell.' Zee stopped explaining her case as she watched her mother almost burst into tears.

Verena stepped forward closing the gap and held the massive wolf's head between her hands, staring more closely into his eyes. She just cried and engulfed his head in a hug, Wolf's tail going mad again. 'Orion,' she breathed.

Zee didn't understand her mother's reaction but at least it was a good one, she guessed. 'So that's a yes? Great! And his name is Wolf, Mum.'

Verena gathered herself as if lost in the moment, wiping away at her face. 'Yes, honey... it's a yes,' she smiled, Wolf's face still in her hands.

She knew. The recognition came to Zee after she had replayed the memory from all those years ago in her head. She knew and she had never told her. The hurt twisted her gut.

'There was nothing she could say, Zee. And, yes, as I said, I'm Orion.' He defended Verena.

'She could have told me,' Zee snapped. 'Said something. I wouldn't have told anyone. I didn't have anyone to tell.'

'She wanted you to have the most normal childhood she could give you. Playing in the forest alone and hunting with a wolf was strange enough, let alone thinking that the wolf was your father.

You have to understand it from her point of view, Zee. How hard it must have been for her to have me back, but not really me.'

Zemira took this in, missing her mother and feeling guilty for being angry with her when she wasn't here to defend herself. 'And Diwa, no wonder she treats you like you walk on clouds. She knows too, doesn't she?'

The hunter felt defeated thinking of all the other things she was totally in the dark about. 'Then why didn't you just shift back at Diwa's? Why wait till now? Why not when the soldiers took Pax? You could have saved him!' An overwhelming feeling of frustration flooded her. Pax would be so worried about her. She hoped he was still alive. Mother, where had the soldiers taken him!

'I couldn't make the shift inside the Rim. I'm sorry about Paxton, Zee. He's a decent young man. When the soldiers came, I wasn't expecting them to be there. I was just so happy you had made it back safe, and I... I was being complacent. It's my fault. I knew the only way to keep you safe from them was across the Rim... and then I could shift to protect you.'

'How did you know I could pass through? What if I was just stuck in the river for the creatures to eat me?'

'I know, Zee, because you're a halfling... a Rim walker. Because you are my daughter. You are human, but also... something more.'

Zee didn't feel like any more answers, the conversation leaving her tired. Yet her remaining questions still flew around in her head like a swarm of small dewbirds. Each answer she was getting was creating ten more questions.

Wolf, sensing her mood, said, 'We should get a move-on if your leg is not too painful. We need to get back inside the Rim. It's alright, Zee, we'll get them both back – your mother and Pax.' He nodded reassuringly.

'My leg is fine, so we can leave whenever you're ready.' She moved to gather her pack that contained the few things from her room she had grabbed. And upon further inspection, also quite a few miscellaneous things she hadn't put in there... Diwa. Her mouth crept up at the corner thinking of the tricky old lady.

'Oh, and I'm not calling you Orion... or Dad... it's weird,' Zee said flatly, still not impressed that all the adults around her had kept secrets from her for so long.

Orion laughed at this, the sound catching Zee off guard, rumbling around the quiet cave and breaking the tense mood. It was a deep, contagious laugh, and Zee forced herself not to join in. The pair stood at the entrance, ready to make their way back.

'Fine,' he said. 'I'm used to Wolf anyway.' He clapped his hand on her shoulder, smiling broadly. Zee couldn't help herself; she let a small grin enter cross features and stared back at him. She could see why her mother chose him... he was very handsome, but there was also something else there... a light that shone within when he looked at her.

A small amount of warmth crept over her, and she immediately felt better about the journey through the outer Rim. At least she wasn't alone. She had found Wolf, and she had found him... her father. As Diwa had said she would. Diwa had surely seen all this coming. She was going back. Back into the Rim. Back to save Pax and her mother. And she was ready for a fight. If the king wanted her, she would not hold back, she would not hide, and she would not go easily. She was Zemira Creedence, and she was finally allowed to be herself, her real self. Not hide away, not afraid of being found, or of being different. And she was going to show them all what she was made of.

The Outer Rim

Lamiria

The outer Rim was completely captivating, and Zemira's body filled with the energy that was present all around her. The forest was illuminated, its bright neon colours nothing like she had ever seen. Every leaf, every small, crawling creature around her had its own special glow. It was so beautiful, the things of dreams made real. How could such an amazing place have so many people terrified of it?

As they travelled through the outer Rim forest at night, Zee didn't feel the fear she knew she should have, but felt invigorated in the presence of the glowing forest. Orion, Wolf in human form, led the way ahead of her, carefully on guard, completely unaware of Zee's absolute astonishment at the beauty all around her. A small creature darted out from the brush in front of her, what looked like a floxel. The fluffy round-shaped creatures with hidden feet made them appear to glide across the ground with only their small echidna-like beaks protruding. But this creature had a longer protruding snout and sparsely spread glowing spikes of every colour nestled in between its fluffy coat. It stopped on the ground before her for a second, sniffed in her direction and then darted off into the forest undergrowth.

'How can something this beautiful be dangerous?' she questioned Orion.

'Don't be fooled, Zemira. There are many deadly creatures in here just waiting for us to let our guard down,' he replied seriously. He had told her it was safest to travel at night in the outer Rim, as most of the larger animals were not nocturnal and would be sleeping, avoiding the iridescent light-show the forest produced at night.

They came up to a small creek, the crystal-clear water flowing down its winding path. The sandy bottom was visible with the lights all around. Small fish darted through the water, their translucent bodies containing highlighted strips along their sides, zooming around like a beautiful little light show. She could also see small yabberis on the creek floor. Yabberis were the small freshwater crustaceans with lobster-like bodies, twelve small legs, four round pinhead-sized eyes and large clawed pinchers lit up with streaks of blue and yellow.

'This place is incredible!' she said while kneeling down and peering into the glowing water world. She waved her hand into the cool water side to side, feeling the pull of the water, taking a deep breath in. It was like a dream made real. She stayed still, taking it all in and fortifying the memory. Storing the feeling of awe and locking it away in her mind. This was one to keep.

Following Orion through the twisting forest of light, she tried to examine every leaf. Every tiny, glowing creature. How had this amazing land been kept secret for nearly five hundred years?

As if Orion could read her thoughts, he said, 'It was to keep it safe, to keep it all safe. Humans couldn't be trusted to preserve any environment after what they had done. So Mother Nature decided to keep her lands and creatures safe, through her Rim guardians and their watchers. She created these with all the energy of the souls she collected after the Oxygen War, which ended the human world that once was in 2032. The surviving humans needed to be kept safe from themselves as well, inside the Rim.'

Zee just listened, still finding the concept of her father suddenly appearing after all this time a lot to deal with. The luminescent forest was a beautiful, distracting buffer for the moment.

'We'll be back in no time,' he assured her as they weaved in and out of the glowing foliage, Orion leading the way.

'How do you know where you're going?' Zee questioned.

'It's a feeling, a magnetic pull that guides your way once you've set your mind to it. Like thinking of the place you long to be and summoning it to yourself. You may be capable of this too. Do you feel the world around you? I've never been able to ask, or to help you hone your skills. I'm sorry for that, Zemira. You've been somewhat left in the dark most of your life, yet somehow you've been able to discover some of your powers yourself. To find the light on your own.'

Zee let his words sink in. She *had* always been able feel things around her, and everything had its own feeling, its own pull to it. The ocean beneath Warwick's boat, the salt in the air, the scent and the feel of the rolling waves... all had given her a certain energy that she had harnessed the night the vipen had attacked. The woverbine, his honest eyes, his coarse, twisted, thick hairs and smooth onyx horns. He had his own particular feeling, connected to the smell of the grass fields and the sensation of the air whizzing through her hair and over her face. An incredible sense of power.

The Rim river, a submerged darkness not to be trusted, produced a cool feeling in the pit of her stomach, not fear but something else - a message to be wary of the power that lay beneath. To respect the river and steer clear. This illuminated forest, it elicited a euphoric feeling, as though she was lit from within, as energy pulsed through everything all around her. As if she could harness the rainbow and lift herself with the millions of connections happening within each being.

'Yes, I can feel everything. It all has its own vibe. The whole environment around me has a smell, a touch, even a certain sound that I can connect with and become a part of. I don't know how to explain it. It makes me feel as though I instantly fit in and become a part of the ecosystem, even though I've never seen it or been here before. But it's like I belong.'

'That's right, Zee. It's the power inside of you growing with every connection, every moment, every memory – strengthening you. Your inner compass can guide you wherever your heart deems most important to go. You have so many rare gifts already, there's no telling what great things you will be capable of and what you will accomplish.'

Zee's heart beat a little faster and even though the air around her in the forest was cool, she felt a warmth inside from her father's kind words. 'First things first, we have to get back and somehow find Pax and then somehow find Mum and save her from a mad king. Sounds easy right... what's the worst that can happen?'

Orion's laugh boomed in front of her as he made a path through the glowing undergrowth. 'Exactly right, that's the spirit, hunter,' he said, unable to wipe the proud smile from his face.

Her legs were aching by the time they reached the deep, dull sheen of blue that emitted from the Rim river. Panic coiled around her stomach like an awakened snake. 'I forgot we had to cross the river again,' Zee stammered, her palms feeling instantly sweaty. A hot flush took over her despite the cool night air surrounding them. 'I can't go back in there.' She backed away from the edge where she stood next to Orion. The three large indents in her calf muscle pulsed slightly with pain... a warning. Danger, danger, danger, her body told her.

Orion sensed her fear. 'I've got an idea. It might be a better alternative to swimming, and we've got to get back faster than this anyway. Give me a moment. I'm a bit rusty.' He stood back from Zee on the river's dark edge, and it looked like Orion was absorbing the glow of energy into himself from the foliage all around them. He outstretched his tattooed, muscled arms, and a blue glow enveloped his body. His outstretched arms transformed with a blast of light into magnificent, giant wings. The wings of a beautiful white eagle.

'Wow,' Zee breathed, awe plastered across her face, which was beautifully lit by the glow of the foliage she stood within. 'Well, I like this idea better than swimming... but I'm still not sure I like it all that much.'

She was utterly blown away by the power he contained, by how amazing it was to see his form shift before her eyes. Orion's giant, stern-looking eagle head twisted to the side, his shining emerald eyes still intact in his new form. He hopped to the side and lowered his head, furling his feathers forward to Zee as if to say, 'Get on, it'll be okay.'

Zee's heart raced now, not with fear but with adrenaline. She was going to fly! Was this even going to work? Orion's eagle form was huge, but was he strong enough to carry her across the river? What if they failed and she was too heavy and they both plummeted into the dark, icy water.

Orion clicked his beak impatiently.

'Alright, already.' Zee hesitated, breathing deeply to calm herself.

He leaned further towards the ground to make it easier to climb onto his soft, feathered back in between the giant, shining wings. Once in place, Zee had her legs comfortably tucked in either side behind Orion's wings and held on securely with two fistfuls of very large feathers. Orion twisted his head back with a look in his eye, 'You rip out my feathers, and I will not be happy.'

'I won't rip any out.' Zee rolled her eyes back at him.

He turned his head forward, shuffled his clawed feet to gain a stable lift-off and outstretched his massive wings. Zee couldn't believe how huge they were or how far they stretched beyond his body. The glow beetles raced inside her chest. This wasn't going to work. They would plummet into the river for sure. She wanted to get off – this was a bad idea. They would find another way. Zee loosened her grip on Orion's feathers and just as she was about to slide off back to the safety of solid ground, he ran very roughly forward towards the river.

Zee grabbed more fistfuls of feathers and squeezed her legs tight, trying to hang on. Oh Mother! What was she thinking! As Orion jumped off the river's edge, they fell, and Zee squeezed her eyes shut, ready for the impact and the blast of cold water, but it didn't come. Instead, she felt a gentle boom of wings lifting, forcing the air downwards with another swoosh. Her stomach cartwheeled inside her and left itself behind as they rose up,up,up. Wind slid over her flushed face, like smooth, cold hands calming her.

She opened her eyes without loosening her death grip on the feathers near Orion's neck. She was sure she may have already dislodged a few. Oh, well. Served him right for not giving her more instruction.

Orion's wings beat higher and higher, and the wind rushed past her now. Her stomach was well and truly left behind. They soared higher over the river, Orion rising then following the river up and gliding down to skim his feet and tips of his feathers along the water as he flew. He let out a screeching caw, Zee guessed of joy. Then he sped upwards towards the stars and away from the river with marvelling speed, considering he had Zee and her pack in tow.

Zemira could smell the sweet night air above the forest and looked down at it to the mesmerising glow of each leaf and plant all blending into one as they rose higher. It was one of the most beautiful things she had ever seen until she looked up. They were in the clouds! The moon illuminating the gargantuan pillows of clouds upon clouds. They made Zee feel like an ant upon a beetle's back. This was incredible!

Orion steadied and slowed his speed, levelling out and gently gliding in and out of the clouds. The mountains of glowing clouds dispersed, and Zee's eyes felt as though she were looking upon diamonds. The stars were brilliant, illuminating the whole sky. She'd never felt so in awe. This was by far the most beautiful thing she'd ever seen. Even she couldn't have imagined it better. She bravely loosened her grip on Orion's feathers and let go, reaching upwards, fingers spread out as if trying to sift the stars through her palms. Taking a deep breath in, she let out a giant, 'Yessss.' Orion joined in with his own cry of pure exhilaration at being able to once again shift and fly. The pair were utterly on a high.

'This is by far way better than a woverbine!' she yelled out, just as Orion dipped a little, indicating for Zee to hang on again. She obeyed his subtle order, drawing in the last of the shimmering sky around her, and hung on again tight. As Orion tucked his wings in and dove down, they spiralled with a speed like nothing Zee had ever experienced before. A scream ripped from her mouth, one of pure elation mixed with terror, her hair streaming behind her. Her body betrayed her with its shaking legs, but her mind was absolutely euphoric. They levelled out just before the forest's glow and before the trees became too distinguishable, with just a hint of the Rim wall's iridescent sheen in sight up ahead of them.

They arrived at Diwa's cottage and floated gently down after passing back through the protective zing of the Rim wall. Diwa, as always, had known they were coming and had food, tea and plenty of hugs awaiting the both of them. Zee was weary now, her legs were achy, and she felt as though she could sleep for a year. She had no idea how Orion had had the energy to fly himself, let alone her, all the way here. Her mind was still full of vibrant images of the outer Rim forests and the absolute exhilaration of flying. Everything had seemed a shade dimmer upon re-entering the Rim. Somehow less... like the magic was missing a little.

Diwa coaxed her to have large meal, a bath and a cup of her special tea. 'You need rest, Zemira, rest for what's coming. When you wake up, we'll talk,' she said in her comforting, throaty voice as she steered Zee away down the tiny hall in the tree cottage. Away to the end of the hall and her own bedroom for Zee to sleep off all the recent events that had occurred. To recover and recuperate her strength.

Diwa returned to the kitchen table where Orion in his large Watcher form sat sipping tea out of a dainty cup decorated with tiny blue flying lizards and fern leaves. The cup looked miniscule in his masculine grasp.

'My dear, how good to see you in your original form again.' Diwa's smile reached her ears, crinkling her shining eyes. She reached out a wrinkled, frail-looking hand with large nobbled joints, and Orion offered his large tan palm to her. Her strong squeeze was hidden underneath the frail appearance as she looked into his emerald gaze.

'What was the cost, Orion?' Diwa asked searchingly.

'Orion replied with a gruff rumble, 'It was worth it, Dee. It was worth it to see her again. And it will be worth it when we find Verena.'

'Will you kill him?' she asked, squeezing her small hand around Orion's a little more, her eyes penetrating into his.

'I will do what has to be done. Nothing more, but nothing less.'

Diwa withdrew her hand, knowing she would not get the answers she sought. 'How is your tea, love?'

Orion smiled, again holding the dainty cup in his hand. 'It's lovely, Dee, just as it always was. And, yes, I will leave the cup when I'm done.' His tattooed brow raised at the sweet being opposite.

'When should we tell her about the boy?' Diwa asked.

'Let her sleep. She enjoyed the forests of Lamiria immensely, and she is just now coming around to trust me and deal with me being back in her life again. We'll let her have this moment of rest and peace and tell her in the morning. Now tell me, how on earth do you make these teas so amazingly inside the Rim? They are just as good as I remember and that was a looong time ago.' He smiled, achingly handsome.

Diwa replied, her mischievous little grin curling up her face and showing her glossy teeth. 'I'll tell you mine if you tell me yours.'

Orion laughed. 'You always were one for a good trade.'

They laughed together and chatted for hours, talking through every situation and what Ravaryn may want with Verena and Zee after all this time while Zemira slept peacefully down the hall. When Orion and Diwa grew dreary, they finally retired to sit in the lounge. Orion left his cup on the table, the leaves collecting together at the bottom in a dark ring that resembled a circle, a hoop, or a hole.

The next morning, Diwa's hands swirled in beautiful motions above the worn old kitchen table in her small cottage, just as she had done before to show Zemira the image of her mother inside the ice castle. This image, however, was one far more gruesome. Orion's hand slid over the top of Zemira's on the table top without asking, and he squeezed it firmly. She didn't pull it away. It was almost a bit painful, but she didn't mind. The gesture made her muscles relax a little and held her there in the moment. Grounded her. The cloud swirled and spun, and a storm of clouds formed within, grey, charcoal and onyx, coming to clear in the middle and showing a pit. No, a hole of thick ice and mud, and a whip slicing through a boy's back. Paxton's back. Blood spilled into the muck as ribbons of flesh were created and cracked yellow teeth snarled with the effort of each swing. Zee's free hand flew to her mouth, and tears welled in her eyes. She couldn't contain the sobs or the feeling of guilt that this was somehow *her* fault.

The Hole

Kymera

The burn of every swing of the pick rippled through Paxton's body as sweat beaded on his brow inside the steamy mine. Upon arrival, he had been shown three things. The pile of frozen bodies just outside the entrance to the large, open cavern called the hole – prisoners who thought they would try their luck at escape, or worse still, that opted for the release the frozen lands would give them upon their imminent death. The second, the mud pit, a slushy, melted area at the opposite side of the entrance to the hole where the thermal warmth from within let ice melt and mix with the earth. In the centre, a single wooden pole was erected where punishments would be carried out and where discipline for disobeying orders was publicly displayed to all the prisoners of the western pits. There was currently a poor soul who had taken double food rations tied to the post, almost freezing to death without food or water for two days.

Paxton was now quite familiar with this area and with what kind of punishments were given for the smallest of infractions. His rippled back stung at the thought of the blacksmith's barbed whip. No wonder so many prisoners had opted to freeze to death. And the third was inside the mines: the hole. No one was given any warm clothing of any kind; it wasn't needed and was the best way to prevent more prisoners attempting to escape. The geothermal heat from within the gaping mouth of the cavern seeped warmth from within its giant, ancient mouth. A glacial stream flowed through a part of one section at the back of the large cave system for drinking, bathing and relieving yourself. It all flowed back underground away to somewhere unknown.

Inside another open cave system, hundreds of coarsely woven hammocks lay strewn about between large stalagmites, some reaching up towards their stalactite partners, which hung down from the gigantic ceiling seeping a steady drip, drip, drip. The dim, musty air and dark environment in the deeper cavern was lit with little glowing creatures that crawled all around at night. They created moving, living lightning, which Pax was sure all the other prisoners were grateful for as the darkness of the mines had a very eerie feeling, and dampened even the smallest spark of hope.

Another swing, and Paxton's back pleaded with his shaking body to stop. The sound of a hundred picks chip, chip, chipping away rattled through his ears and inside his head. 'How much longer till sundown do you think, Tye?'

'Hang in there, not long at all. Just rest while Old Bones there isn't watching,' replied Tye, referring to the tall, wiry guard on duty as they, along with a hundred or so other young bodies, chipped away at the shimmery black walls of the humid cavern.

'You shouldn't be working at all, your back is barely healed,' whispered Tye, frustrated. 'You tear it open again, and it could get infected. I managed to swipe a small jar of mistlefern oil, but if you bust it again, it's not going to be enough.' The worry in Tye's ocean blue eyes poured from him with concern.

'I know, I know.' Pax was huffing, trying to catch his breath in between moments when Old bones wasn't looking his way. 'Thanks, Tye. You didn't have to put yourself at risk like that for me, and you've got to be more careful or it'll be you in the mud yard next.'

Pax, seeing the worry and anxiety suddenly seep into Tye's face, changed the subject. 'Don't worry about me. What's this rock for, anyway? I know it's not coal, as they don't need to burn it for warmth anymore since they discovered that sky pine seeds can burn for an eternity. They don't need the metal for weapons, as they seem to have plenty of them from what I could gather on the way here. Every guard I came across was adorned with knives. So what's it for?' Paxton wiped the sweat from his forehead with the back of his hand, smearing the black-powdered dust on his skin like war paint.

'They use it for the uniforms,' Tye divulged nervously. 'The material is almost impenetrable, but light. And they are building somethin' with 'em. I've heard they are forging them into bricks in some of the other caverns. And they powder it... mix it with other chemicals. It's how he did it. The king. How he managed all those blasts to knock out whole villages and make it seem like an explosion, but it only directly affected the people... some kind of new science maybe? None of the villages were damaged, so there were no rules broken in the code... just hundreds of missing people. Some he even wrote off on old war tech exploding within the ground. That's all lies. He did it... to bring them here to enslave them all, for Mother knows what reason.'

Tye struck the wall with a burst of angry energy as Old Bones strolled past, scowling in his direction.

Pax's mind spun. He remembered his village – there was no damage, it was just empty of all its inhabitants. Like they had all disappeared into the wind. The festival decorations still floated around the streets on their own. He remembered waking in Thorta with the burning chemical sensation that had stung his throat. His burns had been unusual, not like those of fire victims, which had been healed by Jill's kind hands. How Zee had the same smell and taste weeks after the blast. How long it had taken her to heal. Much longer than anyone else, that's for sure.

'How do you know all this, Tye?'

Tye looked nervously to his other side as if checking whether or not some invisible assailant was listening in. 'Because I'm not from Aylenta, I'm from Zenya. I used to work in the ice castle. I used to work for the king.'

'We're taking too long,' Zemira said impatiently.

'We can't risk anyone seeing you gliding in on an eagle's back, Zee,' Orion replied matter-of-factly. 'We are nearly past the border, and when the night comes, we can use its cover in the clouds to make it the rest of the way. Paxton will be okay. I'm sure of it. He's a tough young lad.'

Zee's gut twisted around and around. The image of his blood-stained back falling into the mud painfully occupying her mind without reprieve.

'I'm sorry about what's happened to him, but Diwa wanted you to see the hole, the cavern, the mines and to see what the soldiers will do to us if we're caught.'

'We won't be,' said Zee confidently. 'Our plan is sound, and any soldier that gets in our way won't ever do so again.'

Orion's eyes glazed over in concern. Zee's anger worried him, but he knew she'd be furious at what had happened to her friend. He was more worried that he knew no one would be able to stand in her way, no one was powerful enough to stop her, not now... and not in the future. He just hoped she wouldn't do anything she would later regret. With such power came great responsibility, and consequences. Choices she would make in the present would determine what kind of person she would be in the future. Her actions could do good, or turn her down a dark path. There was nothing he could do or say that would sway her fate; she would have to decide that on her own. He didn't have the right. She was a woman now, an adult, and would carve her own path. He would just stay by her side and trust in her decisions, and be there if she needed him to rely on.

The sun disappeared behind the Wendigo Ranges as they passed the territory border on foot. The thick moscow clothing they had collected on the way in the small town just along the border on the coast fit snugly. Zee was almost sweating within, even with the frozen chill in the air. The beautiful sparkle of the sun's last rays hit the shimmering white snow that covered the land ahead of them like icing. She had a large pack with another outfit for Paxton and supplies they might need, some teas and a salve Diwa had added to the pack, along with various dried fruits, nuts and jerky. They were set. She was itching to go, itching to save Pax, to see him again. She couldn't believe how much she missed his presence. She just prayed he was still alive. She missed her mother immensely, but trusted in the fact that the king hadn't harmed her yet. Zee had so many unanswered questions that would consume her if she let them all in at once. But if she just concentrated at the task on hand, she knew they would all retreat to the back of her mind for a while. Now they had to get Paxton out. They had to save him before he was tortured even more.

'You ready,' Orion questioned.

'Definitely,' Zee replied 'What's the worst that could happen?' Ignoring the fact that they would be heading into an enemy's territory. One who had stolen citizens of Aylenta, enslaved them and tortured them to death in mines, and who had captured and held her own mother hostage. Sure, this would be fine.

183

The sun's weak glow finally faded behind them at the giant opening of the cave mouth. Paxton's body was shaking all over, demanding him to stop. His legs were like jelly, and he could barely lift the pick and carry it back to the racks as they finally finished for the day. The prisoners were left on their own to reach the large cave where rations were dispersed for the day. Then they bathed away the silt, the shimmering Borztan dust that covered every inch of their bodies. Pax didn't know if he could ever wash away the miniscule grains that coated his skin, infiltrated his hair and settled in his ears, nose and eyelashes. Although he tried his hardest to scrub the king's stain away, it was slowly working its way inside him. As was this whole place.

Why hadn't she come? Was she okay? Had she just forgotten about him altogether? Disregarded him as if he were a stray dog following her around? No, Zee would never... she was kind, brave. She would never leave him here in this place to die. He had contemplated running, but what chance would he have of survival in the freezing wastes? Without at least warm clothing? Or a sky pine seed to ignite and keep him warm and alive through the harsh weather and the darker night? No. To try to run now was certain death. He just hoped he could hold on longer in the hole. But his whole body ached and his mind was losing hope.

'Come on, let's get in quick tonight before the rations thin out then hit the bathing stream. You need to wash your back and dry it well. You did well not to rip it open. Not many do so well on their first day back...' Tye trailed off.

He pulled Paxton quickly along through a small tunnel that opened out into where the ration cavern was situated. After they had eaten a bowl of sludgy grey mess from a small bowl with hard seeds folded through the mix, they dragged their weary bodies to bathe before heading back to their bunks for what solace they could gain with sleep. All before another bone-breaking day picking away at the solid, shimmering walls.

'How did you end up in here, Tye?' Pax questioned as the red-haired boy's blue eyes tried hard to focus on Pax's. The warm water had soothed Pax's aching muscles slightly, but the healing slashes stung like hell when he entered the hot water to wash the glittery dust away.

Tye carefully tended to Pax's back, smearing the stolen mistlefern oil all around the openings to fight off any chance of infection. 'Well, as you may 'ave already figured, I'm somewhat of a healer. But my parents scored me a job working in the castle as a cleaner.'

Paxton winced as Tye hit a particularly sore spot, the mistlefern oil biting like a raspor's sting.

'Sorry.' Tye withdrew.

'Nah, it's all good.' Pax clenched his teeth. 'Thank you for helping me.'

Tye's cheeks bloomed, and he was grateful that Pax's back was turned towards him so he had no clue. 'I would help heal people on my nights off in the city. Mostly frostbite, colds, some cuts inflicted from a soldier's blow. A black eye from a club brawl, a broken wrist. That's where I met Jace.'

A small smile filled Tye's face but not exposing his too-large teeth. 'He had some unexplained slashes and said he had barely gotten away from a soldier in the market square. He had been stealing food for his family. The penalty for stealing is to be sent to the mines. But he said his little sister was sick and his mother couldn't leave her, so she couldn't work. He was desperate. Anyway, like the fool I am, I was sucked right in. I started to steal food from the castle kitchens for him. Just a loaf of bread here and there, a few dewfruit. Eggs, nothing too drastic, only a few things I thought no one would notice.

'One night, I met with Jace to give him what I had taken that day. A soldier appeared – he had followed me. I was careful, but

185

not careful enough. Jace ran for it, but I was caught, flogged and ended up here.'

Tye's voice cracked slightly as his throat constricted. 'The worst thing of all is my parents don't even know I'm here. They probably think I've run away and that I don't care about them.' A tear rolled down his cheek, but he quickly wiped it away with the back of his hand, careful not to wipe any of the misltefern oil from his fingers into his eyes.

'That's why I know what they are doing with the Borztan. I used to overhear things... in the castle. No one noticed me, and they didn't bother to think whether or not I would listen. Just some insignificant little servant,' he finished quietly.

'I'm so sorry you're in here, Tye. You deserve better. You're a good person, so don't let a few bad people make you forget that. Just hold on. I know Zee will come. You and me, we'll be out of here in no time.' Pax encouraged light-heartedly, but it took way more energy than he had.

'What about you, Pax? You think your parents are just as worried as mine?'

Pax looked down at his callous black-stained hands and replied, 'Nah, Zee's the only one who'll be looking for me, Tye. I'm an orphan. My parents died years ago.' At least, I hope she's looking for me. Without Zee, I'm nothing. I have no one... she doesn't even know how much she means to me.'

'Sorry, Pax. I didn't know. You're lucky you've got Zee,' he said, trying to patch the awkward silence.

Pax finally replied. 'Yep.' A smile covered his face when he thought of her bright forest-specked eyes and soft, silky midnight hair. 'I've got Zee.'

Lost Souls

The Hole, Kymera

The blistering cold raged past her face, small icicles dangling from the fur around the hood tightly encasing her head. She could almost feel the small beads of ice forming on her eyelashes as they became heavier to lift in the blurry fog of the blizzard. Orion blazed a trail in front of her through the frigid white mess.

'How do you know where you're going?' Zee yelled over the roaring wind. 'I can't seem to feel where the mine is through this snowfall.'

'You have to try, Zee,' Orion yelled back.

The pair were holding each other now and trying to stand against the powerful gusts of the storm.

'I've got an idea!' Zee screamed, barely able to hear Orion now.

She let go of Orion's grasp and removed her large, thick fur-lined mitts, tucking them safely inside the front pockets of her moscow jumper. Her hands instantly froze, the cold creeping up her arms swiftly. She closed her snow-flaked eyes and concentrated. The green flames flickered against the blasts of the wind, barely able to ignite. Zee didn't give up, just kneeled down and placed her shaking hands on the frozen earth where a dull green glow illuminated from under the snow all around her.

Her hands flickered with small flames of magic, and around them, the ice started to melt. She could barely see an inch in front of her face now – the storm was worsening. She could understand now how her father had been lost and swept away in this land all those years ago when he had crash-landed into her mother's house. Zee focused her mind, creating exactly what she wanted below the frozen earth. She was shaking profusely now, her lips and hands turning juneberry, like when she was a small child, and the juice from the ripe juneberries in Diwa's garden would stain her lips dark purple-blue.

A large melted hole appeared where her hands had been tunnelling down into the ground away from the raging storm. She didn't bother trying to yell through the storm again, so she got behind and pushed Orion forward, motioning towards the hole. He complied and barely managed to fit his large form in, just squeezing through.

The underground ice bunker Zee had created was a first. She amazed herself – it had worked! Almost everything she had tried to manifest with her flames had been accomplished. A large blue smile spread across her face as she removed her stiff white hood, hands shaky. Tiny icicles hung all around her hood like beautiful little chrysalises waiting to hatch.

Orion couldn't hide his pride as he stood inside the area Zee had created. The sudden release of the roaring wind from his ears was welcomed. 'Zee, you did well,' he encouraged. 'Now put those mitts back on before your hands drop off!' he commanded in a fatherly tone.

Zee just rolled her eyes. 'Yes, Wolf.'

She inspected the ice cabin she had created more closely, the raging blast of the storm still bellowing in from the smaller entrance hole. She swiped a hand and a thin layer of ice crusted over the doorway, sealing them in and making it even more peacefully quiet.

'This is it,' Zee said excitedly. 'This is how we will get Pax out! They'll think he's run, tried to escape, but if they go looking for him, we'll be safely hidden out of sight. They can look all they want and they will never know we're hidden just below the surface.'

Zee's smile radiated, proud of her own idea and how well she had mastered the powers she still had no clue about, all on her own.

Orion smiled back at her. 'Sounds like a plan to me.'

Nightfall was just upon them. Zee and Orion peered over the small mound of fresh snow outside the entrance to the hole. She could see a dark muddy area, and the image off Paxton being whipped, his blood mixed with the filthy mud flooded her mind, not making her sad this time... but furious. She shook the image from her mind. She had to concentrate.

'You ready?' she whispered to Orion, whose face was close up beside her as they both lay on their fronts in the thick snow. His handsome tanned skin and dark tattoos were a deep contrast to the bright white of the frigid land around them. Kymera. The storm had gone, but the wind was still blowing about enough snow for a fairly good cover. Not that they would need it... Zee didn't plan for them to be followed. She didn't plan for any more harm to ever come to Paxton.

'I'll wait for your signal. If you're not back in half an hour, I'm coming in. Deal?'

'Okay, Zee. I'll find our lad.' Orion smiled as his eyes started to glow, and within a flash, she was staring at Wolf.

'That still messes with my mind, but it's very, very cool,' she said to the large, furry face staring back at her. Wolf took a last look at Zee and disappeared into the snow, blending in completely like a ghost in the night. She just prayed to the Mother that Pax was hanging in there, that he was still okay.

Wolf padded soundlessly in the snow at the mouth of the hole, searching for any sign of soldiers on watch. There was one tall, slim-built soldier at the large entrance, puffing on a dark cigarette and leaning up against the far wall of the cave mouth. Wolf waited. Zee guided her hands before her and concentrated on the air around the lone soldier's form. She withdrew her arms back towards her and took a large breath in, her outstretched hands and invisible tendrils of power sucking the air and smoke straight from the soldier's lungs.

He grabbed at his throat, and after a moment slid down the metallic wall and slumped to the ground, his head lolling to the side. Zee's heart raced. She hoped she hadn't taken too much for too long, and that he had just passed out. She was sure he was only unconscious but something inside her said, 'Who cares if he's dead?'

Wolf looked back at Zee from where she stood and kept guard close to the entrance. He nodded once and loped off into the large cave system to find Pax. Wolf knew he would find him if he were here, his scent firmly in his memory bank having spent many times hunting with Zee, Pax tagging along. Wolf shook away the annoying fatherly feelings of dislike towards the boy. He was simply that, a boy, or young man now, and he had been with Zee when she'd needed someone the most. He'd helped her escape from Thorta and had brought her back safe and sound. Paxton deserved a little more respect and patience from him. He rounded a corner that opened up into a giant cavern strewn with dripping stalagmites and bright crawling creatures. There were over a hundred hammocks with weary young bodies on them scattered about the large opening, and he could smell him. Pax was here.

The slumped soldier didn't move, his cigarette still smouldering away on the cave floor where it fell minutes before. Zee watched and waited, her hands and nose freezing. What a horrible place to be. Who in their right mind would choose to live in such a Mother's damned place? Exhaling a cloud of warm air, she wondered what was taking Wolf so long, growing more anxious with every minute. Just then she spotted another soldier coming from the back of the dimly lit cavern. There were lanterns hanging from some of the walls with small candles burning within, lighting the area just enough to see that the soldier had indeed spotted his comrade passed out and slumped against the slick black wall.

Zee hoped he just thought the guard was having a snooze, slacking at his post. But the still-smouldering cigarette that had rolled away from him suggested otherwise. She had to act. She couldn't let them get caught. They already had Pax, and she wouldn't let anything happen to Wolf. As silently as she could, she darted through the snow and into the dim, ominous opening of the hole. Creeping up behind the soldiers, she tried not to alert the other guard. Placing a hand on the back of his neck, Zee sent a shock of pure power into his system. It felt the same as the power she had used on Winifred 5.

Her hand glowed with a bright white humming light, and the second soldier dropped to the ground. Zee amazed at herself and feeling more confident, decided to see where Wolf had gotten to. Maybe something was wrong? Maybe they needed her help? She crept through the dim and musty corridor leading off to a dark, much smaller cavern, one that had rocks strewn all around. The dirt was well-compacted in this area, with a kitchen of sorts to the back.

Something tugged at her mind... a small opening off to one side of the cavern, one that no one would ever notice if they hadn't already had known it was there. She saw a vision of the entrance in her mind and followed it. Behind a large stalagmite against the dark wall was a curved entrance hidden away in the rock. Faint tendrils of power pulled at her to follow.

Zee couldn't quite place the feeling of energy that was calling to her, but it felt strange. Otherworldly. Against her better judgement, she followed. The narrow passageway started to seep with dark energy towards her, but she couldn't turn back. She knew she shouldn't, but she had never felt this strange pull before and had to investigate further.

She conjured a small, flickering flame within her palm to light the claustrophobic tunnel. Small white, almost translucent, creatures scuttled away on the walls of the passage. Just as she thought she couldn't handle any more of the thick, stagnant air in the cramped tunnel, it sloped downwards and opened up into a flat-floored cave with a fireplace built into one of the walls to her right.

Dousing her own flame, she looked around the dusty den, the energy screaming at her. It was so strong she could feel its presence in the air. The walls of the small space were floor-to-ceiling shelves. Nearly every shelf space was occupied with sphere-like dusty objects. There was a solid metal table in the centre of the room, and the floors felt sticky under her boots. The metallic tang of the air made her nose crinkle.

She tried to concentrate on the force. It was trying to communicate with her via a loud, incessant thrumming though her body. What did it want? She walked further into the curiously dark space, barely seeing much at all as the dull fire cast just enough illumination to see outlines of the room. Zee walked over to the shelves that lined the wall, and the energy hummed louder, much louder. She picked up one of the round dusty objects. As Zee spun it around in her shaky hands, her heart nearly jumped from her chest. It was a human skull she was holding in her hands. The image of a young boy strapped to the table in the middle of the filthy cavern flooded her mind. He was screaming, pleading, as a soldier with a crusty yellowed smirk dissected him bit by bit. The energy screamed into her head with the boy's vision, and his pleads. Zee dropped the skull in shock and horror.

The whole wall was full of skulls. She saw them now as dozens filled the small space. The energy rose horrifically as they all tried to reach for her help. She saw them all as the tears streamed from her face. They were being tortured, raped, dismantled, asphyxiated. They were pleading with her for help. Zee then felt a hand clamp around her from behind. Calloused and foul-smelling, it clamped over her mouth, and the other slid against her waist, immobilising her.

'Well, well, well. What do, we 'ave 'ere?' A deep, husky voice slid into her ear. 'You're a pretty one. I think I'll 'ave my fun with you.'

Zee panicked and tried to wriggle free to swing the body forwards from her, to get away from the repulsive feeling of him pressing himself up against her into her back. She wanted to be sick. How had she let herself become so distracted? How could she have let herself get into this situation. There was no way out... without her hands free she was useless.

The man spun her around forcefully as she desperately thrashed about. He easily restricted her hands, forcefully crushing them together in one palm. He wrapped a coarse rope-like band around her wrists that he had attached to his waist.

The cracked yellow smile breathed vile, warm breath into Zee's face. 'A very pretty one. I'll 'ave to take my time with you.' His malevolent grin was just visible in the minimal light of the cavern. 'Lucky me, I have two treats for myself tonight.'

193

He thrust Zee into the metal table behind her, smashing her side into it. She fell to the ground winded. The vile soldier dragged what Zee thought was a large sack into the cavern and dropped it beside her.

Come on... think, think. The pulsing energy was so loud. All the lost boys were screaming at her, trying to say something... save... save... save us? No, save him. It wasn't a sack at all. It was a body. A boy, bloody and beaten. His fiery red hair was crusted with dry blood next to her, his freckled face pale... unconscious. The lost souls were glowing in front of the small embers in the fireplace. They drew her down... trying to save him.

Her side was still pulsing pain through her as she tried to catch her breath. Her ribs screamed. The soldier stood over her. She had to do something; she didn't care if her hands were tied. Zee would burn this whole sick place down if she had to, to get her and this poor boy out. Looking down at her bound hands, she saw it wasn't rope that the soldier had wrapped them in, it was a whip. The vision of Paxton being mercilessly whipped into the mud pit flashed in her mind, along with the soldier's dank grin and malevolent eyes.

It was him, the soldier standing above her. This disgusting creature had tortured and killed all these boys. Her eyes widened and took him in as he bent down to grab her off the damp floor. She raised her legs and with as much force as she could, kicked out and connected with his foul face. He flew back and roared in pain.

'You little—'

Zee forcefully ripped at her hands to free them, but the whip was bound so tight. Rage ignited inside her, the voices, the pulse of all the energy of the lost boys filling her. Speeding through her veins. Her hands burst into flames, the whip disintegrating within seconds, just as the soldier went to lunge at her again, crawling nearly on top of her with a clenched fist drawn. He stopped, stilling in surprise. Zee lifted her free hands and thrust them right into his

194

gruesome face, digging her fingers deep into his eye sockets and melting his face with a furious blast of fire.

He screeched in pain, the sound ripping from his throat. His hand shot out to grab her forearms, which in turn also ignited. His hands caught alight, and he flew back screaming in pain as his eyeless face gaped, scuttling backwards away from her. Zee felt not one ounce of guilt. Her eyes were consumed with flickering rage. She wanted to end him, her fury was barely contained as she thought about what he had done... to these boys... to Pax... to what he would have done to the red-haired boy still lying unconscious on the floor of his torture room. But she controlled herself.

Death wasn't punishment enough. Zee stalked over to the withering soldier thrashing now with pain, his melted face a horror. Melted skin where his eyes should have been... his hands a mess. He would lose them for sure. But it wasn't enough. He deserved more. The green flames poured from every inch of her along with the power of the boys, their combined energy fuelling her. She grabbed the man's melted jaw in her hands and squeezed it open. With her other hand, she forced fingers inside, past the jagged yellow teeth, and found what she sought.

With one swift motion, Zee roared with the pain she felt from dozens of victims, and ripped his vile tongue from within, just like gutting a fish. His wretched screams became silent as she dropped his tongue to the ground of the cave. Taking one last look at the disfigured, evil soul, she turned and didn't look back. Rushing to the poor boy on the floor, Zee checked if he was still breathing. She pressed her now-cool hands to his face. Come on. Wake up.

His long eyelashes flickered, and large blue eyes stared back at her.

'Come on, we have to go. Can you walk?' she asked gently.

The boy nodded, eyes wide. Zee untied the ropes on his wrists and ankles; they had been drawn so tight that the bruises had already bloomed, along with a brilliant black eye on his young face. The poor thing, he was so thin. But he had fought. She saw that in her mind. Zee grabbed his hand, and they headed out of the dark hole and away, as quickly as their feet could carry them. The voices were now silent. She hoped they could all see what she had done to the blacksmith. She hoped that it was enough to finally give them some peace. And she hoped with all her heart that Paxton was not among one of the poor souls that had been imprisoned within the shelves there.

Escape From Darkness

Kymera

Wolf crept silently through the hammocks scattered all over the giant cave, following the scent trail to Paxton. As he weaved through the exhausted bodies, none of them stirred. They were all so spent, hopefully dreaming of somewhere other than this hell they would awaken to. He closed in on the scent and found Pax half curled in his hammock, fitfully sleeping on his side.

Nudging the young man's face with his wet nose, Wolf gently coaxed him awake. Pax opened his eyes and looked as though he might burst into tears upon seeing Wolfs face.

'Are you real?' he whispered.

Wolf just gave his cheek another nudge as if to say yes, now let's go.

Pax picked his body painfully up out of the hammock, trying to make as little noise as possible. Then hugged Wolf's huge head.

'It's good to see your furry mug. Wait, where's Tye? We have to get Tye.' Pax whispered. He looked back to the nearest hammock behind him to find it empty. Where was he?

Wolf huffed a small sound, saying hurry up, Pax. But Paxton wouldn't, couldn't leave without Tye.

'We have to find him, Wolf. I'll check the stream. Maybe he had to go.'

Wolf followed Pax's lead into a huge area with a trickling clear geothermal stream. There was no sign of anyone. Wolf nudged at Pax again. Time to go. Paxton looked around worriedly.

'Okay, Wolf, but I'm guessing you're with Zee, and I'm not leaving Tye behind. I'll have to get her to help me come back in and look for him.'

Wolf just nudged him again. They both started towards the front mouth of the cave as quickly and as quietly as they could. Pax felt weak, and his back still ached furiously, but he couldn't believe the exhilaration he felt inside. He was so worn and yet so relieved she had come. He forced himself not to cry. He could remember the last time he cried, but that was different. Now he felt relieved, like he belonged again, not like when he lost his parents.

Spying the two downed soldiers at the entrance to the cave, Wolf sprinted outside into the snow, to the mound that he and Zee had promised to meet on. She was gone. Damn it! Paxton followed closely behind, now shivering uncontrollably in the frigid weather. Wolf sniffed around in the snow, the wind brisk and still blowing enough fresh fall around to make vision blurry. He started to dig furiously and unearthed the pack, dragging it up with his mouth and pushing it towards Paxton. Pax immediately dove for the large pack, retrieving the moscow outfit and thick, furry boots intended for him.

'Where is she, Wolf?' Pax shakily clothed himself, his teeth chattering loudly, snow clinging to his hair already.

Wolf just kept his eyes pinned on the cave entrance. She must have gone looking for them because Pax had taken too long looking for the other boy. He was worried and annoyed at the delay. Now Zee was somewhere inside that hell hole. Just as he was about to dart back into the mine, he saw two figures emerging from deep within the dark cave.

Relief washed over Wolf. But who did she have slung around her? He leaped down from behind the mound and padded towards Zee and the figure, his arm draped over her shoulder as she helped drag him out of the mine. Wolf transformed into Orion in a blink as he raced towards her.

'Are you okay? Are you hurt?' Orion asked her, noting the tear stains down her face, concern plastered all over his face.

'I'm alright, Wolf, but can you take him?' She transferred the poor boy over to her father.

His eyes were wide with shock, probably thinking he was now hallucinating as he had just seen a wolf transform into Orion before his eyes. 'Y-you're Zemira...' he stuttered in awe as he glanced between the two. 'You came... you actually came. And you're a wolf...?' he looked as if he were about to faint. The boy was not in good shape at all.

'We have to get him out of here. Did you find Pax?' Zee looked around wildly.

'Yes, but let's go quickly before more guards come.'

'Where were you? What took you so long?' questioned Zee as they made it to the front of the cave entrance, the two slumped soldiers still thankfully passed out. At least Zee hoped they were only passed out. Actually, no, she didn't really care anymore.

'Pax had a friend that he was adamant we had to find. We searched but he wasn't in his hammock, and he wasn't at the bathing stream. Pax wants you to go back in to search for him, but I'll go. You're not going back in there.'

Zee raised her brow at this but held her tongue. She didn't want him to know... but she was definitely more than capable of looking after herself.

Paxton watched, still shaking from the cold but now slightly more shielded from the vicious weather, as Wolf leaped out of the snow. A blue light shone, consumed him, and then the animal morphed into... a man.

Oh, shit. I'm dreaming. Fear streaked around inside him. It was a dream. He felt panicked and couldn't get enough breaths in at the thought of waking to another painstaking day in the hole. It was too much to bear. Yet he watched as the wolf, now man, approached two figures coming from within the darkness at the back of the cave entrance.

Zemira, it was her. He would know her form anywhere. Maybe he was dreaming, but deep down he knew she had come for him... and she had a boy with her. Paxton's legs told him to move. To get as far away from the mines, the hole, the blacksmith as humanly possible. But instead, he sucked in deep breaths and started to walk back towards the entrance and towards Zee. She would understand; she'd help him. He had to find Tye.

He walked faster now, despite his shaking legs and aching back, as she ran to him. Colliding on the snow's edge, Paxton wrapped his arms around her and squeezed her tight, swinging her in his arms, his body instantly feeling lighter. She was real, it was all real. He breathed in her jasmine, pine and mint scent. She smelled of home. His eyes welled up, and he just stood there drinking her in. She had come. She had come for him.

'Did you miss me?' she said as he pulled back and looked her in the eyes, his own shining with relief and happiness.

'Just a little,' he smiled weakly back.

Zee's smile illuminated her face that was flushed with relief, sensing the small joke, her eyes sparkling back at him.

'Me too,' she said, joyful tears slipping out and trailing down over her cheeks.

Orion cleared his throat. Paxton turned, shifting his focus, and looked at the huge man now holding up a dishevelled, pale form. He stared dumbstruck at the man, feeling lightheaded. The man had Wolf's eyes. What was going on here? Then Pax shifted his focus to the weary boy now held up by the man/Wolf. His red blood-stained hair and freckled nose filled his heart with relief.

'Tye! You found him!'

The large warrior that was Wolf just seconds ago, replied, 'Well, that saves us some time then, Well done, Zee. I don't know how you did it, but good work.'

Zee smiled, but it didn't reach her eyes. The horror still raged inside of her at what the disgusting soldier had been doing. She brushed it away. 'We have to get out of here. There will be more guards any minute. I can feel it. We need some moscow clothing for the boy, for Tye.'

She looked at his shivering, now slightly purple face. The soldiers didn't even have any on, maybe in the barracks where they resided?

'Pax, do you know where the soldiers stay?'

'No clue.' He shook his head. 'We could only access the three caverns to work, sleep or eat. We never knew where they went at night, or when or where they would change shifts.'

Zee tried to think. She eyed Orion, his warm moscow outfit. 'We need some warm clothing for Tye.'

He grumbled a reply. Zee smiled a little. 'You'll be warm enough as Wolf. Don't grumble. Wolf is better company anyway.'

'I'll remember that,' he said, offloading the wobbly Tye onto Zee again. He took off his warm clothes, and they helped Tye get into them, even though they were huge on him. Zee's anxiety crept in on her, so she formed an air shield to keep them hidden from sight just in case any soldiers came upon them before they left.

'Let's go, and Zee, you form us a bunker as soon as we're out and safely far away from this place.'

She nodded at him, then with a flash, Wolf led the way.

201

'Well... that's definitely something you don't see every day,' Pax said in awe, still wondering if this was a dream.

'Oh, you have no idea,' replied Zee.

The three trailed after Wolf as fast as they could, leaving the darkness of the mines behind them.

The Sparkling City

Zenya, Kymera

Paxton and Zemira sat side by side in the small ice bunker under the howling storm. Tye curled up against Wolf for warmth, the pair both sleeping soundly. Tye's mouth was slightly ajar, and his black eye was now a magnificent range of colours.

'What happened? How did you find him?' Pax asked the first of many questions milling around his fragile mind.

The four had walked for what seemed hours into the frozen windswept night, trudging on through the snow until Tye couldn't move his legs anymore. Zee had lit up the snow underground with her glowing power, creating an ice bunker away from the incessant blow of cold, and they all wearily crept inside, feeling safer and more secure than they had in months.

Tye had passed out almost as soon as his head had lain down in-side the overly large hood of Orion's moscow suit. And Wolf had curled up near the poor boy to share his warmth with him and to get some much-needed rest, leaving Zee and Paxton together.

'I don't know what happened, exactly. There was this malevolent, twisted energy calling to me. I followed it down a dark corridor into a cavern opening, and then a soldier turned up dragging this poor, beaten boy behind him. There were so many lost souls down there...' Zee stared towards the flickering green fire she had created to illuminate the cave. It didn't give off much heat, but the low light was welcome.

'That soldier, he was so evil. I had to... he was torturing them, killing them, collecting them,' she said in disgust, angry tears slipping from her face.

Paxton had no idea what she was talking about, but he guessed it was bad, and that Zee had saved Tye from a terrible fate. 'Hey, come here.' He wrapped an arm around her, and she buried her head into his chest.

'You're the one who should be a mess, not me,' she said, letting the pain out, letting the tears fall. 'Are you alright? Are you... still you?' she asked quietly.

Paxton stared ahead at her amazing feat of green magic, the small flames dancing beautiful patterns around the ice dome Zee had conjured. His brave, incredible, beautiful Zee. Tears of his own slipped from his face as he squeezed her tight. 'I'm okay now,' he whispered. 'Did Wolf really turn into a huge tattooed man? Or was I hallucinating?' Pax asked weakly, needing the reassurance to calm his frazzled mind and to confirm his reality was not distorting around him.

'Yes, you're not going crazy, but I'll tell you all about it in the morning, I promise,' Zee reassured gently.

They spoke no more, both exhausted. Both utterly spent. They were together again. There was time to answer all unanswered questions later. They just held each other tightly in silence, sharing each other's presence and enjoying the warmth and comfort that came from simply being together.

'I missed you, Zee,' Pax said as he stroked Zee's silky dark hair, just before nodding off.

Zee replied before sleep claimed her as well. 'Me too.'

Zemira swept her hands along the tops of the humseed grass, the small hard seeds in clusters at the top of each strand tickling her palms as she and Paxton followed behind Orion and Tye. At least this part of Kymera was not unbearably cold. They had travelled on foot from the mines through freezing snow and finally reached the warmer area near the coast, with endless fields of humseeds and moscows.

'So how do you do it? Is it from the blast? Do you both have radioactive powers? If I was in a blast, would I get them too? How do you control it? And what are those marks on your skin? Are they tattoos? What other animals can you turn into? How old are you?' Tye was incessantly pestering Orion from behind.

The harsh freeze of the wastes behind them for the moment, Orion had shifted back into his warrior form as they all traipsed through endless fields of humseed grass. Zee and Pax were trying to not burst into laughter at the irritation Orion was clearly not trying to hide. Tye was completely oblivious to it.

Orion trudged on ahead, not answering any of the curious boy's questions.

'Actually, Wolf, that is a good question. How old are you?' Zee yelled out to him from the tail of the line.

'You don't want to know,' he rumbled.

'So let me get this straight. That fairy-tale, the one you told us at Warwick's, it was really your mum and dad's love story? And Wolf has been your dad all this time? And King Ravaryn is clearly pissed and now has your mum hostage, no doubt waiting for you or Orion to come and somehow get her back? And you didn't get your powers from the blast, you've had them for ages, just kept them secret. Aaannd you've been on the other side of the Rim... and survived.' Paxton was breathless after relaying all this in one go.

'Right,' said Zee, feeling slightly guilty at all the information Pax had to digest. 'I'm sorry I never told you that I was different. You have to understand that I promised my mother I wouldn't tell anyone. It was to keep us both safe, and I didn't know if I could trust you. And even I didn't know the full extent of it.'

'I'm not upset with you, Zee. I'm amazed by you. I'm always amazed by you.'

Zee's cheeks reddened in embarrassment. She was sure Pax would be hurt by her mistrust, but she had underestimated him.

'The whole Wolf thing kind of makes sense now that I think about it. He's never liked me being too close to you.' Pax chuckled at the realisation, thinking about all the coincidental times Wolf was there... always in the way the moment Paxton got too close, always hovering protectively near Zee.

'Speak for yourself. I saw what happened to you, Pax. Diwa showed me, just like that night at her cottage when she showed us my mum. I saw that soldier hurting you. I'm so sorry. You are so strong. I would *never* have been able to survive that.'

Pax looked down at the trail that Orion was cutting through the long grass. Tye was trailing him closely, still talking non-stop without reply. 'If it wasn't for Tye, I don't think I would have made it. He looked after me, cleaned my wounds, cared for me. And he's smart too; he knows all about healing. I'm sure I would have died from infection from further punishments were it not for him, I would have ended up in the corpse pile out the front of the hole for sure.'

Zee shuddered. Every inch of that place was evil. She vowed to return and destroy the whole reeking pit of despair. But she had to keep going. She had to find her mother. 'He's a nice kid,' Zee said, 'I think I was meant to find him... I was meant to save him. Those boys down there... they helped me to save him from the same fate..

I'm glad I could help at least one other person from that death sen-tence before we left. One day, Pax. One day you and I, we'll come back... and we'll burn it all to the ground.'

Paxton wasn't shocked by the fury coating her words. He felt his own hatred simmering inside of him. One day they would pay, the soldiers – and the sick King of Kymera.

After a week of travelling and regaining their strength, the four travellers finally reached the sparkling frozen city of Zenya, which towered over the Alvion Sea. Tye's eye was now a faint shade of pale yellows tinged with brown. Paxton's back had knitted together and was healing well with Diwa's special salve that she had added to the pack of supplies Zee carried. Zee felt no ache in her side, and was ready. Travelling unnoticed through the wilds of Kymera, Ori-on had procured Tye his own weatherproof outfit from a small village and regained his own back. The four were now all protected from the still-frigid iciness encapsulating the city.

The sky pines towered high into the air, tipped with the most beautiful blue sparkling flowers like sapphires twinkling in the af-ternoon sun. Buildings encircled the enormous tree trunks that interconnected with sky carts. Flowing bridgeways and metal wires were used for the transfer of goods. The city was like nothing Zee had ever seen. It was definitely something from fairy tales. In par-ticular, her mother's fairy tale that she had told a thousand or more times. Zee had imagined it, but nothing was like seeing it.

Zemira pictured her mother's face and anticipated her warm smile. Verena would be so happy to see them, and to finally see Orion again. It must have felt like centuries for her. Zee just hoped her mother wasn't being tortured, and that she wasn't bloodied, beaten or freezing to death in a cell or something. Her fists clenched at the thought. She had looked unharmed in Diwa's vision, but that was weeks ago. It could have all changed. If the way the boys were treated inside the hole was any indication of how the king treated his prisoners, this did not bode well for her mother. *Come on, Zee, focus on the positive.*

There were no glow beetles crawling around in her stomach this time. Their plan was sound. Tye had told them extensively of the passageways and tunnels leading into the ice castle. Once they reached the kitchens, they knew where they must go. He had said that they wouldn't be holding Verena in the cells below the crystal floor that the king inhabited. They were kept for the worst of the worst, and for Ravaryn to have traitors nearby for torture.

Tye thought the king would be keeping Verena in the eastern wing, opposite his own tower. In the eastern tower, there were multiple rooms for guests. Not that Ravaryn ever had any guests, Tye had explained. During the few years he had worked in the castle, he had never actually seen the king have anyone there. No governors from Thorta, no heads of state from Aylenta. No family or friends that Tye knew of. No one. The boy was terrified of returning to the frozen, glistening prison that was the castle. And rightly so. But he had told them every inch of information he could remember that he thought would be helpful.

'Here's where we leave you, lad,' Orion said, clapping a hand on Tye's shoulder. 'You take care of yourself. Your parents will be lucky to have you back.'

Tye smiled with a large, toothy grin, blue eyes sparkling again.

'Thank you, Tye, for all your help and information on the castle. I appreciate it more than you know. And I can never thank you enough for looking after Paxton for me.' Zee winked at the fiery-haired boy as she hugged him goodbye.

Tye replied in her ear as they had a good squeeze. 'I owe you my life, Zee. You saved me from the mines... and from him.' His voice cracked.

'Try to never think of that place again.' Zee instructed.

'Stay safe, my friend,' Pax said with a warm smile, lit from within.

Tye reached out and gave Pax a long hug. Paxton patted him on the back. 'Thanks for everything, Tye.'

Tye wiped at his damp eyes. He reached up and gave Paxton a hug. 'Thank you, Pax. I'll never forget you.' His tears were now cascading down his face. 'I'm going home,' he choked out.

He then disappeared down the icy trail off into the busy town at the base of the sky pines. Off to find his parents. Off to hopefully have a better life. Mother knows, he deserved it.

The Rescue

Zenya, Kymera

The shimmering black walls of the castle loomed upon them as
night crept in, the moon's glow illuminating the fortress with a
ghostly sheen. It was so quiet. Not a glow beetle hum, not a sliver
of wind. No snow, just the faint crashing of small distant waves.
Even the dark sea was eerily still in anticipation. The trio knew
where the large pipe tunnel under the castle would lead. Tye said
the kitchen would be empty after dinner and clean up. Orion,
Zemira and Pax planned to enter the tunnels and wait late into the
night for the kitchen to be free. Any soldiers or guards stationed
outside of the rooms to the east wing would meet their fate with
Zemira.

Once inside, they would search the entire east wing, and they
would find Verena. Pax was on one side of Zee, and Wolf at her
other. She felt a solid foundation with them by her side that she

had missed so much growing up. Sure, her mother had been her rock, and had looked after her the best she could. She had kept her safe, kept her hidden. But how would she feel after knowing what Zee had done? What would she think of the things she was now capable of? She knew her mother loved her, but a small, heavy seed of disapproval was lingering deep inside Zee. She knew her mother would be mortified if she ever found out what Zee had done to the Blacksmith. And what if Orion knew? He would surely be disappointed. No. No one would ever know. She would tell no one. Zee locked the horrific memory away, deep into the dark abyss at the back of her mind to be forgotten. She didn't even feel bad about what she had done, which was the worst part. No remorse for the sick soul she had punished.

'Zee, are you ready?' Pax questioned, breaking her chain of thought.

Taking one last look at the glowing castle in the bright moonlit night, her eyes hardening like steel, she said, 'I'm ready.'

The trio stealthily made their way through the dark, icy stone-lined tunnel. Orion at the front had decided it was easier to travel through the cramped space as Wolf and had shifted within minutes of creeping through the tunnel. Zee trailed behind him, with Paxton at the tail. The ground under their feet was slick, and it was extremely difficult to stay upright having nothing to grab onto. They passed through the tunnel without any words between them. All Zee could think about was her mother. She was finally going to see her again, and her mother was finally going to see Orion again... not Wolf. She was avoiding the fact that Ravaryn was also inside this castle, and that he was the reason Verena was here in the first place. He was also the reason for Pax's scars. For Tye's near-gruesome death.

Zemira forced the rage down. She had to keep control. She had this. They saw the light up ahead emitting down through a grate into the dark drain. There was a shuffling around above them. Probably the cook, as Tye had said that the staff was minimal at best. That the king never had visitors, so there were hardly any staff. But there were a handful of soldiers and his right-hand commander of the Kymerian army, Caden.

They waited in the tunnels for a while longer before the shuffling and clanking of pots and plates became still. It was quiet. Time to go. In a flash, Orion was in the tunnels beside them, and he reached up and forced the grate above him out of the way. He lifted himself up easily and reached down a large tattooed hand to Zee. She took it, and he hauled her up easily into the dim light of the kitchen quarters. Geez he was strong. He lifted Paxton up with similar ease and replaced the grate.

Orion eyed them both. 'Let's go. Quietly. You see anyone, Zee, you know what to do. And remember to be gentle. We want to render them unconscious, nothing else.'

Zee nodded, looking at the ground. So he had noticed that the two soldiers at the entrance of the hole were no longer breathing when she was done with them. She forced the feeling down. She had done what she'd needed to do at the time.

Following Orion out of the kitchen quarters, she spotted a small, winding staircase. Tye's instructions had been amazingly accurate. They followed the servant's stairs up into a long, icy hall. There was a soldier standing guard at one of the doors. The last door at the end of the massive hallway. Orion popped his head back around the corner into the small staircase opening.

'There's one soldier, Zee. She must be inside that room... remember, gently,' he said to her with an encouraging smile.

Zemira focused on the air around her. She felt the cold of the icy walls and the fresh sea air that blew in through a small opening in the hall. Motioning her hands towards her, she sucked in a long, steady breath, removing all the air around the soldier as slowly and gently as she could. She didn't take too much, but she could feel the urge to. The force, the joy of it running in her veins. *No! Don't take too much.* She wanted so badly to suck the energy from him, to consume his life force, that it scared her.

213

He wavered a bit then grabbed at his throat as if struggling to breathe. Slumping back against the smooth wall, he slid down and passed out on the ground in front of the shimmering black door at the end of the hall.

'Well done, Zee.' Orion clasped her shoulder.

She took a large exhale. Paxton was silent behind the two, not wanting to get in the way. They all trailed quickly down the hall to the dark door. The soldier was still... but he was breathing.

'Zee.' Orion broke through her thoughts again. 'You do the honours.'

'I can feel her. She's in there,' Zee whispered, eyeing her father's face, which was as giddy as a man on his betrothal day.

Reaching for the door to twist the large latch upwards, a shot of pain passed up her arm at the moment of contact with the strange metallic metal. She ignored it and pushed on with all her might. She forced the lock inside the door's mechanism to melt, sweat beading on her brow.

'Something's wrong,' she said, slightly panicked.

Orion, keen to see Verena again, urged her on. 'Try again, Zemira, you've got this.'

Zee wanted to see her mother again so badly. She didn't want to fail, to disappoint her ever-proud father that she had finally been able to meet properly. She forced everything she had into the strange metal, stifling a grunt of pain as the lock finally gave way. With a thunk and a click, the door creaked ajar.

There was an overly large bed in the centre of the enormous room, and a huge window stretched along the opposite wall, looking out to the sea. The moon shone into the room, sparkling over the dark sea. A figure was in the bed, wrapped under the blankets, still. Her dark hair was visible in the glow of the moon. Large crystals hung from the ceiling. Orion raced over to the bed to the figure silently sleeping. He reached up and placed his hand on her shoulder, turning her towards him. She flew up out of the bed, a sharp shard of crystal in her hand that she pressed into the base of Orion's neck.

He raised both hands quickly into the air. 'Verena... it's me. It's Orion.' Verena shook her head, unable to see her attacker. She held the shard firm.

'Mum, no!' Zee said, not yelling but loud enough to convey her worry.

'Zemira, is that you!'

Zee flew to the bed and wrapped her mother in a fierce hug, holding the tears in, she breathed in her scent of jasmine and lavender. 'I missed you so much, Mum. I thought you were... gone.' The tears now slid down her face.

'Oh, my girl, I was so worried.' Dropping the crystal shard, Verena squeezed Zee hard.

'I found you a stray on the way here too,' Zee said, wiping her face.

Orion sat staring at Verena in the dark moonlit room. Gasping with recognition, she raised a hand to his cheek, cupping his handsome face in her hands.

'It really is you...' she breathed.

Orion leaned forward, his lips met hers and they kissed, savouring the seconds. Years had gone by waiting, wanting to have each other to hold again. Orion's face was still in Verena's delicate, little hands. As the pair pulled apart, Verena's eyes were shining, tears brimming, her smile huge.

'How I have missed your smile,' Orion said, unable to pull himself away from her loving gaze. The pair embraced for the first time in more than a decade.

Tears fell from Verena's face. 'I hope it was worth it,' she said, looking into Orion's shining emerald eyes,

'Every second,' he replied.

'Okay, you two, I hate to move it along but let's get out of here and quickly. This place feels wrong. This all feels too easy. Let's move. Now.' Zee was feeling completely spent from the door's mysterious metal.

Verena wiped her face and slid out of the bed, her hand in Orion's. 'You're right, honey, let's go—'

'Leaving so soon? I wasn't even invited to the family reunion.' A deep, velvety voice slid into the room behind the trio.

Paxton stood still and silent as a knife pressed against his throat from behind. The huge man towered behind him in the dark, just inside the ajar door. Orion's growl of fury rumbled out of his throat as he went to lunge at the man.

'Uh, uh, uh.' He pressed the knife harder, dark liquid streaming down the front of Paxton's throat as he struggled against the hold of the tall stranger. His face held the panic in, the punishment and pain from the hole no doubt creeping into his veins.

'Let's light up this momentous occasion.'

Lights suddenly glittered all over the ceiling, illuminated like a million stars. Zee took in the man's dark eyes, his raven hair and pale skin. He wasn't unattractive. Every angle of his face was well balanced, and he would be strikingly handsome if it weren't for the loathing look in his eyes as he started directly at her father. Venom, hatred and loss brewed there. Zee felt it in the air as she saw the blood trickling down Paxton's throat. This was serious. She sensed a killer when she saw one. Reflected back at her, she could see the calculated rage she herself had felt only a week ago when she had disfigured the blacksmith for his despicable crimes against those poor boys.

'Let him go, Ravaryn,' Orion said in an ancient voice, glaring into the king's eyes.

Verena's free hand was clenched in a fist at her side, the other holding fiercely onto Orion's. For support? No, to hold him back.

'You three did well. I'm impressed you knew about the tunnels. And the soldier, was that credited to you, Orion, or your dear daughter?' He kept his voice light, like they were all conversing over a cup of tea. His dark eyes landed on Zemira, and he took her in as if appraising an object for its value.

Zee stared into the dark eyes, her own emerald eyes boring into his. She contained her rage well for the moment. Something about this man was familiar to her. But not that familiar. 'Let him go now, and I'll let you keep your hands,' Zee said, her voice like steel.

'Oh Verena! She's got your fury,' the king said in an excited pitch. 'And her father's eyes. What a shame.'

Ravaryn forced Paxton forward into the large room, knife still at this throat. Caden entered behind him, along with three soldiers. They moved around Zemira and her parents, flanking them while standing still, silent, obedient.

'I heard the news from the Borztan mines. Seems poor old commander Drake is a little incapable of much these days.' Ravaryn smiled at Zee, yet when it reached his eyes, it made him look even more sinister. Handsome, but sinister. He knew what she had done and what she was capable of, yet – he was so cocky? So sure of his victory.

'Let the boy go now, Ravaryn. He has done nothing. Let us leave now. End this, and we will let you leave unmarred.' Orion almost had to choke the words out to hide his rage.

Zee was impressed by his control. She endeavoured to be like that one day. One day, but not today. She faced her palms out and let the rage flow from her core down to her palms, waiting for the fiery green glow of her forest flames to ignite. Instead, she felt nothing, and her body ached the more she tried, while her forehead blistered with sweat. She forced more of her energy, her magic to obey her. She screamed inside her head as nothing came to her command.

Ravaryn bellowed with a loud, booming laugh. 'Do you three fools think I would really make it this easy for you? That I am ignorant enough to have one guard at my prisoner's door? That I wouldn't anticipate the second you had the chance,' he eyed Zemira, 'that you wouldn't melt me into a twisted mess for taking your mother away? For sending you away to Thorta? The walls are lined with borenium. A mix of Borztan, silver and a few other elements I've found to be very effective at minimising certain gifts. Every inch of this room is covered in it and also woven into my soldiers' armour, so your powers won't work. Save your energy.'

Zee was dumbstruck, and that day at the river bloomed in her mind. She could barely move that soldier when he should have been lifted off the ground and flung metres away from her. So he knew. The king knew she had powers.

'Here's what's going to happen. Verena, you can have your lover back in one piece. You two lovebirds can finally have each other to yourselves.' He looked over at Orion and Verena like he was looking at cockroaches. 'And you will stay here with me.' Ravaryn's smile was indecipherable, and directed straight at Zemira.

'Over my dead body,' seethed Orion with a terrifying stillness to him. He looked as though he would shift into Wolf and rip Ravaryn's throat out in a split second.

'I can most certainly arrange that, but if I were you, I wouldn't try anything, dog. Your shifter magic won't work here. Besides, you will now get what you always wanted. Verena. So I suggest you take her and this boy and leave. But you will be leaving your pup. I won't harm her, I swear. Leave before you get what you deserve... before my composure expires.' His eyes simmered with anger as he looked at Orion.

Orion tried to shift anyway, but only a dull glow came from his skin, then nothing...

Ravaryn forced the knife further into Paxton's neck, making him wince in return. 'Try anything and this boy with have an extra orifice that won't serve him well.'

'Stop!' Zee commanded. 'I'll stay. But if you hurt any of them, I swear to the Mother you'll regret it.' Fury flowed from her even without the use of her powers.

'Enough. Caden.' Ravaryn nodded to his commander.

'Now,' Caden boomed at his three soldiers. They moved to grab Orion and Verena, restricting their hands behind them. Orion let them. He saw the blood flowing from Paxton's neck, and knew if Pax was lost, Zee would also be lost – to the darkness. She was at such a fragile stage with her growing powers.

Ravaryn pushed Paxton towards the third soldier. Zee let out a breath of relief as he was released. Her relief was short lived as Caden approached her, holding dark metal bands in his hands.

'Hold out your hands, girl. Now.' His voice was not malevolent, but serious. He attached the sculpted metal around her wrists where they stretched up her forearms, like armour. But they weren't armour; Zee felt the block that the impenetrable void the metal created at the exit point of her energy flow.

'Why are you doing this!' Verena spat at Ravaryn. 'You hurt her, and I will gut you myself!' she erupted.

'Verena, darling, I know you'll miss me, but our time together is up. Your pet will have to suffice for now,' he said, looking at Orion. He was enjoying baiting them.

Orion's jaw tightened yet he stayed stoic. 'Zemira, don't lose your way. I'll come for you.'

Zee nodded, ignoring the panic creeping in around her wrists and circling her core. She knew what Orion meant. 'I'll be fine, just look after Mum and Pax.'

She eyed the king again and as his gaze fell back on her, for a split second, she saw a twitch of his brow, a break in his composure as his eyes met hers. Was that a flash of regret? Guilt? She blinked, and the look was gone. Did she imagine it? His composure was restored, his face back to the indifferent mask. She didn't know why, but she just knew the king would not harm her. Despite his scheming and treachery, she felt a whisper of destiny hovering at the edge of her mind. An invisible tendril, beckoning her. A connection to him that she didn't yet understand. She sensed his strong aura filled with a dark yet unreadable swirling power, masking something else... something more... something hidden.

219

Ravaryn waved a hand, and Caden dragged Zee off out the door into the icy hall. Pax and Zee caught each other's eyes just as she vanished form view. A silent 'it'll be okay' between them.

Verena, however, was furious watching her daughter taken away. 'You'll pay for this, you monster!' she screamed at Ravaryn.

'Tsk, tsk, such lack of restraint. Just as well you never became the queen of Kymera,' he smiled, baiting her further.

Verena spat in his face.

Ravaryn laughed again and wiped at his cheek with a gold embroidered black handkerchief that he materialised from a pocket. 'You've really been a bad influence on her, shifter. Such a shame,' he said to Orion's stony face. 'Nothing to say?'

Orion didn't bite. He just stared eye to eye with the king. 'You'll regret this.'

'You don't scare me, shifter,' he smirked at Orion.

'I wasn't talking about me.' Orion replied, a sneer of his own curling his handsome features.

Ravaryn's own smirk vanished. 'Get them out of here.'

The soldiers dragged the three from the room, the same metallic cuffs now adorning their wrists, which were bound behind their backs. Ravaryn stood in the empty room and stared out to the sparkling black sea. His smug face slumped into an unreadable expression... the smile gone. He finally had her. He was so close. He just hoped it would be worth it. That the girl would be strong enough... powerful enough... to free him from his cage.

Part III

Powerless & Imprisoned

Part III

Zenya, Kymera

Zemira paced back and forth, back and forth. The room was just as beautiful as the one they had found her mother in, with the huge window looking out towards the dark sea. The walls and door were heavily lined with more borenium. How could he have known? She had tried several more times to use her powers, straining herself, only to sweat profusely, gain a migraine and develop dark circles under her eyes. Zee was furious. She was also exhausted. Throwing herself angrily onto the giant, ridiculously soft bed, she planned of all the ways she would maim the king when she was free of the metal cuffs. But as soon as her head had hit the pillow, she slept. She slept and she dreamed.

Zee wandered alone along the small trail through the illuminated forest of the outer Rim. Small, glowing beetles and winged lizards whizzed all around her in the air. Every flower smelled more beautiful, every leaf more intricately patterned than the last. The fresh night air caressed her, gliding smoothly over her skin, sliding through her long hair. She wandered for what seemed like hours, the small, glowing floxel-like creatures darting out onto the trail ahead of her then speeding away into the neon undergrowth. The track twisted and winded, until she came to a small apex of land. An illuminated river ran ahead in front of her, two smaller creeks merging beside her into one larger one.

Zemira could see right to the bottom through the clear water. There were beautiful glowing fish, shooting around in small schools, and yaberris on the sandy bottom, lying in wait, their beautiful lightning streaks of yellow and blue shooting out from their claws. Standing at the apex of land where the two creeks joined, Zee could see two figures, one either side of the river ahead of her. To the left was the most beautiful woman she had ever seen, with earthen hair and sparkling star-speckled eyes. Perfect porcelain skin. The woman was glowing in the moonlight, which hung heavy in the sky above the river between the two figures.

The beautiful woman smiled and reached out her hand towards Zee, motioning her to follow. Zee looked over to the other side of the river. A large, solid form stood there, thick arms crossed over his broad chest. His metallic black armour gleamed under the moon's glow. Thick, slightly curly black hair hung over his forehead just above his ebony eyes. He stared right through Zee, and she looked from him back over to the smiling woman then back to the stoic man.

He stared across the river at the woman as well, looked back to Zee and slowly shook his head. A huge rumbling shook the forest behind the woman, who stood still and pointed at the dark-haired man. As the rumbling erupted from behind her, a huge, grotesque creature on all fours with the disproportioned head of a massive toad-like creature appeared. It roared, exposing jagged, crooked black teeth. Its eyes were coated with a sliver sheen, and it hunched back on all fours then pounced across the entire expanse of the river. Its crusted, scaly hide caught the moonlight, and it landed with a thud, shaking the small piece of land. The man just stood there as the creature dug its huge claws into his flesh, his dark eyes not leav-

ing Zee's as the creature opened his giant maw and tore the man in two. Creaaaak...

The huge door to her room squeaked loudly as it was pushed open, the hinges protesting at the weight of the metal encased in ice. Zee jolted awake and sprang up off the bed, her heart beating fast as it tried to leap out of her chest. Entering the room was Caden, the king's general. Zee, as quick as a floxel, flew past him, darting out the door and running down the icy hall, looking for an exit. She couldn't hear Caden coming after her, and there was no one else in sight. She ran faster than her legs had ever carried her.

Just as she neared the end of the hall, a mass of white fur and spindly legs moved into her path, blocking the whole opening. Zee slammed into the beast, her feet slid out from underneath her and she landed on her backside on the hard stone floor. The creature's giant head bent down to her on its long, furry neck. It had multiple eyes like the vipen but didn't look as sinister. Its fox-like ears and huge body were held up by scaled, clawed feet like that of a bird.

To Zee's shock, the creature produced a thick black tongue and licked right up the side of her face, collecting a thick patch of her dark hair. Zee scuttled back, the multiple eyes all on her, the creature panting like a pup. Wiping at the saliva on her face, she inspected the animal further, noticing carefully concealed wings almost camouflaged down the side of its broad body. Its face was furry and there were no tentacles in sight.

A rumbling laugh erupted from behind the creature, a deep, almost joyful, sound. 'I see you've met Chester,' said the king. The creature leaped away and circled him, coming to stand at his side and sit... like a pet. Ravaryn reached out and scratched under his neck, his large face a good head higher than the king. Chester was massive. 'Be gone with you.' Ravaryn motioned with his hand. The furry white creature trotted out of the hall and into another hallway at the far side of the opening.

'Where in the Rim were you off to so fast, Zemira? Are you so eager to see me?' Ravaryn said, outstretching a hand to Zee still sitting on the floor.

Zee's lip curled up in disgust at the offer of the king's hand. She spun around and pulled her aching body up off the ground.

He just shrugged and pocketed his hand.

'For starters, I was planning to get the hell out of this place,' Zee replied, eyeing the king after the offer of the hand up.

'And what were you going to do with those once you were out of the castle?' he motioned to her hands. The metallic cuffs still encased her wrists and forearms. 'With no powers, you'd surely freeze to death trying to get back to your... family.' He almost choked on the last word.

Zee just glared daggers at him. His eyes seemed to bore into hers as he stared at her.

'Seeing as I'm here, and you clearly have gone to a lot of effort to make that happen, would you mind telling me why?' She hadn't expected the king to be... so... normal. No that wasn't it. He wasn't normal at all, none of this was. He was clearly a monster. But monsters often had the best disguises, as Diwa would always say.

Zee crossed her arms. 'What are you staring at?' she snapped.

Ravaryn looked as though he had just snapped out of a trance. 'Nothing at all.' His face went back to being unreadable. 'Follow me, I'll escort you back to your room.'

Zee was utterly confused. 'And what if I don't want to follow you?'

'I'll have Caden escort you. You can either be civil and stay in the rooms prepared for you, or you can explore the crystal dungeons below the castle if you wish. Mind you, they are a tad colder than inside the castle, and there's also much quieter company down there. If I disgust you so much though, it's entirely up to you.' He just stared at her again, waiting for her reply, his dark eyes not leaving hers.

Zee imagined he was talking about frozen corpses and proceeded to roll her eyes at him. 'Fine.'

'Good,' Ravaryn replied. 'Follow me.'

'My name is Zemira. I'd appreciate it if you'd use it.'

Ravaryn smiled a little, then spun around, hands clasped behind his back and set off for Zee to follow him. The castle's rooms were impressive to say the least. The high ceilings glittered with glowing light-like stars, which reflected off the walls. The floors changed from the icy stone to woven carpets of purple and blue that were spongy underfoot. They entered another huge room with a few sparse lounges that faced another enormous window, looking out to the dark sea.

'Where is everyone?' Zee couldn't hold her curiosity in. Her hatred of Ravaryn almost made her not want to even speak with him, but she had been alone in that room for a long while. She was still tired but needed to find out anything she could about the castle. If she could just manage to get out, she could find someone to help her get these things off. Diwa would know what to do.

'What do you mean?' Ravaryn replied.

'I don't know, like people? Your council, servants? People that would normally be in a castle.'

'There are people here. You're in my castle, aren't you?'

Zee didn't like his familiar tone. He talked like they knew each other, like they were about to have scones and tea.

'Your room, Zemiirah.' He rolled his tongue, making a point of using her name. Ravaryn then outstretched his arm theatrically, inviting her into the chambers. There were no borenium lined walls, and the door was... just a door. The room was incredible. It was like nothing like she had ever seen, with a huge bed sculpted out of crystallised marble. Small carved creatures chased each other on the headboard. Inside the marble were actual crystals, sparkling with all colours.

The ceiling was illuminated with more of the star-like lights. Velvet blankets of dark forest greens and deep purple cushions ordained the bed. There was a whole wall to her right, every inch covered in books. Opposite her, the same glass window covered the entire expanse of the wall. This time it looked out over the city. She was now on the opposite side of the castle. The tall sky pines were lit up with little buildings and sky carts, right up to their beautiful crystal-like blooms sparkling in the morning sun.

The city was alive with movement; the people down on the snowy floor of the town moved around the market stalls like ants. Zee closed her open jaw and quickly regained her unimpressed façade.

'What do you think, Zemirrah?'

That roll of her name again. It made her insides tingle a little.

'Would you like these chambers? Or should I escort you downstairs and see if you prefer the ice dungeon?'

She just crossed her arms and looked out towards the city of Zenya, not bothering to give him a reply. She was tired, she missed her family and she didn't want to play this game with him.

'I see,' he replied after a moment. 'There are clean garments in your bathing room, which I advise you use.'

He had hinted at her state; the days of travelling across Kymera with the men had taken a toll. She did smell, her hair was a mess and her dishevelled moscow clothes had definitely done their job but they were in dire need of a wash.

'You will meet me tonight for dinner. If you refuse, I'll wait until you feel you are capable of dining with me.'

Zemira still had her back to him, staring out into the expanse of bustling city. She remained quiet.

'I'll see you get some breakfast delivered. And Zemira...' he waited for an acknowledgement.

This time, she turned to face him. His dark eyes bored into hers again.

'Caden will be stationed outside your door. But if you feel the need to try and escape, just so you know, there is no living soul in this Rim who can remove those cuffs but me. You leave, and you leave every chance of using your powers again behind. Understand?' There was no sneer or smile behind his eyes this time. He almost looked remorseful.

Zee held in threatening tears as she glared daggers back at him. Her arms were crossed tightly around herself.

'I'm sorry,' he added. 'This is the way it has to be.' He quickly looked away from her and exited the room, closing and locking the large door behind him.

Zee heard lock clicking into place. She turned back to the city and proceeded to sit on the shimmery dark-green velvet blankets laced with gold-threaded vines on the huge bed. Then she placed her head into her hands and cried. She felt like a bird in a very small cage despite the grandeur of the chambers. She was caged and she still didn't know why.

Zemira investigated her room after Ravaryn had left. He was a very unusual king. Nothing in this place was what she had expected. The room was beautiful beyond compare. There was an adjoining bathing room with a gigantic bath, also looking out to the city. And a new set of clothes for her. She hated the thought of having to wear what he wanted her to wear, but the outfit she had on was definitely past ripe.

She thoroughly soaked and scrubbed in the bath, washing away the past weeks. It was no easy feat in cuffs, trying to wash the filthy image of the blacksmith away with his evil yellow grin. She erased it from her mind, filing it away deep down, along with the image of his melted face. Zee's thoughts turned to her mother and Orion, hoping that they weren't harmed, and that Paxton was with them. He was so hollow when they had rescued him and Tye from the mines. His light had gone out a little, and all because of the king. Her fingers burned trying to conjure a flame but she never managed to get past the dulling barrier of the metal cuffs. She sighed and decided to leave the comfort of the steaming tub.

The floors in the bathroom were tiled with iridescent shimmering blues and greens. The taps of the marble basin were gold, and there was a large mirror on the wall above. Zee dressed in the clothing provided. It was all black, like Ravaryn's clothing. She pulled on tight woven pants of the softest fabric she had ever felt. A matching long-sleeved black shirt, black undergarments of the same soft woven material and black boots that Zee utterly approved of completed the outfit. As she slipped the boots on, they felt heavenly on her feet. Lastly, she donned a fitted black jacket with a high collar and black metal buttons to one side.

Zemira looked herself over in the mirror. Dressed in all black with the dark circles under her eyes and her long black hair still slick and wet, she looked slightly menacing. Her dark blue string necklace was now visible, hanging reassuringly around her neck. Why hadn't it glowed once since she had arrived here?

She stared at the mirror. Zee didn't think that she was beautiful. She never had. But Diwa had always told her that she was special, unique. Beautiful. Zemira guessed that's what grandmas were supposed to do. Not that Diwa was her grandma but she was as close enough to it. As close as Zee was going to get. Her stomach growled and felt empty. How Zee missed Diwa. What would she be thinking about Zee in the castle? She had saved her mother but now was stuck here herself... with him.

Ravaryn was unexpected. The way he had been standing there just staring at her. How old was he anyway? He didn't look over twenty-five, but that couldn't be.

'Oh, they fit,' squeaked a high-pitched voice.

Zee jumped, her heart flying from her chest. On reflex, she whipped her arms out in front of her.

The young girl carrying the tray squeaked, 'Sorrrry!' And the tray she carried flew in the air at the same time that Zee had raised her arms out to defend herself.

229

With her now-useless powers, Zee frowned. The girl scrambled the broken plate, teacup and food all back onto the tray on the ground.

'I'm so sorry,' she stammered. 'I didn't mean to alarm you.'

Zee saw the tears threaten on her pale face spotted with freckles, and quickly bent down to help her clear the mess.

'I didn't mean to...' said Zee, stopping what she was about to say mid-sentence. What if she hadn't been cuffed? Would she have injured the girl? Or worse? The thought worried her.

The girl plucked up her courage as they both knelt down to clear up the little pieces on the shiny blue floor. 'I'm Mazda,' she said. 'Do, do you like your clothes? They... they fit really well.'

Zee replied truthfully. 'Yes, they're great actually.'

Pride bloomed on the girl's face. 'Oh good! I wasn't sure of your measurements so I had to guess a bit, but you look, you look w-wonderful.'

'You made these for me?' Zee was relieved she wasn't wearing something the king had handled.

'Y-Yes. I was told you were a hunter and would probably prefer something more manoeuvrable as opposed to a gown or a frock.'

'Hmm.' Thank the stars she wasn't presented with a frock. She would have slid her clean body back into those reeking moscows faster than Paxton would have scoffed down food before she would parade herself in a frock in front of the king. 'Thank you, Mazda, they're actually amazing.'

'I'll be back soon. I'll fetch some more food and tea. I'm sorry again for startling you. I can do your hair for you too when I get back, if you like.'

Zee inspected the girl more closely. She had fiery red hair like Tye, and bright blue eyes. She was young, maybe thirteen or so, not yet a woman. Just a child.

Mazda sped off, tapping at the door twice. It opened, letting her exit, then shut again, and locked. Click, click. Zee was alone again. She hoped Mazda wasn't long. Zee was starving, and it had been so long since someone had done her hair for her. She wasn't sure whether or not to attend the invite to dinner. On the one hand, she might get some answers. Make Ravaryn tell her what on earth was going on. Why she was here. What he wanted from her. Get some food. On the other, he unnerved her. The way he looked at her was like he had found something he had lost a long time ago. His dark eyes had changed from unreadable to... something else. She had an unsettled feeling. He was not what she was expecting at all. Not one bit.

Bones & teeth

Lamiria

Kyeitha's bare feet paced back and forth on the worn patch of earth near the edge of the Lamirian forest. She was waiting for her black wolf, her right hand. He had captured three more forest creatures, this time a battilux, a large, muscled armadillo-like creature the size of an elephant, with a razor-sharp barbed tail. A raspor, and the third, a terrifyingly unpredictable creature she hadn't used yet... a larkaden. Or as the common tongue called them – a mud muncher.

Her fingers dug into her palms as she paced. The moon was just appearing in the distance of the blackened, desolate deadlands. Her left eye had an annoying twitch that was exacerbating her edgy mood. *I will be prepared. I have to make these creatures. They have given me no choice. They will turn on me. They will all turn on me. Just like he did. He deserved it... he made me do it.* Just like always she replayed the memory over and over again. Justifying to herself that she had had to kill him. She'd had to, to protect herself. To protect her son. His father had wanted her power. Men always wanted power. Everyone wanted her power. But she would show them. If anyone dared to try and take it away again, she would have an army. An army all of her own that would decimate any attempt to take her throne away. She was the Queen of the Forest. She was the Rim guardian. The one and only Rim guardian now.

Kyeitha stopped her pacing and walked over to a woven mat of grass on the ground. She lifted it to reveal smooth, hard white objects. Bones. Hundreds of bones. Rubbing her long porcelain fingers over the cold bones, her eyes closed shut. Her immaculate earthen hair shimmered in the moon's glow, now brightening as it rose into the dark sky. Her fingers traced over the smooth bones as she searched through them. Searched the energy they contained. The power they contained. She chose three that would suffice. Yes, these were strong. They would work well.

She swiped her free hand, and the mat slid back over the bone warren. Small vines grew and interlocked over her cache, concealing her treasure. She knew dark magic was powerful, but what other choice did she have? She had seen what they were capable of. The images of the old world were always there in her mind. They would never go away... the destruction... the cruelty. Why had Mother Nature even let humans live? Given them a second chance? Their sins were horrific, unforgivable. Well, she would have to be just as dangerous. These human bones stolen from within the Rim contained immense power. Kyeitha had been using them for years now. To shift, to change, to morph. To create her creatures. Creatures all of her own that she could command. That would be loyal to her. So what if the magic she used was forbidden.

So what if she had taken a few dozen human lives. There were so many within the Rim, so did it really matter? She had taken the middle-aged ones, the strong ones in their prime. That fool Ravaryn had tried to calm the humans' hysteria at the disappearances, saying it was some disease, some silent sickness. Was it really that wrong? All she was doing was exchanging matter. Exchanging energy from one form to another. It was her right as a Rim guardian. They were her humans to watch over. So what if she wanted to use their energy, their life force, in other ways? To shift them, bend them and recreate them in her own way. She was the guardian of this world. She could do what she liked.

The humans had done what they had liked, and the ancient ones had nearly destroyed every living creature in existence. Who cared if she created something new from them? She was a mother, a creator. Her new creatures would be loyal. Would protect her at all costs if the humans reverted to their old ways. The image of the Oxygen Wars exploded in her mind for the millionth time with its death, pain, destruction and suffering. She placed the bones down and dug her long nails deeply into her palms, forcing her eyes shut and grinding her teeth. Her hands flew to cover her ears, and she rocked her head trying to dispel the images. They would never have that chance again! And anyone who sided with them was against her!

A rustling through the trees broke the visions swirling in her mind. A large black wolf appeared, and his luminescent yellow eyes greeted her own sky-blue ones. They were now sparking with agitated anticipation. With confidence. He illuminated and shifted all within a second. A tall, large warrior with dark tanned skin, darker eyes and midnight hair now stood before her.

'My Queen, they are ready,' he said, head bowed as his eyes concentrated on her slender bare feet, waiting for her reply.

'Well done,' she answered, clipped. Short. Unimpressed. So they should be ready; she had commanded it. 'Show me,' she ordered the man. He turned and led her along a track on the edge of the now-glowing forest. Kyeitha clutched the tools that she needed – the bones – and followed. The forest was coming alive for the night, for the moon. Its beauty was breathtaking. Kyeitha ran a hand over the plants, their magnificent leaves shimmering as she passed. *I am doing this for you,* she thought. *To keep you all safe. I am doing what I must.* Her head was held high as she followed her right-hand watcher through the path.

They reached a large opening, and a deafening roar greeted them. Followed by another, more of a terrified screech. In the large clearing, there were three animals bound with ropes and pinned into the earth, barely able to move. A few other watchers were standing guard around the edges of the clearing, in a circle, like they had done each time before, in case any of the creatures were to break free.

The raspor was quiet. It just struggled and panted rapidly against its confines. The battilux roared but was unable to even thrash about, so completely pinned to the ground, its legs outstretched under its huge body. But the mud muncher was furiously screeching an ear-piercing protest. It thrashed about violently within the ropes binding its body. Its large, sharp-toothed mouth snapping between cries.

Kyeitha walked into the clearing and smiled. Yes, these three would be magnificent. She didn't waste any time, the image she wanted to create clear in her mind. She laid a bone out in front of each creature on the hard-worn earth. As if the creatures all sensed even more danger than their present predicaments, they started to thrash about with all their might.

'Hush,' she commanded, after placing the human bones carefully in front of each of them. The screeching stopped immediately. Her hands raised and swept over the bones. A dark blue mist rose, leeching out of the forest's plants behind her, taking with the mist a little of their glow. Kyeitha controlled the mist and trailed it through the air into the airways of the three panicked creatures. They contorted a little more, then a silver sheen spread over their eyes like a shining film. They stopped struggling and lay still. *Good pets, obedient pets,* she thought. A smile spread over her perfect mulberry lips as her brows raised in approval.

She then reached into a small leather pouch attached to a string around her thin waist. Taking out a handful of small, misshapen off-white objects, she proceeded first to the raspor. She held out her hand, and sparkling within it under the moon's ever-watching glow, were teeth. Human teeth. She commanded the raspor, and it obeyed her willingly. It whisked up the teeth with its proboscis and sucked them all down.

Kyeitha moved next to the battilux, and again she commanded the creature. It also obeyed and hungrily ingested the teeth within her outstretched palm. Good. The last was the enormous mud muncher. It was still, but it panted evenly. She removed the rest of the pouch's contents into both her hands and outstretched them towards its mouth. Nearly fifty or so teeth were brimming in her hands. 'Eat,' she commanded. And the monstrous head bent down with its huge mouth agape and very carefully, without even a nick of her skin, engulfed the teeth. Crunch... crunch... crunch. 'Well done,' she soothed.

Kyeitha proceeded to stand in front of the three now very compliant animals. She wasted no time. Their silver-sheened eyes pinpointed on her every movement. Behind her at the entrance to the clearing, her black wolf watcher bent his head towards the ground and averted his eyes. He shifted his stance uncomfortably. Kyeitha raised each bone in the air in front of the raspor, the battilux and the mud muncher. She took in a deep breath and started to orchestrate the bones, moving them with her hands in the air. Elegant movements like a conductor in an orchestra. She slid the bones through the air and started to slice through each creature. They didn't move... they didn't screech or roar or squirm or protest in any way. Blood poured and limbs detached. She sliced and cut and took every piece of them that she desired the most, and sculpted away like an artist to create. To create something new, something deadly and something wholly terrifying.

Cursed

Zenya, Kymera

Zemira admired the long braids in the huge mirror of her bathing room. The smile hadn't shifted from Mazda's face the entire time.

'How did you come to work here?' asked Zee.

'I live here,' Mazda explained. 'I'm an orphan. My parents died from the silent sickness that ravaged Thorta when I was born. The king stepped in and housed and dispersed many children all around the Rim. Some went to orphanage-type homes, but most he tried to place with existing families. He said we had already suffered enough loss, and that growing up without a family was unthinkable. I guess they found it hard to find a family that would take on such a young child, so I grew up here.'

Mazda fiddled with her tiny hands. 'He's not so bad you know, the king. You'll see.'

'I'm sorry, Mazda. I hadn't even heard of the silent sickness until recently. I didn't go to for school for very long.'

'It's not your fault. Besides, not many people know of the sickness... or of the good things the king is actually responsible for. He always says it's the way it has to be. That it's better not to panic the people. Peace above all else is paramount, blah, blah, blah,' Mazda rattled off.

Zemira didn't want to tarnish the idyllic image that Mazda clearly somehow had of Ravaryn, so she tried to keep the topic light. The young girl looked so happy to just be spending time with Zee that she didn't want to ruin it for her. She would get answers soon enough.

'So, what is Chester? And why is he in the castle? And why is there hardly anyone else here?' Zee questioned, trying to change the topic but still glean some information all the same.

'Oh, you've met Chester already! He's a duellerat! A large, flying snow creature that can withstand extremely cold temperatures. Apparently, there's loads of them north of Zenya. I've never seen Chester fly, but he likes to race around under the castle in the icy tunnels and is always racing through the great halls. I don't really know why he's here, but the king likes him, maybe that's why. As for people, the king says he likes to be alone, that people don't like him and he doesn't like them, and that's the way he likes it. He's a bit odd, you know,' Mazda explained.

'I'm starting to gather that.' She was still not convinced that the same king who enslaved and tortured people in the mines, blasted villages in foreign lands and kidnapped children in search of her was the same king that Mazda was talking about. It was all giving Zee a migraine, as were these darned metal cuffs.

Mazda saw Zee trying to twist them around and scratch at the skin underneath with some discomfort. She said with a worried look, 'Don't worry, you won't need them forever, he said he'd take them off. After... he said you're going to change the world. That you're a Rim walker.'

Zee just stared at the red-haired girl as her eyes locked on Zee in wonder.

'Did he now?' The king was definitely a puzzle.

'I have to go, it's past noon! I've got chores. Thanks for letting me do your hair! See you soon, and have a good time at dinner.' Mazda beamed her infectious smile, flew off the bed, gathered the plates and cups on her tray and headed out the door with a double knock. Caden no doubt still standing guard out there.

What did they seriously expect her to do? Pick the lock with a spoon, bust out the door, knock him out with her brush and flee? That duellerat creature would probably hunt her down before she even got close to getting out of the castle, and drag her like a bone straight back to its master. Mazda had a beautiful optimistic glow to her and clearly idolised the king. But she was a child and saw what she wanted to see. Zee was not. But what is it he wanted her to see? What did he think Zee was going to do to save the world? And how did he possibly think she would help him do anything after what he had done to get her here? No, all Zee wanted was to be far away from this place. Far away from him and his frozen kingdom. As beautiful as the view of the twinkling icy city was from above, she knew it was empty. She knew her family were now probably very far away. She was alone in this beautiful yet hollow city.

The light faded from the sky but not from the sparkling city below, the transformation making it seem somehow even more beautiful, but it did nothing for Zee's loneliness. Mazda had left late that morning and not returned, leaving Zee alone again in the large room. As worried as she was about the situation, she slept away the migraine but was not feeling well rested, and she was dreading dinner with the king. She hoped he held true to his word and that

Pax, her mother and Orion were now safely on their way back into Aylenta. Even if she was not.

The door clicked and swung on its large hinges, and Caden stood stone-faced at the entrance to her room. 'Follow me,' he grunted, like she were a mangy dog.

She followed Caden's brisk steps through the glowing halls, and almost had to break into a half jog to keep up. They went deeper into the maze of the castle, not the way Zee had remembered that they had come in. They entered a large room with an ornate balcony overlooking the city, crystal-clear glass all around like they were floating. A small table was set in the middle of the room with two places opposite each other.

'Sit.' Another grunt.

Zee couldn't help herself. 'What a charmer you are. I'd be miserable too if I had to be around the king all day.' Sarcasm dripped from her tongue.

'I see you're in good spirits.' The king's velvety voice slid into the room. He had overheard the limited conversation Zee had tried to have with Caden.

Instant regret and a crawling sensation crept up Zee's spine. Caden turned and left the room at once. Zee's scowl towards the king was louder than any reply she could have voiced.

After being seated, she stared at Ravaryn from her place at the table, a familiar anger rising in her veins. But with nowhere to go, it felt suffocating. He wasn't in his black armoured metallic suit this time. He was still in black but a fine woven loose-fitting shirt and dark pants. His hair was loose, almost messy. If Zemira didn't have so much hate for him, she would almost think him attractive.

He changed tack. 'I hope you're hungry and that Mazda didn't fill you with too many sweets, because dinner is going to be a treat.' His smile was... stunning. Against the contrast of his dark hair and eyes, it lit up his whole face.

He took his seat opposite her at the small table in the oversized room. Fires crackled from two fireplaces either side of it, one behind her and the other behind him. Her hair was intricately braided in beautiful patterns from Mazda, and the black outfit she had on accentuated her eyes. They glowed brighter against all the darkness.

'Wine?' he questioned. She was stuck in this place with no escape and no way of removing the cuffs without his help, so sure, why not get drunk?

'Fine,' she replied shortly. 'So now that I'm here, and you've taken away any defence I may have had against you, or any chance of escaping,' she raised her hands and waved them at him, 'and you've taken my family away from me, are you going to tell me exactly what it is that you want with me?'

He rose from his seat and circled around the table to pour her a glass, standing very closely behind her. 'First, can we just enjoy this dinner?' he asked almost kindly.

Was this a trick? A game to him?

'It's been so long since I've had company of any sort for dinner other than Caden. And he is a man of few words as you may have gathered.'

Zemira was completely unsure of his honest tone, a tired sadness underlining the words. She thought of what Mazda had told her and the way she had lit up talking about the king. Zee relaxed a little and sipped the wine.

Ravaryn was now seated opposite her again and just watched her like a shadowren about to devour its prey. It made her instantly uncomfortable. 'Tell me, how much do you know about the origins of the Rim?'

His question surprised her. She placed her glass back on the table. 'I feel that I should not be the one explaining anything to you. You are the one who needs to explain, Ravaryn.' His name felt strange coming from her mouth. Addressing him by his actual name rather than calling him the king.

'Hmm.' That smile lit up his face again.

He took a sip from his own glass and stared into the contents, seeming to decide his words. 'Years ago, and I mean many, many years ago, I lived outside of this Rim. I was a caretaker, a watcher, similar to Orion. All the watchers had shapeshifting powers, we were born with them, but I had something more. I didn't know my father but I always believed he might have had something to do with these additional powers. That they had something to do with his side. We age so slowly compared to humans, and I was the equivalent to your age when my mother was the Rim guardian. She had trained another to take her place. Kyeitha.

'Kyeitha inherited the elemental powers on becoming the new Rim guardian. I was young then, but I knew there was no radiation left to the east of the Rim walls, and that the humans had lived in peace for centuries, rediscovering how to care properly for the land inside of the Rim. Kyeitha, the new Rim guardian, forbid any interaction with the humans. She commanded that we were to watch and contain, not interact.

'You may have your ideas about her, the Queen of the Forest, as she calls herself, but she is not what you would think. She is twisted... cruel. There was an incident.' He paused, swirling the wine in his glass. 'There was a watcher. She had the gifts of the forest and was able to manipulate plants and trees at her will. She secretly fell in love with a human. A hunter, farmer, a grower and carer of plants inside of the Rim. For we, unlike the humans, were able to pass freely through the Rim wall, as you may now know.

'By the time the lovers were found out by Kyeitha, they had borne a child. A beautiful little boy with eyes of the forest, much like yours.' Ravaryn took another longing look at Zemira.

She stared back into his ebony eyes, captivated by the story. By how handsome he looked when he wasn't playing the part of king. When he seemed to be at ease with himself. Almost genuine. Terrifying, but genuine.

Ravaryn continued. 'Kyeitha was furious, and she had her sentinels drag the watcher, the babe and the farmer to her palace in

Lamiria. We were all summoned. She made a spectacle of it. First she killed the hunter in front of the watcher's eyes as she begged for forgiveness. Then she...' Ravaryn's eyes grew darker if that were possible. He stared away into the fire burning brightly behind her, the flames dancing within his own eyes.

'She ended the babe's life right then and there in front of us all. I can still remember the screams, the wailing of the mother as they dragged her away to the mud cells to rot and become a part of the earth. I couldn't bear it. My own mother told me not to, but I had to do something. I confronted Kyeitha in front of the whole court. I was disgusted, outraged. She had slaughtered the humans that we were tasked to watch over, to care for, to keep safe. And for what? For a watcher and a human loving each other? I didn't understand, but she had gone mad with power, the power she'd inherited when she became the new Rim guardian. The responsibility of it all had broken her.

Kyeitha was furious with me, and we fought. My powers were no match for hers. She was far stronger... and cast my mother and me into the Rim, cursing us. She stripped most of our powers away. She was afraid, I think, afraid of the humans... and of what they might do to her land, her forests, if they were to ever break free from their cage. That is why she forbid us to interact with them. The babe, it was said, was to have great powers that would rival her own elemental powers, a child born from both worlds and with love from both races. A Rim walker... a being of both. The Rim guardian was terrified... frightened of a tiny child. My mother and I have been here ever since.'

Zee just stared at him, open-mouthed. Could this be true? Could he actually be telling her the truth?

'I plan to stop her, Zemira. I plan to free us, my mother and me. And you, Rim walker, you will help me. With your help, we're going to blast a hole in the darned Rim and then we'll see how afraid she is of us... of the humans... of the Rim walker.'

'You're mad.' Zee stated. 'I can't destroy the Rim. I can barely control my powers as it is! You saw what happened to the torturer at the mines. *Your* mines.' She hissed the last part.

'I apologise for him. If I had known what Drake was... indulging in... I would have dealt with him myself.' Ravaryn explained, venom in his voice. 'The mines were a necessity. I had to devise a way of channelling your powers to destroy the wall. I was also temporarily blocking them so you didn't blast me to the stars when I finally found you, by the means I had to use to find you. Your mother hid you well... so the minerals and metal obtained from the Borztan mines were essential. The living conditions, though, I was unaware of how... how dire they had become. I had not left the castle in some time. I will see to it that that is put to an end.'

Zee didn't want to believe him. The anger inside her still burned when she thought of her mother's tears, Paxton's scarred back and hollow eyes and Orion's barely contained anger towards Ravaryn.

'I understand you may find all this hard to fathom, and my history with your parents may come across as damning towards me. But it is all in the past, and as much as I revelled in making them furious upon seeing me again, it was all an act. I once thought I was in love with your mother. I thought our child may be the saviour, the Rim walker child the new world unknowingly had been waiting for. I was hurt when she left, but now I see that you were meant to be. That everything has happened the way it should have. And I should have listened to my mother.' Ravaryn chuckled. 'The irony is seriously unbelievable.'

Zee didn't have a clue what he was now explaining, but some of the light returned to him upon talking about his mother. 'Where is she, your mother?' Zee inquired.

'She left here long ago. I believe she went somewhere... warmer.'

The dinner was delicious. A short, round lady with more silver than gold to her hair served them. She reminded Zee of Jill, coming in with pots and bowls of all kinds of foods Zee had never seen before. The servant had them on a large wooden trolley that she wheeled into the room. There was no one else. No other servants. Zee thought it strange that a king would have such a normal dinner setting.

'Thank you, Ilga.' Ravaryn smiled warmly at the older lady as she walked out of the room.

The fires burned, warming the icy air around them as they ate. Ravaryn was still unnervingly watching Zemira, but she didn't care. She ate and ate. After all, the food was amazing, and she would need her strength for whatever was coming. They finished the meal, and Ravaryn refilled Zemira's glass. The perfect gentleman.

'And what if I refuse to help you?' Zee asked. 'What if I think your words are worth less than an oxel fish and you are mad to believe that you can kill Kyeitha. And by starting a war with her, you will cause more damage than good. Maybe things should stay the way they are.' Zemira took another sip.

'Firstly, oxel fish can be worth quite a lot, I've heard, in the right situation.' He raised an eyebrow. 'And I will start a war if I have to. I will rid the world of her poison, and I will make us all whole again, even if I have to kill every last one of her creatures to do it. And I say that you will help me whether you like it or not. I'm sorry, Zemira, but you don't have a choice.'

The gentleman was gone, and the dark king was back. Zee's heart sank, and her stomach turned a little. All pleasantness was gone from his voice. How could the forest mother be what he said? She maintained everything. She watched over the Rim, protecting everything – us. Zee didn't know what to think. She didn't know what to make of Ravaryn, neither his story nor his up-and-down personality. All she knew was that she wasn't going home anytime soon and there was nothing she could do about it.

'So would you care for dessert?' He smiled, completely changing the subject and mood again, his tone light.

'No, I think I'm done,' she said flatly, pushing her glass and plate away from her, feeling a sudden loss of appetite.

'Oh, don't be so morose. It's not all that bad,' he comforted, sipping his wine.

He's absolutely nuts. Probably years of isolation had done it. Great, she was stuck here with the mad king, and they were off to play a game of 'let's destroy the wall and the queen of the forest'. She changed her mind and drew the wine glass back towards herself. At least she was going to get a well-earned sleep tonight.

'So now that I've explained everything, it's settled then. We leave tonight.'

'What?' Zemira practically screamed. The sleep would apparently have to wait.

248

The Rim

The Rim Wall, Kymera

The rumbling buzz of the carriage hummed against the roar of the wind that blasted thick and white outside its windows. It was towed by what Zee could only guess was a herd of dullerats. These beasts had magnificent wings tucked in perfectly, locking into their sides, almost camouflaged. Not like Chester. His mustn't have formed properly. It made sense now why he was the only one inside the castle, why he was somewhat of a pet. The others possibly not accepting him, maybe sensing his deformity as a weakness? She couldn't be sure.

Something Mazda had said clicked in Zee's mind. 'He's not so bad, you know.' Zemira spun back around from the front window to face him. Ravaryn. The King of Kymera. He didn't seem all that terrifying now. He was tall and muscular though and took up the

Renee Hayes

most part of the opposite side of the carriage, his dark eyes still focused intently on her.

'Ugghh, what are you staring at?' Zee's patience was wearing thin. 'And where are we going?'

'I was just wondering how such a small individual can produce so much drool while sleeping in a moving carriage.' Ravaryn's eyebrows lifted, his face wearing a smug teasing expression.

Zee was not one bit embarrassed. 'Just another one of my many talents. Besides, have you no idea how little I've slept in the last three weeks? You're lucky I have these on.' She shook her wrists out in front of herself the cuffs still encapsulating each of her wrists. 'Otherwise, I would have ended you already just to get a good night's sleep.'

The carriage flew over a large hump in the icy road, flinging Zemira from her seat straight over onto Ravaryn's lap. She scrambled to get herself upright, his large hands helping her right herself, cocky smile plastered on his face.

'Zemira, if you think you'd have a more comfortable sleep over here, all you had to do was as—'

He was cut short as Zemira's hand brushed his own upon her trying to right herself. A surge of power shot up his arm, an image of her crumpled body lying in the icy mud of a field, her eyes lifeless... arms without the metal constraints. Ravaryn sucked in a short breath as if in pain.

Zemira quickly righted herself. Angry at his stupid remark, and about her tumbling from her seat opposite him. Her body was sore and weary and screaming for more sleep. 'What?' She had noticed his change in demeanour as she righted herself and sat back in her original spot. His expression was aghast.

'What is it?' she demanded, spooked at the change in the air.

'I just saw an image. Did you also see it? Just now, when our hands touched.'

Zee's eyes suddenly found something extremely interesting to study on the floor of the carriage. 'Maybe you're the one who needs

250

a good drool sleep, eh?' Zee replied sarcastically, now staring out the window and pretending there was something other than a white blur to look at.

'Fine, if you don't want to talk about it.' But Ravaryn was rattled. Possibly by his own guilt at what lay ahead. 'Have you had any dreams, Zemira? Of, of her?' His voice sounded... worried? 'I promise you what I've told you is the truth. Believe me or not. If you ever have the unfortunate experience of meeting her, just promise me... promise me you won't underestimate her ferocity. She will slaughter her own kind, her own watchers and creatures of the outer Rim and forests of Lamiria, just to protect herself. Just... just don't forget yourself.'

'Just what did you see?' Zee questioned, her eyes burning into his.

It was now Ravaryn's turn to look out the blurry window. 'Just something I've been dreading for a very long time...'

The carriage bounced roughly down an incline as the roaring wind eased outside, revealing a sparkling image of an icy wasteland. A pristine white expanse. Up ahead, there it towered, the Rim wall, a stormy vision of black clouds rumbling and twisting beyond it.

'We're nearly there,' Ravaryn announced, sombre.

They sat in silence the rest of the way. The dullerats slowed as they reached the edge of the Rim, the wall that had stood for centuries. The wall that Zemira was supposed to somehow destroy. Caden, wrapped in a thickly furred white Moscow suit, opened the carriage door. He produced two black moscow coats, one smaller than then the other.

'I suggest you put that on, or I'll be removing those cuffs later from an ice biscuit.'

Zee looked at him in disgust, with no answer. She had been too tired to care this whole time about her own safety. With her mother, father and Paxton gone, presumably safe, she hadn't so much as worried about herself. But as she stepped out onto the frozen ground, the temperature dropped.

Zee stared at the looming wall in front of her. There was a platform erected of the shimmery metallic metal with a huge circular metal ring outstretched from it, directed towards the wall.

'This is where we part,' Ravaryn said, standing behind her and also staring out at the structure. 'I'm sorry it had to be this way, Zemira, but you need to do this. You need to help us get through the Rim wall,' he whispered into her ear.

Ravaryn turned and boomed a loud, demanding order towards Caden. He then marched off into a neatly erected black tent with the royal insignia stitched into the side. The same all the army of Kymera carried: A large pair of golden wings encircled by a serpent.

A chill ran down Zee's spine. And not one from the cold. Sorry! He was sorry! She was furious now, but Caden had secured her hands together and was now leading her through a crowd of busily preparing soldiers towards the structure.

'Caden, please, this is ridiculous. I've done nothing to deserve this.'

He just grunted, not making eye contact, and led her through the mass of black tents.

'It won't work. It will probably blow us all to the stars, if anything.'

He ignored her. She was started to panic now. Her magic coursing around in her veins was a familiar feeling, but this time with nowhere to escape to... no out. They reached the huge metal structure and climbed what felt like a thousand stairs to reach the top platform. Luckily the wind had died down or Zee probably would have been blown away with how weak her legs now felt. They were liquid underneath her. But the massive expanse of the view that greeted her at the top took what was left of her breath away. It was beautiful. The feeling of flying entered her mind. The amazing perspective of being on an eagle's back. Orion's back. How she missed him. How she missed them all. But he wasn't here to save her now.

Zemira took in the strange metal ring protruding from the structure to the other side. Metal rods traced back from it all to one point attached to a pillar in the middle of the metal deck. The ring faced the wall and the roiling black clouds rolled ominously behind it. And there at the end of the platform was a figure... standing, waiting. His pinched features sent shivers down her spine, his small, beady eyes hiding behind the shine of the round glass lenses. Greymouth. A malicious grin crept over his saggy old face at the sight of her.

Nowhere to Run

The Rim Wall, Kymera

'Zemira Creedence, it's so good to see you again and in such good health since the last time we met.' Greymouth's voice dripped with sarcasm. 'And after such an abrupt departure from my facility in Thorta.' He tisked as if a teacher were disapproving a student's behaviour in class. 'Fortunately, I had gathered all the required information from your bloods and lab tests before you decided it was time to leave. You've taken us all on quite the floxel chase.'

A real shiver now spiralled up Zee's spine. She wanted to run. There was no use trying to fight. Caden was twice her size, and even then, there was nowhere to go but down. Without her powers she was helpless. Zemira doubted that even with her powers she would be able to somehow sprout wings and glide on down.

'I don't know what you think you're going to accomplish here, but I cannot destroy the wall. I'm not powerful enough, and you'll probably all get blown to bits by trying! I won't do it!' Zee struggled against Caden's grip.

'Oh, you stupid girl, you don't have a choice.' Greymouth countered, sneering.

'Caden, don't listen to him. It won't work. You have to help me. This is wrong.'

The commander stared straight ahead, tugged at her clasped hands and led her to the pillar in the middle of the platform. Two metal-clasped hoops locked Zee's wrists into place. She stood at the centre of the platform, metal rods flowing out in front of her, connecting to the metallic ring facing the base of the Rim wall.

'Caden please, help me! You can stop him, please.' She was begging now.

Greymouth let out a dark laugh. 'No one is going to save you, Zemira. You needn't worry though; after I'm done with you, there's a possibility there won't be much left to save.'

Caden turned to leave, avoiding Zemira's eyes.

'Caden,' she whimpered, panic streaming through her. Her hands were locked in front of her.

'I'm sorry, miss,' he said sadly. 'Just following orders.' With that he turned and walked away towards the stairs that led down from the platform, without a single glance back.

Greymouth produced a small vial filled with dark red liquid. He flicked the corked lid of the vial with his thumb while holding it in one hand. The other hand snaked its way in through Zee's braids as he forced his frozen fingers around her neck, forcing her head back.

'Drink,' he ordered, not an ounce of patience in his tone.

Zee forced her mouth shut and ripped her head away from his grasp, knocking the hand with the bottle of dark liquid away and almost spilling its contents.

'Drink it, girl!' he seethed.

Greymouth slid his arm around her neck in a headlock and breathed puffs of vile breath into her face from above. He squeezed her throat and forced the liquid into her mouth. It was foul, and tasted of metal, smoke and burned organic matter. A heavy thickness coated all her senses. She spat the remainder of the substance out onto the metal floor of the structure. But not before her head started spinning.

'You'll regret this!' she spat in anger.

His laugh just rattled around the empty platform once more.

'Let's begin,' he seemed to say to himself, ignoring her. He attached some metal clasps to the rods protruding from where Zemira was secured and pulled a big metal lever. The metal rods sparked to life, sizzling and spitting with an electrical current. The small snake-like shots of lightning crept in through Zemira's secured wrists, swirling around her body as if collecting her powers from within. She couldn't stop it and felt pain zinging all around her.

Everything was blurry, and her head felt as though a pillow had been stuffed inside it. Her body slumped on itself, so she was now resting on her knees, barely conscious. Zemira just made out a blur of green exiting her hands. Her fingers were on fire. The electrical waves snaked up the metal rods and swirled around and around the giant metal ring, Zemira's green flames following them. She watched as they danced away from her, almost laughing at the absurdity of it.

The hunter felt wholly and completely empty. She was also giddy with whatever Greymouth had forced her to ingest. She couldn't move, couldn't think. She just watched her powers being taken from within her. Completely drained. All the flames left her, the last of them sliding up the metal rods and joining the rest. They mixed with the electrical charges swirling round and round the metal ring, growing brighter and brighter. The speed of the magical energy was now shaking the metal structure. The force of the swirling vortex nearly blew her limp body away from her. Her eyes stung with the brilliance of it. Her hands were still attached to the metal clasps in the middle of the tower, holding her there.

257

Greymouth struggled past her to the front of the deck, the force of the vortex blasting him back. He just managed to pull down another metal lever, the structure wailing its complaint at the force, then it screeched and released the swirling mass. Just as she thought she couldn't hold her consciousness any longer, she saw the enormous swirling circle of her powers spin away from the metal ring with ferocious speed. The vortex of swirling energy blasted away from them and pummelled directly into and through the Rim wall. The entire tower they were on blasted back and Zee saw herself as if time had slowed down in blurry slow motion. She was thrown backwards in the massive explosion. Her hands were ripped from their restraints and her body flew... and then she fell. Metres to the icy ground below.

'Your majesty.' The watcher bowed his head towards Kyeitha. 'We must act now. I've just received intel that the Rim wall has been breached.'

'Send them all.' The queen of the forest was shaking from head to toe, barely containing her rage, fists clenched at her sides. 'Every last one of my damned creatures. Send them to destroy everything.'

The black wolf watcher hesitated, but knew better than to question his queen. He feared the frail control of furious energy she contained, ready to break through the thin surface at any moment.

'Your majesty, as you wish.' He bowed his head again, then turned away from her and leaped into his wolf form. He ran fast through the glowing forests of Lamiria to the outskirts of the radiation wastes to rally and collect the damned. He wasn't sure what he feared more. Kyeitha's rage or the terrifying creatures she had created that lay in wait.

Orion, Verena and Paxton had been unharmed and escorted, if not pleasantly, but safely to the Aylenta-Kymerian border at the base just outside of the Wendigo Ranges. The soldiers' escort of moscows left them with two days' worth of supplies and a woverbine transport to use as they might see fit.

After the king's soldiers had left them, and upon entering into Aylenta, Verena pleaded with Orion, 'We have to go back for her! I have to know if she's alright. What he must be doing to her?' She was frantic. 'My love, she's not strong enough! She won't—'

'Verena.' Orion cut her off, his two large hands cupping her shoulders and holding her still. 'She is stronger than we know... and she will get through this.'

'How do you know?' Verena was taken aback by his calm assurance.

'Diwa. She told me this may happen. We need to get back to her cottage now.'

Paxton silently watched the pair argue. An ache from years ago as he remembered his own parents squabbling filled his weary mind. A hole was growing inside of him from being away from Zemira, and it seemed to get bigger the further away he got from her.

'Paxton, lad, we're leaving. You ready?' Orion addressed the now very quiet young man.

Pax nodded and proceeded to climb atop the brightly coloured woverbine. This one's hair was shades of ocean blues and forest greens, with horns of smooth grey river rocks. Verena just huffed and admitted defeat. If Diwa had said something that would indicate they should head back, she would. Diwa was always right.

'It'll be alright,' Orion assured her. 'She'll come back to us. I know it.'

Verena dropped her head to his chest, pressed her cheek against him and shut her eyes firmly. Orion wrapped his arms around her, encasing her firmly. They held on to each other, savouring the moment.

Looking at Paxton sitting astride the woverbine, after some difficulty mounting it, Orion said, 'She's the strongest person I know. Cheer up, lad. We're going home.'

'To Kali, please,' Orion boomed to the motionless beast chewing a mouthful of grass. The three shot backwards as the woverbine took off at marvelling speed, just as a loud boom pierced the air and rippled through the land around them. A dark green glow could be seen flashing through the clouds behind them in the distance. But the woverbine didn't miss a beat. The three hung on for the ride, knowing they would soon be back in Kali, back at Diwa's and would await Zemira to somehow make it back to them. The disconcerting ripple through the land followed them from behind.

Carts of large shiny metal bricks were being laid all around the gaping hole that seeped black mist into the Rim from which Zemira's combined powers had created. The metal bricks seemed to stop the encroaching magic of the Rim trying to heal itself.

'Faster!' boomed Ravaryn's voice. 'We mustn't let it seal. We will not get another chance.'

Soldiers scurried back and forth lugging brick after brick. Caden approached Ravaryn overseeing the efforts of the soldiers creating the tunnel through the wall.

'How is she?' Ravaryn rasped.

'She has not awoken,' Caden replied, stoic. 'Her injuries are...'

Ravaryn stared ahead, watching the bricks fall into place. The decimated tower and bodies of a few soldiers that were too close to the blast had all been cleared away. A pulsing fury of dark power coursed through Ravaryn's body. The curse was broken. Finally, after all these years, he could feel his magic, his energy returned to him. And he was going to get revenge... for his people, for his mother, for himself and for Zemira.

Kyeitha was going to die.

Black Wings

The Black Forest, Aylenta

She was there with her, the flowing hair encircling her in the dark forest.
Her face was illuminated with beauty. It was the woman from the river
dream... had she tried to warn her about the king?

'Come to me, child. I will help you. I will save the Rim from him and
his destruction.' The sweet voice sounded positively angelic... and yet her
soft, silky hands were wrapped tightly around Zemira's throat.

'Let me put you out of your misery, child. Let me end your suffering,
young Rim walker.'

'Stop. Please.' Zee thrashed, trying to force the woman away. Her
hands, her magic... her wrists were free of the metal cuffs. Green flames...
no, green vines crept forth out of her hands towards the woman. The ten-
drils of power wrapped round the woman's hands, tearing them away from
her throat. The vines became uncontrollable; they grew and grew, travelling

down her arms, into the woman eyes. The woman reared back, scratching at her face, the vines were everywhere, and she screamed...

'Zemira! Zemira! Wake up. Wake up, Zee.' Strong arms shook her. Every inch of her body felt broken. In her blurry vision, she couldn't make out the face, but she guessed they were in a tent.

'I'm so sorry.' Hard, cold metal was released from her limp arms. She couldn't move. There was barely enough life in her to open her heavy eyelids, then a thick blanket was swaddled around her, strong arms wrapping her like a child in a nest of soft warmth. Then it seemed the sky opened up and they were floating... floating away. Cold snowflakes blew by, and she felt the darkness say hello again.

Zee sensed the hard earth underneath her, her body cushioned by gentle plants, the smells... they smelt of home... rosemary, jasmine and cinnamon. There was no longer a cold rushing breeze. She was still wrapped in the warmth, and the sweet smells told her to drift back to sleep, away from the pain her body was ravaged with. She saw the figure leaning over her, large dark wings behind him. He leaned close in the darkness and placed a kiss on Zemira's forehead before tucking it into the warmth of the blanket again.

Three loud, sharp bangs shook Diwa's cottage door, and the occupants all leaped to their feet. Orion, fast on his feet, flew to the door, but it was Diwa whom was closest, and she yanked the door open. She saw a figure, dark wings flying away into the night, out of her grove. They were a familiar set of wings to her... and then they were gone. *So it is done then.* She sighed to herself, rushing over to her patch of nasturtiums where Zee's broken body lay wrapped in a black blanket with a set of golden wings just visible, surrounded by a golden serpent.

Orion had burst out the door and raced to his daughter.

'Pick her up, bring her inside, quickly, put her on the table!' commanded Diwa.

A rush of wind burst through the grove and straight into the old woman. Magic coursed through her, and breathing deeply, she felt it pulsing through her veins. Zemira had done it then. The curse was broken. Thank the stars. 'Hopefully, it's enough...' she mumbled to herself, still standing in the dark garden and breathing in the power, stilling herself, recognising her old self, her full power, before the curse had stripped it away. For Diwa was once the Rim guardian and still contained immense power. 'You did what you had to... All being well, I can heal her,' she said aloud, then turned and hurried into the cottage after Orion.

Diwa's hands glowed brightly over Zemira's skin, hovering up and down every part of her broken and bruised body as she sang in a language that none of the others in the cottage had ever heard. Orion hugged Verena to him as the tears fell from her pale face. Paxton just watched in horror, taking in the devastating state Zemira was in. Diwa's gnarled hands shook as the light streamed out of them like vapours, swirling out, around and into the injuries, clearing away the damage to Zee's body, healing her.

A rumbling shook the tiny house as a storm rolled in, lightning flashed in the tiny windows and the heavens opened up. The atmosphere grew louder and louder as Diwa's voice competed with the rain outside. Finally, shaking and weary, Orion caught the old woman just as she was about to drop.

'I've done all I can,' she croaked out. 'Rest. We... need... rest.'

Orion scooped her up and returned a minute later for Zemira. Dark circles encased her eyes, but her wounds were visibly healed. Black patterns twisted up around her wrists as she slept, and swirls of tiny snowflakes in beautiful dotted patterns entwined around the mysterious patterns. Orion growled furiously as he watched them, but laid Zee down next to Diwa in the old woman's bed and tucked her in, where they slept deeply.

The morning's sun shining bright and warm through the window of the cottage forced Zee to open her eyes. When she did, she was met by a sparkling grey pair opposite hers.

'Hello, Zemira,' the old woman said softly.

'Diwa!' Zee exclaimed. 'Is this another dream?'

'I don't know, Zee. How do you feel?'

'Great, actually, so it is a dream then. I fell... I felt the skin ripped from my wrists, the power sucked out of me. But I'm glad you're here now.'

'It's not a dream, my dear girl, we're here together in my cottage. You made it.' Diwa said, smiling. 'I knew you could do it.'

Zee's heart burst with happiness upon hearing that she was alive.

'Should I make us some tea?' the old lady asked, still smiling, head on the pillow looking into Zee's deep eyes that reflected the forest outside.

'Tea sounds wonderful.'

She felt light, she felt whole. She felt herself again. Eating breakfast in the small cottage with her whole family together, was this even real? It had to be. Verena and Orion were both paler than she remembered but some colour had returned to their faces after she had awoken. Warmth infused her whole body, igniting her core upon seeing her parents together. She couldn't savour her mother's hugs enough, she couldn't take her eyes away from her family all together in one place. The way her father looked at her mother, the way Diwa glowed while fussing with tea and food for everyone.

The tree even felt as though it were alive with happiness, swaying with hardly any wind and causing the cottage to creak and squeak a little. Zee took in a deep breath and cemented the feeling and memory like gold in her mind. Her dreams made real. She felt like she would float away upon looking at her parents together at last, all her worries nearly melting away. And Paxton was on the mend too, the crushing hug he had given her had said as much. The light was returning to his amber eyes. He doted on her hand and foot that morning. She could get used to this.

'We have to go to her,' Zee said after breakfast. 'Kyeitha. We must warn her. Ravaryn means to start a war, and he's going to kill her, along with every creature that gets in his way. He must be stopped. Maybe she can stop him before any more lives need to suffer?'

'Absolutely not!' Verena protested 'You will not leave this forest again. I forbid it!'

'Calm down, Mum. I didn't ask permission. I'm an adult now.'

Verena let out a surprised huff, worry brimming in her eyes.

Zee shifted her gaze. 'I was talking to Wolf.'

Diwa eyed Orion, and a slight nod caught his eye.

'It's too soon! You just woke up from near death. Diwa, Orion, please! Someone talk some sense into her.' Verena was aghast.

Paxton sat quietly at the end of the table, watching the conversation play out. The sadness in his heart felt like a heavy stone, a giant, heavy stone threatening to drown him. She was leaving again, and would she even come back this time? Pax kept his feelings inside. He didn't get a say. He knew Zemira was determined and wouldn't listen to him either way.

'I think they need to go, Verena. Something has to be done,' Diwa agreed.

Verena couldn't believe what she was hearing, and tears pricked her eyes. 'No. I-I just got you back...' her voice broke.

'Mum.' Zemira left her spot at the table to console her crying mother. 'I'm fine, really. I feel great, good as new, and besides, I'll be safe. Wolf will be with me, and I'm tougher than you think. I've been past the Rim before.' She hugged her seated mother's head in her arms.

'Please trust me. We have to do something. But I promise you we'll both come back safely. Together.'

The Battle of the Damned

Rim Wall, Kymerian Border

'Sir, the arch has been reinforced, and the hole in the Rim is stable.' Caden's level voice echoed inside the dark tent erected near the Kymerian border closest to the eastern edge of the Rim. Hardly any light entered as the cool, crisp day blossomed outside, spreading beautiful colours across the snow as it rose. But Ravaryn didn't feel anything beautiful, neither the cool nor the calm. Inside, his rage burned. Burned for Kyeitha.

'I didn't hear you return, sir. Is she—?'

'Well done, Caden.' Ravaryn spoke finally. Abruptly. 'We must hurry. The creatures will be along soon. Tell the soldiers to remember their training, and to remember that the creatures they will be fighting are not of this world. They will destroy and rip apart any human they see. Be ready. They must be stopped.'

The wind picked up as the last of the borenium blocks were carried into place, solidifying the pass. Shimmering. Metallic. They were almost beautiful in the morning sun's rays. The black fog swirled on the other side of the hole, spiralling in. But dissipating on entry as if it were never really there at all.

'Once we enter the outer Rim, keep your eyes peeled. Some things will not be what they seem. Remember your training. But do not doubt your wits, men. Be vigilant! FOR KYMERA!' Ravaryn boomed to his hoard of awaiting soldiers. The air vibrated with their keen nerves.

'FOR KYMERA!' They raised their borenium swords into the air and returned the sound, full of promise.

'Onward into the outer Rim!' Caden ordered the first onslaught of soldiers to go through. They marched in perfect unison into the dark unknown, their suits shimmering together like a wave.

Standing in the eerie smog, the soldiers' eyes darted all around trying to determine their surroundings. It was like entering a dark, thick cloud. Still and silent. Not even the air moved around them now. They proceeded on, yet the only noise was theirs, with their movements and armour shifting as they marched forward. The ground was hard and dead. Cracked, dried black earth was beneath them. There was an odd twisted dead tree here and there. No animals. No creatures. No life at all, it seemed. The fog seemed to be clearing ahead of them. And there stood a figure, a shape, silhouetted in the distance. It materialised as if out of thin air. A lone black wolf standing on the rise of a slight hill.

'Halt!' commanded Ravaryn. The pair locked eyes. Wolf and king in a silent understanding. The creature turned and bounded away to the south. Then nothing. The soldiers waited in silence, only the breaths of their comrades sounded around them. Minutes passed, until a rumbling sound echoed around them. The earth shook and the cracked mud jittered the small stones on its surface. Huge, disfigured creatures bounded over the hill rise ahead. Towards them.

'Ready, men!' Caden shouted, steadying his stance in front of his men. Ready to fight. To protect.

The creatures headed towards them were gigantic. Some had disfigured faces of recognisable creatures attached to large foreign-looking bodies. Some slithered, some flew overhead. They were almost upon them. Close enough to see that they all had a silver sheen coating their eyes, giving them an even more terrifying, ghostly feel. Then it was chaos.

The bodies of the soldiers were thrown into the air while screeching and ear-piercing roars from the creatures filled the stagnant air around them. The giant mouth of a bat-like creature with the body of a large lizard ripped into a soldier's shoulder nearby. His cries of agony were sickening. Blood poured from the creature's silver-toothed maw. Ravaryn swung his sword high and forced it down over the creature, decapitating it with one mighty swing.

The soldier was torn from his grasp by another flying creature just as Ravaryn reached to help him. His body was ripped away from where he was standing in a split second, the clawed feet tearing the soldier's injured body in two and dropping the remnants into the battle below. Ravaryn took a deep breath and carried on. He spotted Caden in the fray and fought his way toward him. A slithering creature popped its lion-like head up from the ground on its only two feet at the front of its body, and reared up at him. Ravaryn swung this time at a leg, avoiding its snake-like strike.

The creature screeched in pain as the leg flew from its body with one strong, swift motion from the borenium sword. Reaching Caden, Ravaryn plunged his sword deep into the heart of a huge bear-bodied creature with the head of a scaled toad, just as it was about to tear into Caden from behind.

'Thanks,' he panted, withdrawing his sword from a vipen-like creature's large eye socket. The sword having reached its brain, it was now twitching in a large pile on the ground.

'Rally the men for a circle!' the king yelled over the din.

'Yes sir!'

But the chaos went on... and on. Creatures of all kinds imaginable kept coming, kept rising from behind the ridge. The soldiers formed large circles, fighting as one. Their backs protected from the creatures by their brothers. A creature tore its teeth deep into Ravaryn's upper arm and chest. Its fish face slapping tentacles into his face. He forced the sword into its goat-like body, praying to hit the heart and hoping it was where he guessed. Ravaryn cried out with the effort and the pain of the creature's bite.

Caden twisted away from the animal he had just slayed and swung his sword into the beast. It was enough for the creature to release its grasp and screech back in pain. Caden swung again with an almighty effort and removed half of its head. Black blood sprayed over both of them.

'Nice move,' Ravaryn grunted.

Caden's grin was wide. He was alive in the spirit of the battle and moved like a precision athlete. 'If you've got my back, I've got yours!' Caden roared. His face was menacing through the black blood splatter.

Ravaryn's chest and arm stung beyond belief. 'I knew I kept you around for something!' Ravaryn bellowed amidst the gore and chaos of the battle, feeling pure adrenaline, feeling utterly alive. Comforted by the presence of his comrade in arms by his side. His brother, his friend. One of his only friends. Suddenly, a look of horror swept over Caden's hard face. His eyes widened and fresh crimson poured from his mouth as a sharp barb pierced through his body from behind and slid back out again in what seemed like seconds. He fell to his knees, eyes locked on Ravaryn's. Looking for... strength? Peace? A goodbye?

Ravaryn froze, his heart pounding in his chest, his ears. No! Caden's smile returned for a moment, his bloodied teeth appearing. But before Ravaryn could reach out, his body was jerked back and ripped away... ripped in two... before the king's eyes. A monstrous scorpion-like creature with the face of a vipen tore him apart like a ragdoll. Ravaryn's voice roared his pain. His body rebelled, the pain

272

coursing through him pushing him onwards. He charged the beast, flying towards him, his sword in front of him like a joist, with unbelievable speed. He plunged the sword deep, almost to the handle, into the creature's face. Black liquid oozed from its mouth. Its severed brain gave way and the giant's body fell to the ground. Ravaryn refused to looks at Caden's remains. Tears streaked down his furious face. He forced his body on, to obey. She couldn't win... she wouldn't win. He would fight until there was nothing left. She deserved death. She deserved worse. He would win. They would win. He carried on.

Descent Into Madness

Lamiria

Zemira and Orion flew through the night at break neck speed, the wind streaming around her and whistling loudly past her ears. Below the fighting was a patchwork of still bodies and violent chaos as creatures clashed with soldiers, leaving a large smear of black and red on the earth as they rushed past overhead. They made it to Lamiria in record-breaking time, Orion thoroughly spent. Zee had to steady herself to gain compose after the speed of the flight, happy to have solid ground under her again.

They landed just outside of Kyeitha's temple in the meadow clearing, in the pass between the mountain entrance and the entrance to her temple. Zee again marvelled at the colours, the life, the beauty floating all around her. Animals of all kinds mulled peacefully about the clearing. The smells of sweet, intoxicating perfumes filled the air, and her body breathed it all in, the pure adrenaline of the ride still thrumming through her veins now sprinkled with the awe of the meadow. There were more flowers than Zemira could ever count, some blooming right in front of her eyes, and little wisp creatures with tiny transparent wings trailed beautiful orbs of light behind them in rainbow mists.

'Come on,' Orion urged her after shifting from his eagle form and catching his breath. 'We must hurry. We need to stop Ravaryn.'

They hurried out of the meadow and trailed through a path of woven vines and heavy forest, coming up to a clearing of what looked like an ancient stone building. Huge ceilings and pillars of sandstone held up a structure overlooking a more extraordinary lake filled with more of the rainbow wisps. These ones were playing around with floating orbs of light-filled water above immaculate lily pad blooms of every colour imaginable.

Zemira was speechless. This place was incredible. The beauty was intoxicating. And Kyeitha... there she sat on her giant stone throne, an amazing floral display spearing out behind her head – a colourful headrest of more amazing flora. Trails of small glowing fungi swirled around the moss-covered areas of her throne as she sat there. Waiting. Zemira had never seen a more beautiful person. This was the woman from her dream. Her hair was perfect and shimmered in the moonlight, giving it the appearance of silk. Her skin was flawless; there was not a spot, or trace of a line. Her eyes were the brightest blue of a gorgeous spring day but somehow speckled with stars. They bored right into Zemira's emerald ones. The dark juneberry of her lips curved upwards, producing a glow-ing, flawless white smile.

'Zemira, darling... finally. Welcome to Lamiria.' Kyeitha's smile was not at all inviting despite her sweet voice. The words felt... false. She glared at Orion. He came closer, standing protectively beside Zee.

'So Orion, this is the little mongrel you were so obsessed to find.' Kyeitha's smile grew, but her eyes stayed fierce.

A dark feeling swirled in Zee's gut. Run. Ravaryn had been right all along.

'What in the Rim has caused you two to dare infest my home with your stench,' she seethed.

Zee's palm twitched. Kyeitha was not at all what Zee had expected. 'We needed to tell you...' Zemira spoke hesitantly, almost fearful now of Kyeitha's harsh words. 'There is a war brewing, and we're here to warn you. Ravaryn is coming, and he wants you dead. He plans to take the entire Rim into his control and who knows what else.'

Kyeitha just sat and started at her, expressionless, before turning to Orion. 'Now that I've actually seen it,' she waved a hand dismissively towards Zemira, 'I am even more disgusted than I was before.'

Zee's jaw dropped open. 'Did you even hear what I said? Ravaryn has an army, he is decimating your Rim warriors as we speak! It's a bloodbath out there! And you just sit here in your temple while they die!'

'Zemira,' warned Orion, a hand on her arm.

Kyeitha stood, her figure-hugging silver and green gown shimmering in the moonlight with her movement. She walked effortlessly and without a care for what Zemira had just said, completely ignoring her very existence, and headed towards Orion. She was so tall she actually looked down on him. 'I can't deny your treacherous act any longer, not with your filthy offspring standing right in my halls. If you weren't indebted to be my right hand, I would carve you up where you stand. My son, my greatest disappointment—'

'Enough.' Orion's voice was firm. 'There's no time. You need to stop this. There are hundreds of innocents dying out there. There is a hole in the Rim, and it will all descend further into chaos if you don't do something now.'

Kyeitha burst into a mad laugh, yet still no emotion touched her eyes. They gave nothing away. 'How DARE you filthy, lowlife forms enter my temple, and tell ME WHAT TO DO!' she screamed into his face, her mood swinging madly. 'You two fools presume that I, the queen of the forest, have no idea what is going on in my own world? I know about Ravaryn's feeble attempts to spread his rule through the Rim. I sent my warriors to wipe out his little attempt at escaping the Rim. I saw what your interbred offspring did to the wall. You two think you're warning me? I. KNOW. ALL! And you, my son, this is the last time you disobey me.'

Kyeitha grabbed Orion by the throat, lifting his body off the ground. His feet swung madly, lashing out at her.

Zee was utterly shocked. The queen was clearly derailed. Her spiteful words were zinging around in Zee's skull. Kyeitha was not going to help them. She didn't even care. Her creatures were dying... she had sent them to their death.

Kyeitha's malicious grin seethed into Orion's face. 'I... own... you.'

'STOP!' STOP IT!' shouted Zee. 'You don't have to do this! Put him down!' Green flames ignited from her palms and swirled upwards around her arms. Zee could see that Ravaryn was right. Kyeitha was evil; she had lost her mind. She wouldn't let her harm Orion, she wouldn't lose him again.

'STOP KYEITHA!' Zee roared in a voice she didn't know she owned.

The ethereal goddess twisted around and grabbed Zee's forearm with her opposite hand, extinguishing the green flames in a split second. Zee felt a strange pulse through her arm as Kyeitha's magic entered her body. A silver tendril slithered inside her, crawling up her arm, across her shoulder and entering at the bottom of her neck into her mind. All the negative moments of her life bloomed viciously inside her head.

The lady from the markets screaming at her as a small child for breaking a vase she had picked up to admire its sparkling swirls. 'You stupid girl! You've broken it! Your parents should flog you!' seethed the stall holder. Lawrence kicking her, sitting on her after school, bullying her always when there was no one around to stop him. 'What's the matter, you little roach? Sad you don't have any friends? No one likes you here, you should just leave,' he spat. Greymouth staring down at her in the mud, still and broken. 'What a shame such great power was contained inside such an unworthy, useless little vessel of a human.' His slithering voice cut into her, beady eyes beaming through the round lenses. More silver tendrils spread from Kyeitha, locking into parts of Zee's brain and forcing their way in like spikes.

'Argh,' she cried out in pain. 'STOP!'

Another memory. Paxton's horror of her for breaking a hole in the Rim wall. 'Zee, what have you done? You've broken the Rim.' He faded, only to be replaced by the tall soldier by the Rim river. 'We've been looking all over for you. All this trouble for a scrawny little village feral.' Her mother's disappointed face the day she came home and heard of the incident with Lawrence. 'You mustn't return to school, Zee. You've broken my trust.'

Kyeitha's voice was now strong inside her head. 'Well, well, well, it seems all you can do with your gifts that you stole from me is break things. You break everything you lay your dirty little human hands on, don't you, Zemira?' She hissed like a serpent. A vision of Verena screaming as tree wisp warriors tore Orion away from her entered Zee's mind.

'You even broke your own mother's heart... just by existing. It's all your fault. You've broken everything and everyone around you. You're nothing, a mistake, a burden on the lives that have to withstand your presence around them. Worse still, your friends. Poor Paxton.'

Paxton appeared in the mud, tears streaming down his face, the whip slashing his skin as his body trembled with the blows, reaching out for her, calling out her name to save him.

'Also all your fault. The king would never have raided your village looking for you if you didn't exist. And Paxton would have led a happy, safe life, but now he is broken because of you. Your father is now mine, because of you. I finally own his life – his soul. He is mine, and I will do with him what I wish. Orion is indebted to me, all because he begged for his powers back to save you.'

Zee screamed at the mental attack. She could feel the queen's powers snaking into her arm and into her head, the silky tendrils sliding all through her body, stinging at the point of entry. A dark black force grew within her. Zee knew the feeling – the self-doubt. It was all her fault. She was all of those things Kyeitha had said she was. And her father. No! Why had he bargained that? He would be gone for good this time.

'Zemira, do you really think you're a powerful warrior? A saviour? You've broken the only thing protecting those humans, those vermin, from the outside world. My world. My creatures will decimate any of the fools who try to defend themselves. I will not let them poison me again. Humans. They are helpless without the protection of the Rim, and you, you stupid girl, have blasted a giant hole in it. Zemira, the girl who breaks things. You're nothing, you're worthless. Less than worthless. You're destruction... you're a destroyer of things... a parasite to those around you. A mistake.'

Images of people's disappointed faces swirled around in Zemira's head. She was a creature that should not be.

'And you will destroy everything and everyone that loves you simply by existing. Zemira. The girl... who broke... the world.'

'ENOUGH!' Zee screamed.

Orion was still in Kyeitha's grasp, struggling against her grip, his face turning a slight shade of mistflower blue. Zee had to save him. She could not lose him again. None of this was her fault. The queen was wrong. She was infected somehow with hate, rotten to the core. Zemira could feel it now. She reached for her side, the queen's hand still grasping her arm. She was still forcing images into her head, now of her mother dying old and alone. Paxton being beaten to death by the soldiers circling around him, kicking him into the ground, his blood spraying everywhere. Diwa being stabbed by Ravaryn. Zemira's own hands coated in all of their blood. And the creatures of the outer Rim coming in to devour the bodies of them all, her loved ones, her family.

STOP! She knew it was all an illusion. It was not real. Not real. It's not real!

The queen's powers of manipulation were so strong that Zemira Creedence, destroyer of worlds, saw a vision of herself in a decimated land with no life, nothing. In the radiation fields, she stood all alone. Zee felt the hilt of the knife in her right hand through the fog of Kyeitha's powerful visions. The tears streamed down her face, yet she fought back. Inside her mind, she sent her own vision to Kyeitha, one tiny green tendril of power growing into Kyeitha like a vine.

'If you think I care what you think, you're wrong. I know I break things, and I don't care.' The green flames ignited around Zee's hand, burning inside her mind and travelling through her veins, chasing Kyeitha's silver tendrils out of her body and forcing them back inside the queen. Up into her hand still clamped around Zee's arm, her green flames, vines of power, entered Kyeitha's body. Surging up, up, up into her mind.

Zemira saw the early days of the Rim. Kyeitha standing next to another woman, a young woman with a huge smile and bright face with shining silvery-grey eyes. A dark blue stone necklace hung around her neck, and a small boy clung to her leg. The boy had black hair and eyes to match, his pale skin a stark contrast to his curls, and he had small black wings tucked in behind him. She saw Kyeitha and all her creatures in Lamiria. They were healthy, not the savage and contorted images of the creatures fighting against Ravaryn's army now. The image faded. She then saw Kyeitha fighting with the woman and banishing her and her son to the inner Rim... the boy now a young man.

Kyeitha was screaming in front of her court while a woman and child kneeled before her, begging for their lives. The man with dark hair was held back... held back to watch as Kyeitha slaughtered them both. His agonising screams filling the air. Another vision of the same dark-haired man defending his mother, shielding her from Kyeitha as she banished the pair away. Kyeitha alone, crying on her stone throne. Then she saw Orion, her father, kneeling before Kyeitha as she sucked the power from within him. His screaming form writhing in pain before her on the stone floor of her temple. His form transforming into Wolf. Another image of the queen raging while the black wolf warrior stood guard as she raged, smashing through the temple with her power. Destroying, killing innocent bystanders as she went. Slaying her creatures, her loyal Rim watchers in her rage. Members of her guard. Zemira projected her own voice inside Kyeitha's mind, her green vines digging into all the memories, the secrets she had hidden. 'You are the one who has driven your family away! You are the one who breaks things. You are the one who is *broken*.

Kyeitha's grasp on Orion slipped, and he dropped to the ground motionless. She turned to face Zee, her grip stuck as the pair internally exchanged forces. Their powers tied together and tangled within for the moment. The Rim guardian's eyes opened wide in shock as she stared at Zemira, horror creeping into her perfect face, features contorting.

Zemira saw the queen's fears... the destruction that the past humans had wreaked on the world. The death, the devastation, the famine, the war, the pollution, the diseases. The destruction and death of the animals and the environment. Her deep-rooted fear of humans. Zemira didn't care, she felt the evil within. Kyeitha was rancid. Centuries of hate and fear had turned her into a creature of her own destruction. She withdrew her green vines from Kyeitha's mind, surging them out of her body back through the hand she had wrapped around her forearm.

Then she forced everything she had, every ounce of power she drew from everything inside her being, and forced it up her other arm into her hand, through the knife and into Kyeitha's stomach. Forcing it up, twisting it into her ribcage. Silver blood poured out all over Zemira's arm, burning her, but she forced it up higher to where she knew Kyeitha's heart would be. She let all of her power explode within the broken queen. Kyeitha's face contorted in more shock if that were possible, and her grip went weak... and slipped from Zemira's arm.

Green flames flickered within the queen's pupils from within and glowed out of her open mouth. Zemira looked into her eyes, her own searching for any remorse within the soulless queen. She found none, and said with a dark voice to the twisted being before her, 'You are the one who is broken.'

A last surge of power sent Kyeitha bursting into green flames. They engulfed her body, the light pouring from her eyes, her mouth, bursting out of her chest where Zemira had pieced her heart. Her body crumpled to the ground and turned black, the flames extinguishing as her body disintegrated into a pile of ash. Zemira panted, forcing a strong breeze to course through the temple's open pergola to sweep the ashes out onto the beautiful pond. A pond that Kyeitha had once stared at in wonder, before transforming herself into the sick being she had become. She was gone... to forever be a part of the world she had created for herself.

One last image burst into Zemira's mind of the battle... the creatures' silver-sheened eyes vanished. They stopped their violent and vicious attacks, some being slayed while others came to a realisation and ran from the fight, no longer controlled by the forest queen. The Rim wall's shimmery iridescence dissipated, vanishing from all around the whole expanse of the Rim. The Rim was gone... The vision cleared, and Zee rushed to Orion. He lay on the cold floor, his face pale, his huge body limp.

He wasn't breathing.

Saving Orion

Lamiria

Panic filled her every cell. 'Wolf! Orion, get up!' Tears streamed down Zemira's face. No, no, no!

'Dad, wake up.' She shook his lifeless form. Her head pressed into his chest, and she calmed her mind. Using the same magic that Kyeitha had unexpectedly shown her, she reached inwards for her tendrils of green vine power, sending them into Orion's body and into his chest, reaching for his heart. Her eyes closed, her energy searching not into his mind but sprouting her vines around his heart and squeezing. She forced what was left of herself, of her power, into his heart.

Zee thought of every memory of herself and Wolf, the day he saved her from the black tree serpent, her mother's tears of joy at realising he had come back to her. Orion, herself, Pax and Tye, joking, laughing, teasing inside the ice igloo Zee had made after rescuing the boys from the mines in Kymera. Verena's joy at finally being reunited with Orion when they had found her safe inside Ravaryn's castle. But it wasn't working. Zee's face was slick with sweat, and his heart was still dormant. Why wasn't it working! Her panicked eyes poured with tears now.

'No,' she croaked, her throat barely able to speak, so constricted it was with fear and pain. She forced every happy moment she could muster from her mind into her father's heart yet still nothing worked. Zee didn't even feel the stir of a rhythm from within him, a movement, nothing. She had failed. She had yet again broken something else. Her hands pushed harder into his chest as she wept. 'Wake up!' she screamed through her burning throat, her body aching with the effort.

'Why? Why aren't I powerful enough?' she wept. 'I told her we would come home, together.'

Zee was desperate. Thinking of anything, every moment they had shared. Orion had told her, 'I was always with you even when you felt you were completely alone.' She felt absolutely alone in this moment right now, crying over her father's lifeless body. Her tendrils of power still squeezing his heart, she forced everything she had into his chest, searching for something, anything. But then she felt her magic reach upwards, guiding her. She let the tendrils explore inside Orion's body. They travelled quickly now searching, searching, searching... up into his mind.

'Of course!' sparked Zee's mind. My memories are my own... attached to my own emotions... my own power. They're not enough. I need Orion's. She reached inside with a green fern-like tendril of power. And memories exploded all around her. Orion crashing into a veranda in a vicious storm, his heart skipping a beat as he locked eyes with Zee's mother for the first time. Orion and Verena on a woverbine's back, racing through fields in Aylenta, smiling, laughing. Verena throwing her arms in the air as Orion held her waist steady. Visions of Orion building a small house on the side of a hill in a quiet forest. His hands slowly caressing a swollen belly,

Verena's eyes full of happiness and shining with love at him. A baby in his arms, tears of joy as he held her. The day he had finally returned, but as Wolf, his happiness at finding his girls. Saving Zee from the serpent, then making a huge mess of their cottage with his huge form upon reuniting again with Verena.

It was working. Zee collected all the light, the power from the memories and surged them into Orion's heart, forcing the vines tighter and willing a response. It was working! A slow beat started to pump a weak rhythm, but she needed more. Zemira searched his mind frantically for more joyful memories of him and Verena, but they were few as he didn't have many years before Kyeitha had taken him. The small beat was dying... fading.

'NO!'

Zee searched harder. 'Come on!' Her hands pressed harder into his chest, more tendrils of herself entering, searching his mind. Then she found him. Wolf. And a million moments exploded around her like stars glowing with all the happiness and love of a galaxy. They were all memories of her. She saw herself chasing floxels with Wolf, fishing by the river as Wolf watched. Hunting deer together. Crouching silently together, stalking brustlehens in the forest. Trotting together along the worn track to Diwa's. Crouching, ready to pounce and scare Paxton unawares. Wolf lying comfortably by the fire with Zee patting his large head. Zee cuddling Wolf as he squished in between herself and Paxton on mattresses on the floor of Diwa's cottage. His happiest memories, his brightest and most powerful reasons for his being... were her.

More tears streamed down Zemira's face as she sobbed with happiness. She was never alone... he hadn't left her. He did want her. Her heart exploded with her own new happy memories and she grabbed them all, she collected every sparkling essence of power and withdrew every tendril containing the small gems, forcing them all around his heart and coating it with light.

The rhythm grew stronger. She felt the steady thump growing. Stronger and stronger. Yes. It was working! Relief flooded her body, her hands finally easing the force on his chest but still remaining over the steady rhythm that had returned. His heart was now encased with the memories of light, their power seeping into it. Orion's eyes started to flutter. His skin was still pale, and dark bruises laced his neck where Kyeitha had held him. But his eyes opened, he coughed and drew in a deep breath.

Orion saw Zee sitting there, her hands still in vigil over his chest, afraid the thump, thump would disappear again. He rattled out with a hoarse, deep voice, 'My little wolf... you did it... you freed us all.' A strained smile beamed up at her.

'Oh, Dad.' She threw herself onto him, weaving her arms around his neck and cradling his head. Tears poured from her face and she didn't care; she let them all trickle down like raindrops. 'I thought you were dead. She-she was poisoned... from the inside. I had to... I'm so sorry,' Zee sobbed. 'I killed her... I had to. I had to save you. I couldn't lose you again, Dad. I didn't want to be without you.' Zee cried into his chest.

Orion coughed. 'Oh, so now I get called Dad.'

But Zee's tears didn't stop.

'My girl, you did the right thing,' he whispered through his strained throat. 'I'm so, so, proud of you. I could see what she was doing to you. I saw every negative image that she twisted into you, and I could do nothing to stop her. I'm so sorry I couldn't save you, but you did it... you overcame even your darkest demons, and you did it, you stopped her.'

Tears slipped from Orion's eyes and trickled down his face. 'Look at me, Zee.' His emerald eyes searched her own shining forests of green as he stared at her in awe. 'I'm so proud of you. You saved me... you saved us all. You healed the world, my girl.' He smiled at her his brave daughter. Who no one needed to save. She had saved them all... and she had managed to also save herself from her own darkest demons.

Balance is Restored

Shifting into his eagle form, Zemira and Orion left Lamiria, both worn, and they gently glided over the forests and mountain pass. Past the battlefield where hundreds of bodies lay, both humans and Rim creatures, the vines already growing around the bodies to digest and recycle their souls into the earth. The destruction was devastating and nothing like Zee had ever seen. They found the entire Rim wall gone. Zee had destroyed the whole Rim wall, along with Kyeitha. They headed for Diwa's cottage in the tangled ancient woods - home - this time together.

Ravaryn returned to his castle, his curse broken. Zemira had done what he had wished for. His mother had been right, she had broken the curse, and his powers had returned more powerful than ever. Diwa Mumasumi, former Rim guardian and his crafty old mother, must have healed the girl. Diwa was so powerful before she gave her title over to Kyeitha, along with the elemental powers of the forest. But she had kept her own powers gifted from Mother Nature herself, that of a seer and a healer. Diwa was one of the most amazing women he had ever had in his life. She had protected him all those years ago when Kyeitha had cast them into the Rim and cursed them for his mistake. When the forest queen had killed his beautiful wife and babe. He had only told Zemira part of the story. It hadn't been a female watcher that had fallen in love with a human farmer inside the Rim, it was he, Ravaryn, who had fallen in love with a human woman.

The memory still felt heavy, making his heart ache. His eyes brimmed with tears and shimmered in the fire at the thought of them. But Kyeitha was gone now. She couldn't harm any others. Zemira, that miraculously brave girl, had somehow done it. Ended Kyeitha's reign. His stomach twisted with guilt over what he had had to do - the part he had to play - all this time. But his sins had been forgiven. The people taken from Aylenta had been returned, the mines shut down. All the planning and manipulation to get Zemira to do what had to be done to break the curse without being able to tell her... that was the hardest part.

He guessed it had been the same for Diwa too... the not being able to speak, to explain, to have to twist words. That was the thing about Kyeitha - if it hadn't been cruel, it hadn't been fun. It was possibly the worst thing about Kyeitha's curse to not be able to tell Zemira the truth... to have to have lied. But maybe, just maybe, she would forgive him. Chester let out a long, quiet howl into the icy room around them. It echoed eerily. His huge head rested on Ravaryn's lap. The fireplace opposite them reflected the flickering light in their shinning eyes as Ravaryn thought of Caden, also now gone, along with his wife and child from so long ago.

'I know, buddy. I miss him too.' Tears slid down the lonely king's face and dropped in the dark red liquid inside the wine glass he held to his chest. At least he still had a chance to see his mother again.

Diwa sat in her warm cottage and thought of her son. So alone for so long but he had played his part well, and maybe one day he would again be happy. She remembered Kyeitha's cruelty, but her fellow Rim guardian was no more. In banishing them both to the inside of the Rim for caring too much about the humans, she had inevitably doomed herself. Diwa knew her apprentice had gone mad with her task of containing and looking over the humans for all this time. But eventually the Rim had to be removed. The humans and outer Rim inhabitants were one day to live together in peace. Kyeitha would never have let this happen. Without Diwa there to continue to mentor her, to make sure the balance inside her was not tipped over the edge to the side of hate and paranoia, the queen's fear of the inner Rim inhabitants had spiralled out of control.

But Diwa hadn't been able to bring herself to stop her; her heart was too soft and her powers too weak. No, Zemira, the Rim walker child, had done what Diwa could not. What a beautiful, caring young soul. Tears brimmed around the old woman's eyes. Tears of joy, of pride. Zee had finally played her part and thankfully won. She had fought the darkest demons imaginable... the ones that lingered inside one's own mind. Diwa sipped the last of her tea and looked into the old, worn cup spotted with orange fruits and little white flowers. The rim was lined with chipped gold, and it was one of her favourites. The tea leaves within swirled in strange patterns before her eyes, and then stilled. She saw it, a wolf and a dragon danced around each other in perfect balance. Diwa smiled.

Diwa had healed what was left of the mark on Zemira's arm, and as she had healed it she had told Zemira of her son, Ravaryn. The sweet boy who had grown up as a watcher of the Rim, and who had fallen in love with a human inside of the Rim. He had broken Kyietha's rule, to never interact with humans, and had hidden the relationship that had brought forth a beautiful baby girl. Kyeitha had been furious when she discovered the truth, and she murdered the child in a rage in front of all her watchers.

Ravaryn had exploded in agonising rage, attacking her with dark swirls of magic that no one knew where they had originated from. They had fought with their powers, but Kyeitha being the Rim guardian won, her elemental powers stronger. Diwa had held Kyeitha back from killing Ravaryn as his broken body had lain unconscious on the temple floor. If only she hadn't chosen Kyeitha as her predecessor, none of it would have happened. Why hadn't she foreseen it? How had she gotten it so wrong?

Kyeitha had finally backed off after looking into the old woman's eyes, but still furious and seeping with rage, she banished the pair to the Rim, stripping them of nearly all their powers. They were to remain apart in separate territories inside of the Rim, never to see each other again. Diwa's guilt still felt heavy inside her soul, like a weight dragging her down. She had failed her son. Had he forgiven her? Would he ever forgive her?

The hand print of Kyeitha's remained on Zemira's arm. It turned black to tell a story like every other scar, but there were no beautiful marks. Nothing appeared. Just the dark handprint remained. Zee didn't tell Diwa that it had started to grow... to change... to ache. Sharp pangs would sting her arm at times. No, she hid the scar wanting things to go back to normal... wanting things to be easy again. Maybe she had asked for too much, having wished for a little adventure in her life. Well, she had gotten adventure alright, but along with it came a river full of pain.

Zemira wanted Kyeitha to stay in the past. Far away from her. But the nightmares raged when she dreamed. In them, she was seeing the world as Kyeitha must have seen it. The dreams were nearly all of Kyeitha, of the fears she had of the old-world humans before the Oxygen War. Zee had seen what they had done to the planet, the plants and the animals. She would awaken sweating and panting as if she had been running, a sinking stone weighing heavily in her stomach.

Zee wouldn't burden everyone's happiness by sharing her dreams; she didn't want anyone to worry. Kyeitha was gone. She couldn't hurt anyone anymore. Ravaryn's forces withdrew from Aylenta. The town's people all returned, and the world miraculously righted itself. Zemira was a hero, a saviour... but she didn't feel like it. *Murderer*, a voice in her dreams whispered. But there were other dreams as well. Dreams of a dark-haired man. With large dark wings... and darker eyes. And a charming smile.

Epilogue

One year after the blast that had turned her life upside down, Zemira had grown into a lovely nineteen-year-old young woman. 'The moon festival is on tonight, and I'm actually going to it. Can you believe it?' Her sarcasm was still intact, thankfully.

Diwa's hearty cackle filled her cottage as her quick, spindly fingers worked beautiful braids into Zee's long, shiny hair. Paxton's wolf mask awaited in the beautiful ornate box he had presented her with exactly one year ago, on her eighteenth birthday.

'It feels like a lifetime ago... and I feel a lot older than nineteen,' she confided.

'You are older, dear, much older, I think.' Diwa mock gasped. 'I see a grey hair in here! Hehe!' she teased.

Orion and Verena arrived ready to go, arms linked and love in their eyes. Verena's stomach grew larger every day. Zee watched them, sharing the moment, happiness filling her beyond expectation.

'You two are gross, keep your kissing to yourselves,' Zee joked. So happy that for a night she could feel free and slightly normal.

'Are we ready?' asked Orion. 'No need to sneak out this year.' He eyed her with a knowing smile and a wink.

'What do you mean, sneak out?' Verena said.

'Nothing, Mum, he's joking! Don't stress her, Dad! I don't want to have to share my birthday, as well as the two of you, with the baby!' Zee retorted playfully.

'Don't fret, the baby's not due for a long time yet! I just look huge very early.' Verena mock-glared towards Orion.

'No, my love, you look radiant! Are we ready to go? That young man will be sweating every minute we're late.' He laughed.

'You sent the invites, right?' Zee asked her mother.

'Yes, darling, and I must say I can't wait to meet Jill and War-wick. And thank them for their bravery and help in keeping my girl safe,' Verena affirmed.

'Zemira, my girl, you look beautiful.' Orion smiled at her, crush-ing her into a giant hug. 'The perfect mask for you,' he said proudly, nodding in the direction of Pax's wolf mask.

'Thanks, Dad.' She glowed. 'Let's get going! I don't want to miss a single thing!'

The music floated through the neon-painted pathways of the beau-tifully lit streets in the small village of Kali. The smell of herbed breads, roasting meats, sweets and jasmine carried in the warm night air. The bonfire glowed as Zemira rushed through the festival, trying to see as much as possible with Paxton's hand in hers while being towed excitedly along.

A dark figure watched her from the distance, his large form half tucked behind a tree. Zee sensed the being watching her before she even spotted the figure. A cool rush blew over her face, cooling the sweat on her brow from the heat of the fires.

'I'll be back soon,' she said to Paxton. 'Grab us a wine, and I'll meet you by the largest fire.' She smiled reassuringly.

He hesitated, not wanting to leave her. 'Where are you going?'

'Not far. Geez, a girl's gotta pee sometime,' she said to embarrass him.

'Oh right, sorry. Let's hope the wine is better than Jill's whiskey!' Pax winked at her, perking up.

Zee laughed. 'Oh stars, we can only hope!'

She felt bad lying to Paxton, but she didn't want to worry him. He was a little more fragile these days, more then he would ever let on. She wouldn't be gone long. Zee made her way, slipping through the crowds and padding silently out into the moonlit forest where she had seen the figure behind the tree. It wasn't long before she felt the cool wind and a—

'You look simply stunning tonight, Zemira.' The deep, silky voice caressed her senses.

'You were quiet making your way through the forest,' she replied, turning and taking in his black suit, muscular form and golden mask. The sides were upturned with golden wings, a serpent wrapping in and around his dark eyes.

'A wolf, how fitting,' he said sardonically.

'I saw you, in Kyeitha's mind... before, before I—' Zee rubbed her arm, the black mark stinging, and she searched the ground to avoid his gaze. 'Diwa told me everything... about the curse, about Kyeitha, how long you've been alone...'

'Don't you ever look down upon yourself.' His strong, smooth hand cusped her chin, lifting it up. 'You saved us. You saw her, saw what she was capable of.'

'But I—' she cut in.

'But nothing. We've all done terrible things we didn't want to do, that we've had to do. What's done is done, and no one, not even you, the great Rim walker, can change the past, only the future. I'm sorry, Zemira, that it had to be you.' He looked longingly into her eyes as they sparked with flame behind her mask.

'You lied,' she said, pulling back. 'They were your family, your... your child, your partner. And Kyeitha, she...' A tear slipped rebelliously down her face. '

'I told you what you needed to hear. And I was cursed. Not able to tell you anything that could aid me in breaking my curse. I'm sorry we had to manoeuvre you, to guide you towards what had to be done. It was unfair and painful to orchestrate, believe me. And yes, long ago, it was my family that Kyeitha murdered. It's been nearly fifty years since Kyeitha took their lives, Zemira, although I haven't aged, even with the curse. It was a lifetime ago, yet feels like yesterday.' His voice cracked.

Zee felt his pain and wished she could do something to ease it.

'Thank you, Zemira. Thank you for ending it. My curse, my mother's curse. The Rim's curse.'

Zee looked at his remorseful eyes, the slightest glint of silver specks lined the rims of them in the moons glow. She hesitated then said, 'Well, your mother is one crafty old fox.'

Ravaryn lit up with a hearty laugh. 'So you know her all too well then.'

'Yes, I saw that too, you protecting her from Kyeitha, and you both being banished together. How she came to find and protect you. I'll never know it all, but you could fill a house with books on the things we don't know about that woman.'

He smiled lopsidedly, making him truly handsome in the moon's glow. 'I'm glad she could save you. And I'm eternally sorry for the pain I've caused you, and others that you care about.'

Ravaryn looked down and took her small hands in his, closing the gap between them. 'And these...' He turned her wrists over and inspected the tattooed scars from the cuffs he had fashioned and forced her to wear.

'I kinda like them.' Zee shrugged her shoulders, deflecting, voice light. Feeling the closeness of his large body next to hers, the tingle that was shooting up her hands from where he held her. His were warm, slightly calloused and strong. She pulled her hands gently away from his and took a step back.

'Wings, hey?' she deflected further, slightly awkward. She didn't want to even start to decide whether or not she had it in her to forgive someone like Ravaryn and what he had done. For what he had needed to do. She needed time to process all that.

Another deep laugh came from him. 'Yes, wings.' His shoulders rolled and two very large black wings sprung out from behind him.

Zee gasped. They were truly magnificent, shimmering and powerful.

'Would you like to come flying with me sometime, Zemirrra?' His tongue rolled out her name with a caress. A wide, handsome smiled lined the bottom half of his visible face. She couldn't be sure, but she guessed he raised an eyebrow beneath that golden mask. And was that a slight tremor in his hand she spied?

'Hmm, I'm not sure how I would go explaining that one to my parents. But I am an adult now, so it's not like I exactly need their permission.'

He nodded, and the wings disappeared in an instant. 'Of course, they would both likely have heart attacks. And your father...' Ravaryn almost cringed. '...let's just say I'm not looking forward to seeing those two again.'

It was Zee's turn to laugh out loud. 'Yeah, you're in the shit there.' The whole situation was somehow oddly hilarious all of a sudden. 'They will literally chop you to pieces if they ever get their hands on you.'

'They'll have to catch me first.' His dark eyes shone brighter in the moonlight, a mirror image of Diwa's mischievous look. 'It's nearly midnight. I shouldn't keep you from the celebrations.'

Zee looked down at the festival from where they stood, somehow not wanting to leave Ravaryn behind. There was an odd pull towards him, like she could stay and talk with him all night.

'I have a gift for you, Zemira, if you will except it. I completely understand if you don't,' he said almost nervously, the cocky, arrogant king gone.

'Well, it is my birthday, after all, and you did ruin the last one by pretending to blow up my home, steal my mum, torture my only friend, kidnap me, make me destroy the Rim etcetera,' she said sarcastically.

'Let's not linger on that, shall we?' he said quickly, sweeping the literal shit show the last year had been very quickly under the rug, so to speak.

He reached again for her hand, and she jerked back a little at his touch, still not trusting him. But she took a breath and steadied herself.

'Sorry.' He looked as though his guilt would drown him in an instant. He slowed his movement, and as gently as he could, placed something on her finger. 'It's only a ring,' he explained as he placed a small gold ring with a dark swirling crystal inside it on her finger.

Zee didn't know what to say. She was flattered but also didn't know whether she should except the gift or not.

'If you ever need me... or my help... or a good laugh.' He winked under the immaculate mask. 'You send a spark of magic into that ring and I will come. I will find you.'

'Hey, we all know how that turned out last time. Sure you're not just trying to make it easier for me to blow stuff up for you again?'

He laughed at the irony; it was a warm laugh, lifting Zee's insides.

'No, Zemira, you have the power this time, and I promise you, I will not bother you again unless you want me to. You should get back. I'm sure your friend is looking for you.'

'Is that a hint of jealousy I detect.' Zee glowed.

'I don't get jealous.'

'Ha!' Zee smiled. 'You're a strange soul, Ravaryn.'

'As are you, Zemira.' His eyes sparked as her name rolled off his tongue.

'You can call me Zee.'

Ravaryn's face lit up behind the mask, even though Zee was sure he thought it was hidden, she didn't miss the look. 'Thank you, Zee, for everything.' He leaned in close and kissed her cheek under her glittering mask. His breath was warm on her skin, and he smelled of pines, salt and something more.

Sparks shot through her body, and her heart raced. He spread his huge wings and with one giant swoop of air he was airborne and into the night. Zee recalled a dim vision of the night he had taken her back to Diwa's cottage and laid her in the garden. She looked down at the spiralling swirl of black inside the gem on the ring, and her heart fluttered. She felt guilty at her own feelings. Her cheeks were flushed, and she couldn't wipe the stupid smile from her face.

'Zee? That you?' Paxton's voice broke her from the moment. She jumped like a small child being caught red-handed in the cookie jar.

'Coming!' She skittered from the forest, heart pounding, and looked back to the sky once more. She saw a dark figure hover over, then fly away.

'Where have you been? I've got your drink.' He smiled.

'Thanks, Pax.' She returned his smile with warmth. 'Cheers to another year, may it be a darned sight better than the last!'

'Cheers.' Paxton clinked his metal cup with hers. 'Come on. What's the worst that can happen, right?' he said with a laugh.

'Hey, that's my saying!' She playfully bumped him with her shoulder. He wrapped an arm around her slender frame and they walked together into the celebration, enjoying the easy comfort of each other. The dark scar that Kyeitha had left on Zee's arm surged a little more painfully, deeper into her skin. She grimaced silently, Paxton not noticing. Rubbing the vicious mark that seemed to grow more and more every day, she tried to ignore it...

After all, what's the worst that could happen?

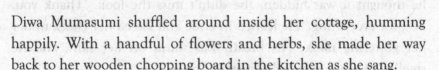

Diwa Mumasumi shuffled around inside her cottage, humming happily. With a handful of flowers and herbs, she made her way back to her wooden chopping board in the kitchen as she sang.

'Teaa, tea – lemon or burgundy? What will it be, blueberry, rosemary...' Diwa sang merrily while she chopped and shredded various herbs.

'Oh yes, that's a great idea. The juneberries will definitely be ready soon! But not now. Yes, I know they are her favourite,' she said aloud to the old fig tree woven through her home.

'I know, I know, it all happened so fast. She's so strong. I knew she'd be strong. Tea, teaa apple or elderberry? Jasmine or mint, give me a hint... I'm so glad she has time to just rest now... yes, yes she knows about Ravaryn. My poor son. No, I don't think Verena knows the extent. And with Kyeitha gone, the world can right itself again for a little while at least. A cup for me, a cup for you, lemon, apricot, mistleberry too!'

She stirred the pot and took its contents to rest on top of her oven, stirring and stirring.

'The damned? Yes... those poor creatures are all out of her control now. They are free and can wander and roam, hopefully away to find their own peace. Turmeric and sage? Ha! Not at this stage... teaa teaaa. No, she doesn't know.'

Diwa flung the lid on the pot and reached up to the old shelf painted with beautiful, worn little stories. She searched with her eyes shut, hands floating in front of all the choices and finally reached for two teacups. One had small sprouts emerging under rays of a bright sun. The other had a silver wind rushing around the cup in beautiful swirls, leaves of all colours caught up in it. A small chip in the base.

'Teaa, tea, some for you and some for– NO! I will not tell her yet! She needs time! Now enough! Zemira will be here soon. I will not tell her about the other Rim world and that is final! Don't you fight with me. I'll prune you! I swear it!' Diwa poured the contents of the brew into the delicate cups, carefully chosen for each of them, the purple liquid spinning around inside, carrying tiny fragments of herbs, just as a knock sounded at her cottage door...

Acknowledgements

Writing a book is something I've always wanted to do, but the challenging road life has taken me on hasn't afforded me the time until recently. After suffering a debilitating back injury and being bedridden for months, I lay there feeling very much like my own modern-day version of Frida Kahlo and thought the universe had given me a very back-handed gift, which I was determined not to waste! So I started to write and materialise this story.

A massive –massive thank you to my amazing editor and independent publisher Dr Juliette Lachemeier... you're an absolute legend. Thank you for believing in me and telling me you loved my story. There is no greater gift than someone lifting you up and telling you that something you created is worthy.

Thank you to Judith San Nicolas for the awesome book cover and map illustration.

Summer, my angel, my daughter, thank you for looking after me, putting on my socks, bringing me vegemite toast and watching movies with me while I was recovering. Thank you for your gorgeous, bright, happy light that you've brought into my world. I love you more than anything in this entire universe and I always will. This book is for you.

Thank you to Josh/George, my sturdy rock, for your unwavering love, and for your patience of a Jedi master.

For Sadie, my rescue greyhound, for your constant company and cuddles, sharing your retirement with us.

Katie, for putting up with me in this life and the next. There is nothing more amazing than having a sister, someone who knows you inside-out and has been with you through the rocky path that life has made us walk., and can still laugh about it all.

Kaitlynd, a girl couldn't ask for a better friend. You're a gift that I will never let go of! You're stuck with me forever. I don't know how you create your amazing light but I'm glad you share it with me. I thank you and Davo for being my first readers. Your words of encouragement have helped me more than you'll ever know.

For Liv and Annie. Thank you for being the most loving and selfless mothers to me. Your belief in me and encouragement have changed my life, you were there when I didn't even know how much I needed you both.

Uncle David, for giving me a home and a sanctuary when I needed it most. I don't think you'll ever know how much you changed my life for the better.

Jess, your bright soul, and never fading confidence in me. Your light always fills me up whenever I see you. You make every room brighter just with your presence alone. I'm so lucky to have you in my life.

Ruby, for your brilliant aura, your ability to tell the best stories and to shine positivity on even the most horrific situations and turn them into a good laugh. Thank you for always having my back and your ruthless honesty.

My three awesome brothers, who all in their own way have taught me to be tough in this life. Growing up with brothers is a gift not everyone gets and I'm so lucky I have you all!

Kerry and Ben, for always being there and offering a helping hand without hesitation.

And thank you to the rest of my amazing women that I hold so dear to my heart and that lift me up and fill me with happiness and love. I don't know what I would do without you all: Kirsty, Edie, April, Laura, Myra, Jayme and Sofie. You are my secret weapons to tackle life, and I thank you with all my heart for accepting me just the way I am.

Mum, for letting the fairies live in the garden, I hope they are still out there with you.

And to everyone who reads this little piece of my heart that I have finally let free onto paper... thank you so much. This book is for you. I hope you get lost in it and forget real life... for just a moment.

ABOUT THE AUTHOR

Renee Hayes grew up in Tropical Far North Queensland. Reading fantasy was an invaluable tool of escapism from the troubles of real life. Her imagination and vivid dreams coated almost all of the memories that she has from her childhood.

Animals, gardens, swimming, pushbikes and reading were a big part of her happier times, growing up with her four siblings. Now Renee's life has finally swung her on a path where she can pour her dreams out onto paper and write.

Her own fantasy stories continue to come to life, and the magic is growing with them in her new house and her new stage of life, and she can't wait to see where it leads her...

Enjoyed the book? You can follow Renee Hayes at:

Facebook: www.facebook.com/profile.php?id=100086763157926

Email: rennnay@outlook.com

If you liked the book, please leave a review on Amazon, Goodreads or with the author directly. Reviews are invaluable in supporting an author's hard work and are greatly appreciated.